THE
SHUTDOWN
LIST

ALSO BY SHARON DUKETT

No Rules: A Memoir

Published 2024

Printed in the United States of America

ISBN: 979-8-9899479-0-4 (paperback)
ISBN: 979-8-9899479-1-1 (e-book)

Library of Congress Control Number: 2024906629

For information, contact:
SharKen Publishing
900 Washington St #1033
Middletown, CT 06457

Interior design by Damonza.com

Printed in the United States of America

THE SHUTDOWN LIST

SHARON DUKETT

SHARKEN PUBLISHING

For my grandchildren

and yours

CALIFORNIA

GLASS SHATTERED OVER Steven's living room floor when a baseball bat hit his window, followed by a firebomb hurled through the opening. The bottle smashed into the first of three computer servers Steven had recently brought home from the data center to keep safe. In milliseconds, flames engulfed all the servers, the surrounding furniture, and spewed clouds of black smoke.

Steven's pulse soared as he grabbed his laptop and dove for the floor, devastated that the download hadn't completed. All the work was lost. Everything.

He scurried toward the patio screen door on hands and knees, inhaling fumes, coughing, and gasping for air. Smoky fog blinded him. He pulled his T-shirt over his face to filter the air, abandoning the laptop in his confusion. Sparks scattered across his path, stinging his skin. The ugly smell of burning hair reached his nose before he felt the flames.

As he fought to survive, that last text he'd received taunted him:

Shut it down, Scarecrow, or I'll throw you a little fire.

CHAPTER ONE

WASHINGTON, D.C. TWO YEARS LATER

Anita Forester rode on the Red Line train into Washington, D.C., staring at her husband Julian's reflection in the rain-streaked window. He hunched over his phone, his forehead wrinkled with a pained expression she recognized, while she herself endured a familiar ache in her gut. She longed to reach out to Julian, but knew it was pointless. The silence of their broken marriage was impenetrable with the memory of their dead son sitting between them.

Today's trip was the first outing they'd shared following their son Steven's death in a wildfire two years earlier—if she could even call it an outing. To her, it was more like attending a memorial service. The somber journey was anything but pleasant.

"We should go together. He would want us both to be

there," Julian had said days before, in a rare moment of speaking with her. Anita imagined he was right about attending the demonstration, so she agreed to join him despite the apathy overwhelming her since Steven's death. This demonstration was something she cared about. She knew doing nothing had consequences, but she was exhausted: the kind of exhaustion that hovered around her like a shroud.

Now, on the train, a memory of Steven gnawed inside her chest—riding with him into Washington, D.C. to a different protest three years earlier, when he was twenty-six. She'd been proud of his drive and determination to make a difference. Watching Steven, Anita had believed the future held promise. Instead, her future had brought her pain so pervasive, that shutting down her emotions was the only way she could cope with it.

The phone buzzed in her purse announcing a text message from her best friend Stacey, who was joining them:

Across from the Peace Monument facing the Capitol. Text when you arrive.

If anyone could improve her day, it was Stacey. Anita slipped the phone into her jacket pocket and zipped it shut, thankful for the distraction.

"Tenleytown-AU," the stop for American University lit up on the display in the front of their car, signaling the next station. Julian rose from his seat and moved into the aisle.

"I'm meeting friends at A.U.," he said. "I'll see you down at the mall about one o'clock."

Anita furrowed her brow, confused. "What? I don't understand. You said we were going together."

"Stacey's there. You'll be fine. We'll be there soon."

Julian reached into his pocket and thrust a folded piece of paper at her. Bewildered, Anita took it.

"If anything happens to me, these email addresses might help. But be cautious."

She was stunned as her mind raced over this sudden disclosure of potential danger. "What are you talking about? What might happen to you?"

He frowned and turned away as the metro slowed to a stop.

"Julian, talk to me. What's going on?"

He ignored her and stepped off the train.

"Damn you, Julian," she muttered, vacillating between wanting to follow him and knowing he'd be mad if she did. He'd never introduced her to his friends at American University or invited her to join them. Although it hurt, she'd accepted that he had this other life without her.

The doors shut. Her eyes tracked his thick, graying head of hair until he met up with a Black man in a dark jacket, a bushy beard trimmed around his cheeks. They exchanged a few words before turning to stare at her through the window. Anita scrutinized his face, hoping she might recognize this stranger, but didn't. He nodded as they spoke. The train pulled away as they rushed from the station, Julian moving as nimbly as he did thirty years ago when they'd first married.

Angry that he was keeping her in the dark about his activities today, she balled up the paper and clenched it in her fist. The possibility of him being in danger was far too important to not tell her until now.

Recent memories of their stark conversations offered no

clues about today's plans. Part of her wished he would get in trouble. He deserved it.

No. That's not right, she chastised herself, flushing from a tinge of guilt. Maybe he was a jerk for leaving her out of his life, but she'd feel terrible if he was in jeopardy.

Her fist loosened. Smoothing out the crumpled paper, she read the list of cryptic emails containing no clear names, recognizing none. This time she folded it and slipped it into a zippered compartment in her handbag to keep it safe.

Whatever Julian was up to, she hoped she wouldn't need to resort to this list.

$\approx$

"Anita!"

Stacy's voice sparked a rush of joy as she turned to greet her. Strands of Stacey's dark hair dripped from beneath her hood when she leaned in for a quick hug, their soaked jackets sticking together when they separated.

"I'm so sick of this weather." Stacey's eyes darted about. "Where's Julian?"

"Something weird is going on with him." Anita explained about his sudden departure from the train and the email list. "I don't know why he didn't meet his friends here."

"I thought you said he wanted you to come here with him?"

"He did." Holding back tears of disappointment, Anita locked eyes with Stacey, who pinched her lips together. "Why do I even bother trying?"

Stacey gave her a sympathetic shrug. "Maybe when he gets here, he'll explain. Let's go find the speakers. I'm not sure who they have coming today." Heavy wind and rain caused Anita to pull the straps of her hood tighter.

Stacey nudged her in the direction that the others were walking. A small crowd of about a thousand people had gathered despite the storm. Some carried signs, but far fewer participants attended than the last time Anita had come with Steven when tens of thousands showed up. Today, there probably were not even enough to make the news. Occasionally, someone's eyes met hers as they walked, giving a quick nod, and she returned the acknowledgment. Capitol Police spread out along the sidewalk, behind the barriers in front of the Capitol steps and scanned the gathering from beneath hooded ponchos.

"I'm surprised so few people are here," Anita said. "Was this well advertised? I haven't been paying attention."

"Didn't see anything on social media. Maybe the weather scared people away. But I'm glad you finally came today. You need to get out more."

Anita nearly smiled at the phrase Stacey had often used over the last year. "Get out more." What she meant was get out at all. Beyond grocery shopping, visiting Stacey's house, and a forced trip to the gym twice a week, Anita seldom ventured anywhere. Julian was gone all the time between his professorship at Gettysburg College and the group of friends he congregated with around American University. Not even work occupied Anita. Three years earlier, she'd sold the technology consulting firm she'd spent years building into a successful enterprise.

They hung their heads against the driving rain as they fell in with the crowd walking toward the Capitol, all cloaked in foul weather gear. The wind and rain dulled the sounds of their voices.

"By the way, I've been meaning to tell you about something." Stacey leaned in close. "One of the other teachers in my school can't find her daughter. Turns out, she was arrested during a protest last month, but when her mother contacted the police to find her, she wasn't there. They said she was given a warning and released. But her daughter never came home."

Anita's stomach churned from a familiar anguish she'd experienced herself. "That's scary. Were they close?"

"Very. Her daughter isn't the type to take off and not tell her mother. She even filed a missing person's report. Nothing."

Swallowing as her stomach acids threatened to revolt, Anita relived the day when she'd learned of Steven's death. Horrified by the news as the fires had spread through his area, she had tracked the websites showing those who'd checked in safe and never found his name, called him over and over until his phone rolled into voice mail. Now she bit down hard on her inner cheek until she tasted blood, attempting to stop herself from sinking into a dark place.

"You okay?" Stacey asked after a minute. "That was stupid of me. I wasn't thinking."

"Don't worry about me. I'm fine." Anita licked the inside of her mouth, soothing the hurt spot she'd bitten.

The sky darkened and tiny hail fell. A groan rose around her. People huddled together, pulling their hoods forward. Anita checked her watch. It was 1:15. Had she missed Julian's call? Stopping and turning her back to the wind, she fished her phone from her jacket and shielded it from the hail. No missed calls. No texts. Julian was late. And he was never late. Her jaw clenched tight enough to break a tooth.

When she looked up, Stacey was no longer next to her.

Those nearby all looked alike, a maze of black hooded jackets. People jostled her as they pushed by, their arms and shoulders bumping against her as they surged toward the Capitol building, but no Stacey. Her pulse raced. How stupid she'd been not to tell her she was stopping.

A cheer rose from the crowd, and Anita flinched. She pivoted toward the building and witnessed two hooded figures leap a barrier, sprinting up the steps of the Capitol as the police raced toward them. Before they reached the top, they turned and unfurled a massive flag above their heads, struggling against the weather to hold it open. It was an Earth Day flag. On the dark background of space was the giant blue marble photo of Earth taken during an Apollo space mission.

What are those fools thinking? They're going to get arrested, Anita thought.

Hundreds of hands pointed phones at the action. People chanted, "*STOP THE LIES. NO MORE OIL.*" As the police converged on the rebels, they pushed off their hoods, exposing their faces to the cameras and thrusting fists into the air.

Anita gasped. One of them was Julian.

She forced her way between those blocking her path to the stairs. One person yelled at her, and another pulled on her slick jacket, but she wrenched it away. At the barricades, she watched helplessly as police dragged Julian across the stairs while he wrestled against them. One of them tased him. His body stiffened, then went limp before they hauled him over to a van and shoved him inside.

"Julian," she screamed, horrified.

Another officer spotted her and jogged down the steps toward her. Before he got close, someone's hand grabbed her upper arm and yanked her back into the crowd, dragging her behind a wall. It was the Black man with the bushy beard whom Julian had met and walked away with at the Tenleytown station.

He leaned in near her face. "Run! Don't follow him. It's dangerous."

"That's my husband. Why did he do that?" Her fear left her breathless. "Do you know . . . why he . . ."

"I know who you are. He asked me to watch for you and give you these." He pushed a set of keys into Anita's hand. The blood rushed to her head as she recognized they were Julian's set for their EV, his key fob and house keys attached to a plastic Gettysburg PA souvenir key chain. The car was plugged in and parked in the lot at the Rockville station where they had boarded the train today. He'd driven, but she had her own keys in her handbag.

"Why? Who are you?"

He shook his head. "I've got to go. He left you five thousand dollars in his laptop bag in your front closet. Take it and hide. They'll come after you, too. Leave." He gripped her shoulders and turned her toward the road with a shove.

Before leaving, Anita stopped to ask him where they were taking Julian, but the man had vanished into the crowd.

Why would they come after me? I didn't do anything.

The D.C. police van drove away. The risk of deadly side effects from Tasers caused her stomach to twist with worry.

The rain continued pounding on her until she sheltered beneath a group of tree branches hanging over the wall. She located the number of a nearby police station and inquired about her husband.

"What's his name and date of birth?" the clerk asked.

Anita told him. After a long wait, he spoke again.

"He's not in our system yet. Protestors from the Capitol are usually given a summons with a court date and released. Wait until you hear from him. He'll have a chance to call if he's arrested. It can take a couple of hours."

"He was tased. Will they take him to the hospital?"

"Yeah, if he was injured. Call back in a few hours if you don't hear anything."

"What hospital?" But he'd already hung up before answering.

Anita cringed at the thought of waiting for hours. Jitters prevented her from standing still as the rain falling through the tree leaves soaked her. She phoned Stacey. No answer. Then Julian, and he didn't answer either. Her grip on the car keys hurt her hand, reminding her of the man's warning to run.

CHAPTER TWO

THE TRAIN

THE IMAGE OF Julian being tased replayed in Anita's mind. Panic rippled through her as she visualized his body going limp before being placed into the van. Her jaw tightened, her head throbbed, and her breaths came faster and faster. *Please don't be dead. Please.* Closing her eyes, she focused on deep breathing, ignoring the odor of mildew on wet jackets surrounding her on the crowded red line train. Counting each breath, three counts in, five counts out, her breaths began to slow. She'd become adept at this over the last couple of years. Following a few cycles, she was able to concentrate again.

Since this man with the bushy beard had met up with Julian when he left the train, and handed her Julian's car keys, she believed he was telling the truth. *He said to hide. From whom?*

A few stops later, the crowd dwindled, and she took a seat.

She retrieved her phone to search for lawyers in the DC area, wondering what kind Julian might need. Was this a criminal act? Or one of constitutional rights? Her lawyer handled her business dealings, but nothing like this.

Several missed call notifications from Stacey popped up. *Damn.* Anita's ringer was shut off. As she prepared to call back, her phone rang displaying Julian's number. *Thank God.* Her pulse ratcheted up. "Oh my God, where are you?"

"Hello, Mrs. Forester." She didn't recognize the man's voice. "This is not Julian, but I have his phone. I need to ask you some questions about your husband's activities."

Anita cupped her hand over her mouth and the phone, using hushed tones to prevent the other passengers from hearing. "Is this the police? I've been waiting for his call. Is he okay?"

"I'm a private investigator whose client has requested I speak with you. I'm not at liberty to answer your questions. I apologize."

Her chest tightened.

"Who can answer my questions? Where did you get his phone?"

"Let me begin. Who helped him plan that exhibition today?"

"I have no idea. I didn't know anything about it."

"Who are you trying to protect?"

"No one." Her face wrinkled in confusion. "Why can't you tell me where my husband is? I need to talk to him. I have a right to."

"As I said, I'm not at liberty to answer your questions. Let's continue. Who are his close friends and associates?"

"I don't know. We don't talk. Why don't you look at his phone and see who he calls?"

"Then tell me, who are your close friends and associates?"

"None of your business. What kind of scam is this? Are you looking for money?"

She wanted to scream at this man, scream at anybody. Holding in her anger caused her head to pound.

"I can assure you, this is no scam and has nothing to do with money. You can answer these questions on the phone or come here and answer them."

"Where is here? If you have my husband, I'll go there. But I'm bringing my lawyer."

"Only you are allowed to come. We'll pick you up. I see you are heading north right now. Red line? We'll have someone meet you at the next stop."

Her breathing accelerated. They were tracking her. Who had those capabilities? And so quickly? From the work her consulting company had provided, Anita knew intelligence agencies did, but they identified themselves. The words of the man on the mall came back: *They'll come after you, too.* Whom had Julian become involved with?

She disconnected the call and tried the police again. This time, they had a different answer. "He was given a summons to appear in court in two weeks and released about a half-hour ago."

A tingle ran up her arms. She powered off her phone hoping no one could trace her. The police didn't have him, and now she had no way to reach him—wherever he was—since this mystery man had his phone. *He left you five thousand dollars in his laptop bag. Take it and hide.* There was one way for her to verify this was true. Get the laptop bag. If it held five thousand dollars, she would hide.

But she didn't know where to go, or if these people would continue to track her. Using credit cards was out of the question. Financial transactions were like dropping breadcrumbs for those who might trace your movements.

Suddenly she remembered the email list Julian had given her and pulled it from her handbag. This time she turned it over and found writing on the back in smudged pencil.

Howard Street Bed and Breakfast - Newport, Rhode Island.

Maybe this was a place she should go for help. Unless this was some old paper Julian had used. Even if that was the case, it was still a place to hide. They knew no one in Rhode Island, so no one would look for her there.

At least I have a destination. She stuffed the list back into her bag.

At the next stop, Anita kept her head down, turning her face away from the open door in case anyone was searching for her. Her arms trembled while people boarded, wondering who might approach her. To steady her nerves, she jammed her fists into her pockets and squeezed them close to her body. A girl who looked like a college student got on and sat next to her. Setting her backpack between her feet, the girl put her phone in her pocket and opened a book. Once the train took off, Anita unclenched her fist and gazed around at the other passengers. No one was paying her any attention. Her breathing slowed. Several minutes later, Anita was calm enough to speak to the girl beside her.

"Would you mind if I borrowed your phone to call a friend? My battery died, and she's supposed to pick me up from my stop." Lying went against her ethics, which she was forced to overlook.

The girl hesitated, shrugged, and handed it to her. "Don't go anywhere with it."

Stacey had been her best friend since college in Washington. She'd memorized her number years ago. As it rang, Anita worried she might not answer an unknown number, then heaved a grateful sigh when she did.

"Stacey, I . . ." she began.

"Holy shit!" Stacey said. "I can't believe I lost you, and Julian shows up acting like he's Abbie Hoffman. I looked for you and couldn't find you anywhere. Why didn't you answer when I called?"

"My ringer was shut off. I can't remember why. There was this man with his keys . . . the police took him but released him . . . now some creepy guy has his phone. May even have Julian."

"You're not making any sense. Are you okay?"

"No. Not at all. I can't explain right now but I need your help. Can you round up some things from the house and meet me in the parking lot of the Middle School?" She dropped her voice. "I'm so scared."

"Don't worry. I still have your key. I'll bring what you need. I should beat you home, assuming the roads are clear. The weather's still rough."

The college girl sitting next to Anita was looking sideways at her now. Anita turned away and whispered into the phone.

"There's five thousand dollars in cash in a laptop bag in the front hallway closet. Bring the laptop, too. Throw it all in a suitcase with some clothes.

"Why the hell do you have five thousand dollars in cash sitting around?"

"Julian left it for me. I'll explain when I see you."

"I can't wait to hear this one."

At the end of the call, Anita handed the phone back to the girl who stuffed it into her backpack before getting up to move to another seat. Anita couldn't blame her for not wanting to sit next to a panicky woman who sounded paranoid.

At her stop in Rockville, she pulled the waterproof case off her phone and dropped it into a sewer drain.

CHAPTER THREE

NEWPORT

STACEY JUMPED OUT of her car where she was waiting in the Gettysburg Middle School teachers' parking lot and slid into Anita's front passenger's seat, "I brought everything I could think of and it's all in your suitcase."

"Was the money where I said?"

"Yep. Just like you told me. I didn't count it, but it looks like a lot. What's going on?"

A lump formed in Anita's throat when she heard the money was there. This stranger had told her the truth. For the past couple of hours, she had pored over the possibilities of why Julian had put himself at such risk, and what might have happened to him. He was a history professor in a stable, tenured position, a man not prone to extreme actions. Skiing was his most daring activity. Since their son's death, he'd changed, and was now spending all his free time with those people from American University. Where he'd once loved to share deep intellectual discussions, he now shut her down with sarcasm or shut her out with silence. Silence at least allowed Anita's wounds to scab over. Now, in her car with Stacey, anger bubbled up, causing her to squeeze the steering wheel until her finger joints cried "uncle."

"I thought we were going to stand around in protest like everyone else. Instead, Julian shows up and practically begs to be hauled away! Why?" Anita told Stacey about the man with the keys and the call from Julian's phone.

"This is flipping me out." Stacey's eyes widened. "It's almost like he knew this would happen."

"Like he planned it." Anita slammed her palm on the steering wheel and broke into tears, then collapsed into Stacey's arms, while her friend rubbed her back. She'd come to rely on her through these dark times, on Stacey's ability to rescue her when she began slipping underwater. Now Anita had to leave and abandon contact with the only person keeping her afloat.

When she was able to stop crying, she pulled away from Stacey's embrace.

"It's bad enough we barely talk anymore." Anita fished the paper out of her jacket pocket and held it up. "But he has the nerve to give me this list. And without any explanation, like it's my responsibility to save him from his stupidity. I think he just wanted me there as a witness. He didn't care about us going together."

Anger was burning through her chest.

Stacey slipped it from her fingers and opened it.

"Damn him! Where the hell is he? Why are they after me? They must think I'm involved in whatever this is," Anita said.

"Who do you think is after you?"

"It's not the police. They didn't have any interest in me. The man who called me on Julian's phone wanted to pick me up. Had some client apparently but didn't say who. He was tracing me, so I ditched the phone."

Stacey's brow furrowed as she read over the list before handing it back. "Don't you dare let them pick you up. Where are you going?"

Her heart hurt because of what she needed to say. "I can't tell you." She avoided Stacey's face. "It might put you in danger, too. I need to disappear until I can figure out what's going on."

Her eyes welled with tears again. Stacey took Anita's hand in hers and gently rubbed it. "I'm always here. Call."

They locked eyes for a moment, sending unspoken emotions to each other the way close friends do. Then Anita flipped up her jacket hood and opened the hatchback, while Stacey grabbed the suitcase from her car and lifted it inside.

"I put your passports in there too, along with some of your clothes and the photo of Steven from your desk. I knew you'd want it."

"More than ever. I can't thank you enough for all of this."

They held each other in a long hug until the wind whipped Anita's hood from her head.

♠

Hours after darkness fell, Anita crossed the Pell Bridge into Newport, Rhode Island. Traffic lights were working unlike other areas she'd driven through on the way from Pennsylvania. The wind had eased up in Connecticut and the rain was more of a shower than a deluge. Using her car's GPS, she located the Howard Street Bed and Breakfast, backing up the driveway to conceal her license plate. Pennsylvania didn't require them on the front. Without knowing whom she was hiding from, Anita didn't want to risk the police scanning her plate into their system. That man with Julian's phone was vague but had some powerful tracking abilities. If he tapped into a police database, he'd find her.

Rain drizzled down her neck as she unloaded her suitcase, throwing her jacket over her arm. From the laptop bag, she grabbed a handful of twenty-dollar bills and stuffed them into her pocket, then locked the bag inside the trunk.

A floodlight by the back door kicked on and lit the sidewalk as she rolled her suitcase behind her. There was no doorbell. Anita knocked a few times until a light switched on. An older man walked through the kitchen toward her with a frown on his face. When he reached the door, he squinted outside at her through the glass.

"Can I help you?" he shouted.

"I'd like a room, please."

He opened the door and motioned her inside.

"I'm sorry I didn't call first." Anita stepped into the kitchen, pulling her suitcase over the threshold. "I lost my phone earlier today. I realize it's late."

"That's okay." He reached his hand out to shake hers. "I'm Paul Tanner, the owner. Welcome."

When he smiled for the first time, she guessed he was around her age of fifty-five. His white hair made him appear older from a distance, but his skin didn't show deep wrinkles. The warmth of his hand surprised her. She drew back and shivered, pushing her damp hair behind her ears.

"All my rooms are on the second floor and there's no elevator. Are you okay with stairs?"

"I'm fine. How much?"

"Ninety dollars a night. How long do you plan on staying?"

Anita had no idea. For a moment she stared at him, not knowing what to say, as she tried to keep her breathing calm. "A few days, I think."

His eyes narrowed. "You can pay for the first night now, and we can settle up the rest when you leave. Is that okay?"

Nodding, she pulled the cash from her pocket, trying not to fumble and expose her nervousness. If he kept asking her questions, she wouldn't have answers.

On the registration card, she wrote Janice Knowles under her name and made up an address of a town she had driven through earlier.

⁓

Despite her exhaustion, Anita had difficulty sleeping. The bed was comfortable enough. The blue and white trimmed room had a pleasant nautical theme—sailboats interspersed with helms on the matching bedspread and curtains. The wind was still blowing hard, however. Tree branches grazed the side of the house, jolting her awake whenever she began drifting off.

When she finally fell asleep, her dreams were filled with images of flames leaping around her as she screamed for Steven, desperate to find him, but he never answered her cries.

She awoke with a start and flipped on the light—her face wet with tears. Inside her suitcase, she rummaged for the photo of Steven, then sat back in bed with it, staring at her son's handsome face. An ugly grief uncoiled itself from the pit of her stomach where it lived most days. Afraid he was fading from her memory, she buried her face in the pillow and sobbed. Some days his photos were all she could remember of him.

The last time she'd seen him, they'd waved goodbye as he stood smiling on the front steps of his new house at the edge of a California forest—a forest which burned to the ground a few months later when a raging wildfire spread too fast for escape. The geo-coordinates of his house were now in her will, with instructions for her ashes to be spread where his remains would lay scattered forever. Julian had done the same.

But now Julian had screwed up everything. Sitting up straight in bed, she gulped back her tears, wondering if any news about the protest was on TV. The television remote control sat on the white wicker end table beside her bed. She flipped through the news channels, but they all reported similar stories — the amount of damage done by the storm across the East Coast, with record power outages, flooding, and downed trees. Reporters likened it to a hurricane in the amount of damage it had created over four days.

"Yesterday afternoon, the President held a press conference to discuss the storm that stalled across the northeast until late last night," the announcer said. "Here are the highlights."

The newscast shifted to the President as he stood at the podium in a room full of reporters. His perfectly groomed gray hair was parted neatly down the side. He wore a dark gray suit with his signature red, white and blue striped tie scattered with stars.

"My fellow Americans, ladies and gentlemen of the press. I have asked you to join me to reassure you that where a state of emergency is declared, those states will have financial aid rapidly deployed to repair power lines, roads, and bridges. We've all been through storms like this over many decades and we have your back."

"Not as bad as this, you ass," Anita said to the television.

"I also want to say how proud I am of all the first responders who put their lives on the line every day for our citizens and have been with us throughout this storm rescuing those affected by flooding and wind damage. These brave men and women deserve our thanks, along with all the linemen out there restoring power. Let's all say an extra prayer for them tonight."

He smiled at the reporters.

"Ask him what he'll do to slow the climate crisis, so these storms won't keep getting worse," Anita argued out loud, but reporters didn't ask those kinds of questions. Or if they did, they never made it onto the news, despite the fires, storms, and flooding that shut down entire regions with increasing regularity.

Anita cursed him.

The newscaster moved on.

"In other news, the Senate and the House agreed on and approved revisions to existing legislation on Friday afternoon to prevent discrimination against the manufacture and use of gasoline powered trucks and automobiles. This will help to both preserve jobs and provide consumers with lower-cost fossil fuel as alternatives to expensive green technology."

Anita shook her head. The protest changed nothing. They'd passed the legislation anyway. Julian stood on the steps with that flag for nothing. All the legislation passed by the prior administrations, all the money she'd donated and phone calls she made over the years were for nothing.

She shut the television off, swallowing down a sour taste in her mouth, angry at the news and angry at Julian. After losing Steven, Julian was all she had left, and this scared her. In their final moments together, Julian reached out to her for help. Wherever he was, she needed to try to find him.

Fear gnawed at her innards and whispered in her ear. "You're all alone. You can't do this. You'll fail."

CHAPTER FOUR

ARGENTINA

Douglas T. Hayes boarded his Boeing 777-9 at Dulles Airport and walked over to his creamy white leather recliner across from U.S. Senator John Colton and Secretary of the Interior Michael Bernard. The two men stood to greet him, pumping his hand while Doug returned a pat on the shoulder to each of them.

"Hey, sweetheart," he called over to the attendant, a blonde former model who'd worked for him the last two years and stood waiting by the liquor cabinet at the back of the cabin.

"Bring us some of that Pappy's 20-year-old for me and my guests, would you, dear?"

"Sure thing." She pulled out the Pappy Van Winkle bourbon and poured it into three glasses on a tray. After adding fresh cherries and pecans to three separate bowls, she carried them over to where the men sat and served each of them.

"Captain says we're cleared for takeoff in ten. Can I get you anything else before I strap in?"

The two guests stared at her body as she stood above them in her form fitting sleeveless dress.

"Thanks, dear. This ought to do us until we're in the air." Doug got a rush out of watching the guys devour her. They probably thought there was all kinds of hanky-panky going on between them. He wouldn't mind if there was, but he didn't make it a condition of employment.

"What time do you want Sergio to put on the steaks?" she asked Doug, resting her hand on his recliner. "Captain says we should be in Buenos Aires in about nine hours."

"About an hour from now ought to do it. Then we can have some shut eye before touching down."

"Excellent. The guest rooms are made up whenever you're ready, and your luggage has been placed inside them. I have to ask you to buckle up for now. Once we are underway, it's your choice, but I suggest you keep your seatbelts on in case of turbulence. We have a couple of tropical storms out in the Atlantic which could shake us up as we pass."

The senator raised his eyebrows. "Late for tropical storms, isn't it?"

"Not so much anymore." She pouted and shook her head. "They're pretty common in November now."

The men followed her instructions. Returning to the back of the cabin, she took a seat by the window, fastened her seat belt and slipped on a pair of noise-cancelling headphones.

Doug raised his glass toward the other two men, who followed suit.

"Thanks for getting it done, buddies." Lifting his glass to them, they all took a drink.

The senator let out a long exhale. "Damn that's smooth. My daddy would say it's as fine as cream gravy."

"Only the best for the best. All this 'go green' bullshit has been a thorn in my side for too long," Doug said. "It's about time we put a stop to that legislation. I'm sick of goddamn Musk walking around like his billions are cleaner than mine. Anyhow, it's my party now. Oil is back in style. Wahoo!!"

"Wahoo indeed," the senator replied.

"I want to thank you for alerting me to all those dirty assets I added to my portfolio a few years ago," Doug said to the senator. "When the power companies started dumping them like hot cakes, I picked up some real bargains. As of today, they've skyrocketed."

Senator Colton was one of Doug's favorite senators, as he had strong connections throughout the energy industry. Lining John Colton's pockets with campaign funds was one of Doug's best investments. John would bring him potential deals he was privy to which benefited each of them.

A few years earlier, companies were under pressure to move polluting power plants, aka "dirty assets," off their spreadsheets, so they could report their status to shareholders as becoming green. Rather than eliminate the polluters, the fastest and most lucrative exit strategy was to sell them, and Doug was privately buying. At a reduced rate, of course, but with the goal of changing laws to favor fossil fuels under a new political administration. Right now, it was all coming together nicely.

Doug tipped his glass toward the secretary. "Let's speed up those drilling and mining permits. Can we cut the approval process in half? Double the number of permits? I'm anticipating a very good year."

"I'll talk to them when we return. Find out what we need to move those along. I'm sure we can trim off some of the bureaucracy." He winked at Doug.

"Here's to some challenging golf, a little polo, and fun after dark," Doug said, toasting.

They laughed together as the plane began to taxi. "I had my chef fly in some prime Argentinian steaks so you can preview the upcoming pleasures. Then we need to discuss how to handle the other issue on my agenda that's been causing me headaches. I'm sure you'll have some ideas by the time we return."

When the plane arrived in Buenos Aires, Doug was rested from a solid six hours of sleep in his onboard master bedroom and had already showered, shaved and was ready for a full day. He had a car and a driver waiting to transport them the forty minutes to the Alvear Palace Hotel in the Recoleta neighborhood. His usual suite and those for his guests were already arranged, including private butlers who would unpack their luggage—except for the leather gym bag he kept close. No one would be unpacking that.

When they arrived at the stately Belle Époque style hotel, their luggage was whisked inside by the staff and the reception desk had their keys waiting for them. Moments later, Doug was in his suite on the top floor. His guests had suites on the floor below him.

Doug looked over the platter of homemade pastries and

fresh fruit his usual butler had set out for his arrival. He selected a *medialuna rellena* stuffed with creamy chocolate from the silver platter and poured himself coffee into a china cup. Reaching into his pants pocket, he pulled out a blue pill and swallowed it with the coffee. On the glass-topped desk he found a set of car keys atop a rental car folder, with a Post-it note describing where it was parked. He smiled. The receipt showed the charge was billed to his butler's credit card, as per usual, which he would reimburse in cash along with a hefty tip. Doug appreciated the way his butler kept everything discreet.

Stepping into the bathroom, Doug lifted the fresh flowers from the vase on the counter and slipped them into a clear plastic bag his butler had left for them next to the sink. Then he picked up the gym bag and set off for the car, certain his guests could occupy themselves for a few hours.

A block away at the Plaza San Martín de Tours, his rental car was parked in front of a café on the corner. He hopped in and cranked up the air conditioning, thinking how hot it was for November. Must be an early summer.

Driving in Buenos Aires was a challenge, but Doug's pulse sped up as he readied for the adventure. Cars cut him off. He blew by others getting in his way, adrenaline pumping through his veins. He'd always imagined being a race car driver and loved the competition with other cars. Unlike in the U.S., drivers here had no fear, just like him. For a moment, he wished he'd rented something sportier than a Camry, but he didn't want to attract attention.

It took him only a half hour to arrive in Martínez. *Almost a personal record*, he thought, breathing deeply with satisfaction. On the one-way street, he pulled into a parking spot in front of a two-story gated brick house. With the bouquet in his hand and the gym bag over his shoulder, Doug tapped an access code onto the security panel. The gate clicked and he entered.

The property was perfectly manicured as always. A patch of ground cover filled a bed edged in brick, and a three-foot-high statue of Buddha sat serenely between two potted plants. He imagined Elena doing her yoga and smiled.

Before he knocked, the front door opened and the Italian beauty he still found gorgeous at fifty-four stood before him. He'd never believed it possible. She was almost timeless, maintaining herself like a woman half her age. It pleased him immensely.

Elena gave him a broad smile as he handed her the flowers. He admired her wavy dark hair caressing her shoulders and her trim shapely body. In particular, he loved the aura of sophistication she always displayed in her elegant choice of clothing, confident posture, and eye for detail. She arranged the flowers in an empty vase of water sitting on a polished wood table in the foyer. It pleased him that she knew he'd bring them, that she counted on him treating her well. Setting the gym bag on the floor, he wrapped his arms around her, and she pushed up against him. Her kiss stirred his inner teenager who was starving for her body.

"I missed you," she whispered into his ear, flicking her tongue on his earlobe.

"Elena, my love, I miss you every day." A familiar pang of regret ached in his chest. In another lifetime Doug might have married her, but he'd already been married to the woman whose family dominated the oil industry. There was no giving that up.

Smiling, Elena walked him out to the patio where they sat on a wicker sofa by the pool. On her side table, she placed ice cubes into two glasses, filled them half with Fernet-Branca, and covered the drink with Coke until the top frothed. By throwing one more ice cube in each glass, she tamped it down.

"Welcome home." She handed Doug his glass.

The drink tasted like home—like Elena. He leaned over and inhaled her scent. *Coconut.* And another aroma which was distinctly her. His thoughts blurred as desire coursed through his body.

"I thought we would go for a swim." She removed her sundress and tossed it over the back of the seat. Underneath she was naked and perfect.

As he pulled off his clothes, she dove in and emerged halfway across the water. He watched her sweep the hair off her face, then cup her hands under her breasts so her nipples rested above the waterline. Tilting her head down, she gazed up at him with a coy smile. The blue pill worked its magic before he dove in after her.

"Our son called," Elena said as Doug sat on the bed putting on his shoes. "He needs to talk to you. I told him I would make sure you called him."

Doug never liked it when she called him "our son." It made him feel like he owed the man something or should experience some connection that eluded him. Now that their son was an adult, Doug was glad he was no longer around when he visited. Children were not his thing, but it mattered to Elena, so it had to matter to him.

His legal son, Doug Jr., who worked in his business, was a different story. Without an heir to take over the family dynasty, his in-laws might not have let Doug take control. Heaven forbid if they ever found out Doug Jr. had a bastard half-brother.

His fingers tapped on the table next to the bed. "I don't have time to talk to him now. I have a tee time with my guests. Give me the number. I'll call when I'm back in the states."

She dropped a new iPhone into his lap. "It is an Argentine phone. He has one too, as do I. Just use it to call him and me, and we can use it to call you. No one will spy on you because no one cares about two Argentines speaking to one another. Complete privacy."

Doug looked at the phone. She's smart, this one, he thought. He liked that about her. Usually. Not that he was crazy about either of them being able to reach him any time, but it was a good way for them to talk without anyone knowing. He slid the phone in his pants pocket and pulled her onto his lap.

"You have a solution for everything, don't you? I promise I will call him on Wednesday morning, when I'm back."

"I will know if you do not." She glared at him with accusing eyes.

"Okay. I'll call. But not now." He kissed the top of her nose.

Across from him on top of the dresser, he studied their son's graduation photo from St. George's College North, the private, bilingual, day school a few miles away which Doug had paid for. He couldn't have his son speak like some street urchin. The kid spoke fluent English now and blended right in when he moved to the U.S. for college. Elena must realize how much he'd done for their son—made sure he understood discipline too, like Doug's father did. Made him tough. A boy needed that, so he didn't become some disgusting namby-pamby like Doug Jr., whom he'd left to his wife to mold.

"I put his number in your contacts, so you have it." Elena jumped up off his lap. "Will I see you for dinner while you are here?"

"I'm saving Sunday night for you. Wear something elegant."

Her smile returned.

At the door she gave him a slow goodbye kiss, pinching him on the butt as she did. He jumped and let out a laugh.

"Goodbye, darling. I'll dream of you tonight," she said as he turned to go, leaving her the gym bag full of cash.

CHAPTER FIVE

HUNTING

DAYLIGHT APPEARED THROUGH the blinds of Anita's room at the Howard Street Bed and Breakfast. After watching the news, her churning stomach kept her awake, fearing for Julian and missing Steven. Now she chastised herself for wasting hours dwelling on her anger and grief. She opened the blinds, encouraged by the sunshine streaming through the window.

In the past, she'd been skilled at tuning out what was bothering her and focusing on solving problems—using her business sense, she'd call it. That's what she had to do now: figure out how to find and help Julian. Since the police had released him, she had no idea where to start looking. She wanted to crawl back into bed and bury her face in her pillow, a luxury she didn't have. Instead, she opened the list of email addresses and started to formulate a plan.

"Be cautious," he'd said.

That didn't bode well. It suggested those on the list may not be trustworthy.

It was Julian's laptop she'd asked Stacey to retrieve. She'd tried accessing it once last year, curious if he was hiding anything from her and to learn about his life, since he never spoke to her. It was password protected and none of her guesses worked. It wouldn't offer her any clues now either, but she didn't want whoever held him to find it if they searched their house.

Anita had rarely used a computer since Steven's death and no longer owned one. Social media, the news, almost anything could trigger her grief to erupt. Stacey let Anita use hers when necessary. Her phone provided everything else important—her photos of Steven, his emails and text messages, and his voice messages when she needed to hear his voice. Now her phone was gone, but she still had her Google account. She didn't dare log in, but hopefully she'd be able to recover her messages on a new phone, once this problem with Julian was resolved. A deep ache tightened in her chest at the thought of losing Steven's voicemails forever.

For now, to contact Julian's list of email addresses, Anita would need a new account on a different computer. During her years as the founder and owner of her information technology consulting firm, with clients across agencies throughout Washington, D.C., she'd learned logging into Google was too easily traced. Her consultants wrote some of the tracing and blocking code that security agencies use now. She wondered who else might have this type of access.

The smell of coffee drifted up from the kitchen, enticing her to venture downstairs, but first she needed to shower off her sleep-deprived night. Anita grabbed her towel from the rack at the back of her door and peeked down the hall. The bathroom door was open.

An hour later, as Anita sipped coffee and read Paul's newspaper at the kitchen table, he stood at the stove cooking scrambled eggs and home fries. Since she was the only guest for breakfast, she'd asked to sit in the homey kitchen, rather than the dining room. Its cooking smells and blue gingham tablecloth gave her comfort. Sliced fruit, buttered toast, and two small bowls, one containing marmalade and the other strawberry jam, graced the table. A coffee pot remained on the counter for refills.

Paul cooking breakfast gave her a tinge of nostalgia. Julian had often cooked breakfast for her and Steven on the weekends. During the week, she hustled off to her company headquarters in Rockville, Maryland before anyone was awake, before working from home became an option. Julian taught at Gettysburg College near where they lived, so he had time to handle the morning routine, including getting Steven ready for daycare or school when he was little. Because Julian could always be there for Steven, it allowed her to take advantage of lucrative federal contracts and build her business into a formidable player around The Beltway. Her consultants had sterling reputations when it came to computer applications and security for those applications.

"Do you know Newport?" Paul scooped the eggs and home fries onto a plate and placed them in front of her. "I can help you out if you need any suggestions on restaurants or what to do while you're in town. I've only run the bed and breakfast for two years, but this was my summer house for twelve years before that."

Anita had no plans to venture out around Newport, but she wanted to learn more about him, to figure out where he fit in this puzzle, so she closed the newspaper. "What did you do before you ran this B and B?"

"I was a research scientist. Worked at a company down in Philly. It was shut down so there didn't seem to be a reason to hang around. It wasn't like anything else in my field was going to open up, so I came here to open the bed and breakfast. I was going to do this after I retired anyhow. I just started sooner."

She was afraid to ask if he knew Julian, since she needed to figure out if he was trustworthy. She stared at him, searching his face for a clue, but his expression was unassuming.

"What field?" Several companies around Philadelphia had closed because the current administration defunded green technology research, so she took a guess. "Energy?"

Paul pulled out the chair across from her and sat, nodding. "Yep. Photoelectrochemical water splitting. Ever hear of it?"

"Vaguely. I thought it was pie in the sky. The perfect solution in the far-off future."

"That's what a lot of people thought, so not many were working on it. But we had funding and were making tremendous progress."

"Can you explain how it works?" Anita asked, both curious and hoping for a clue about his stance on climate issues.

"In simple terms, we were capturing solar energy using proprietary equipment we created to split the chemical bonds in water molecules into hydrogen and oxygen atoms. In a cost-effective manner, too. They've done it for years using electricity, but it's expensive. This way, the hydrogen becomes fuel without generating any carbon. It can power vehicles, even ships and jets. We can make it anywhere with a water source. We were on the verge of seeking a patent when the funding was cut."

She leaned back in her chair. If this was true, if their research was solid, it could be world changing. "Impressive," she said, but her inner skeptic waited for the catch.

"Basically, we'd be able to wean ourselves off oil."

Anita remembered hearing the government was cutting funding for green technology research, using the justification that government should not favor one type of private development over another. She'd been in a daze of grief and hadn't paid much attention. Now, while Paul sat across the table from her explaining the loss in concrete terms, a flush of shame crept up her chest, realizing how much she'd ignored.

"So this knowledge goes to waste while you stand here cooking me eggs and home fries. I mean, it's not like we have all the time in the world to devise new energy solutions."

Paul shrugged and stood up. "It sucks alright." The frying pan sizzled as he ran water into it and scrubbed.

Anita resumed eating. Paul shut off the water and picked up a dish towel.

"Do you have a computer here I can use?" she asked.

He frowned. "What do you want to use it for?"

"I just need to send some emails. I left my laptop at home."

He hesitated and she tried to interpret the frown. Maybe she sounded suspicious. Maybe he was hiding something.

Finally, he spoke.

"I was in the middle of my accounting when I came up to

make breakfast but give me about an hour and you can use it. I'll create a guest account."

❧

Paul returned to the kitchen where Anita was still reading the newspaper. "I have the computer ready for you in my office."

She followed him down the stairs into the basement. A small room was partitioned off where a computer and a printer sat on a desk against the outside concrete wall. The room was lined with shelves that contained cans of paint and brushes, various tools, jars of nuts and bolts, and pieces of sandpaper in a pile. Along the floor was a bicycle pump, a couple of folded beach chairs in bags, and a Shop-Vac with attachments. A swiveling office chair was under the desk.

"It's all yours. The guest account login and password are on the Post-it note."

After verifying she had access, Anita thanked him, and he left.

Since Anita's company's clients had largely been government agencies, she'd discovered how little privacy a citizen has when someone investigates you. If you needed to hide, you had to be smart about communication.

First, she set up a Proton Mail account, which was still considered one of the best in secure, untraceable email. Next, she wrote cryptic messages to each of the addresses on Julian's email list, hoping whoever received them could decipher them.

"Hi old friend," she typed. "It's been a while since we talked. I'd like to connect and reminisce over old photos from our hike in the Alps. Our mutual friend Jay Eff has dropped out of the scene, and I need to help him become engaged again. Are you interested?"

Was Jay Eff recognizable as J. F., aka Julian Forester? She assumed all these people were connected to Julian and they would understand who she was referring to.

She made a note on her list and continued.

In the next one she wrote "Hey amigo!! I'm catching up with folks I haven't talked with lately. Remember the time you, me and Jay Eff got ourselves lost in the woods? We should do it again if I can drag him away from whatever is keeping him occupied these days. How about it?"

Maybe these were too ambiguous. They might think she was emailing the wrong person and delete it.

One of the emails bounced back immediately, notifying her the address wasn't found. Anita double-checked the spelling and was disappointed when she had to cross it off. The other nine didn't receive error notifications.

Once she was done, she cleaned her search history data from the computer so Paul wouldn't see what site she had visited and logged out.

CHAPTER SIX

MIKE

Anita pressed her palms to her forehead, trying to ease the growing headache. She'd slept a little during the afternoon but wasn't refreshed. Now, back at Paul's computer, she had only two email replies.

"I think I can help," read one of them. "Can we meet in Boston to talk? Tomorrow around lunchtime?"

The other email asked for more information, but she didn't dare provide anything without knowing who sent it. She replied, asking the sender for proof they were trustworthy.

She'd always prided herself on being decisive, which served her well in business, but her decision about her next steps might endanger her and Julian. Her head pounded with worry as she thought about trusting this stranger in Boston, but she had no one else. At least one of them had offered to help.

Julian had admired her risk tolerance, and wished he was more courageous. Now her cautious, level-headed husband had put them both in danger, and she wondered why. It had to be something those buddies of his at American University got him involved with. Maybe some of those emails went to them. But surely the guy with the bushy beard knew what was going on, and he wouldn't tell her.

As she stared at the computer screen, Paul stepped into his office behind her.

"Bad news?"

She jumped at his voice and shut off the screen before turning around, wondering what he might have seen. "I'm worried about a friend of mine. I haven't been able to call her since I lost my phone. And she's not answering emails."

"You can borrow my mobile if you want."

"If she doesn't answer, can I ask her to call me back on it?"

"Sure. I'm going to be around the house most of today, so it shouldn't be a problem." He handed her his phone as he turned to leave. "I'll give you some privacy."

She punched in the number expecting Stacey wouldn't answer again, but she did. "I borrowed a phone so I can't talk long."

"Thank goodness. I've been so worried about you. And about . . ."

"Stop. Let's just say "him." No names." She guessed Stacey's number was also on Julian's contact list, although he never called her.

"Of course. What's going on?"

Anita hugged the phone to her ear. Talking to Stacey was both comforting and frightening, as she feared whoever had Julian might be tapping Stacey's phone.

"I'm safe for now. Have you googled him? I'm afraid to."

"I have. There's nothing about him in connection with yesterday's event. I drove by your house. It looks empty. Maybe he's hiding out, too."

For a moment, a flash of hope hit her, but it didn't seem likely since that man had his phone. "I'm going to send you a new email address for me. Use it if you find anything at all. No names. Make it look casual."

"I'm on it. Please be careful."

"Thanks. I love you dearly. Don't call me on this number though. It belongs to the owner of the place I'm staying. I'll notify you when I have a new one."

"I'll be thinking of you."

Speaking with Stacey lifted the heaviness from Anita's chest. Just knowing she cared gave her the boost she needed to keep going.

❧

Anita found Paul sitting on the leather couch in the living room, watching football. She mouthed the words *thank you* when he glanced over and put his phone on the glass coffee table next to his soda. His attention to the giant screen resumed, but Anita didn't move.

After a couple of more glances her way, he hit the mute button. "What can I do for you?"

"Can I pay you to drive me to Boston tomorrow around lunchtime? I need to meet someone, and I forgot my car charger. That's the downside of these all-electric vehicles."

Smiling, she hoped she looked casual and honest. In reality, her charger was in the trunk, but she didn't want her license plate to show up on a police camera.

"In fact, I'm going to bring my suitcase too. If all goes well, I'll be staying in Boston for a day or two. I'll pay you before I go just in case. But I'll be back for my car."

Paul's eyes narrowed as he studied her face. "You're very forgetful, aren't you?"

Anxiety stabbed her in the chest. He was getting suspicious. "It's been a difficult time for me. Family problems." Perhaps her reply would garner sympathy and prevent him from prying further. Besides, it was the truth.

"I can spare a few hours to help you out. Just fill up my gas tank."

"That's very kind of you, Paul." The tightness in her chest relaxed.

◆

With its high-end shops and restaurants lining both sides of the road, Newberry Street in Boston was the ideal place for Anita to meet her email contact. Lots of witnesses would be around if he tried anything.

Be cautious. Julian's words kept running through her head. The headache was returning, despite finally sleeping last night.

Paul left his car in the parking garage with her suitcase in the trunk. He would wander around some bookstores and a few shops until he heard from her. They'd stopped at a Walmart on the way there, where she'd picked up a prepaid phone and stored Paul's number, along with that of her contact.

Corey's Bar and Grille was a popular spot for people-watching due to its huge L-shaped bar along the street. The sliding glass windows were open today because of the good weather. While it was too warm for November, having sunshine following the lengthy storm was invigorating. Anita took a seat next to an empty barstool where she placed her jacket, then ordered herself a chardonnay and an IPA for the empty chair. She texted her contact:

At the bar by the street. Got you a barstool and a beer.

A man wearing a Red Sox hoodie and jeans approached her, pulled out the barstool next to her, and took a seat. With wavy dark hair and hazel eyes, he was much younger than she was, but not as young as her son would have been. Thirty-something probably. He scanned her like he was evaluating her attractiveness, making her uneasy. Some men were like that, always focused on a woman's body as if their intelligence were irrelevant. Right away, she disliked that about him.

"Hi. I'm Janice."

"Nice to meet you. I'm Mike. Thanks for the beer." He raised it toward her like a toast. "How'd you know my brand?" His laugh sounded like he was flirting, and a knot formed in her stomach.

Had he misunderstood what she was hinting at in her email? Maybe he thought this was a hookup. Or perhaps he was pretending to flirt as a cover for his real reason to be here. He spoke with an odd accent, almost English, but not quite. She couldn't place it.

"Tell me about Jay Eff," he said.

Anita wanted to trust him. She had no one else to help her find Julian yet. One of these other emails might produce results, but she couldn't count on it.

"I haven't heard from him since Friday. After being arrested at a protest at the Capitol in Washington, D.C., the police said he was given a summons and released. Meanwhile, someone called me on his phone asking prying questions, refusing to answer any of mine. JF continues to be missing. He'd given me your email address before this happened, claiming you might be able to help."

She didn't mention the nine other emails on the list.

He leaned his elbow on the bar. "Have you tried calling the police?"

"I told you, they said he was released." She wondered if he was as dumb as he sounded. Or maybe he was testing her.

"Yeah. Cops aren't very helpful in this type of situation."

"What type of situation is this?" Her eyes narrowed as she stared at him, wondering what he was inferring. He glanced outside for a beat before turning back to her.

"I'm just guessing right now, but if I'm right, I'm the guy you're looking for. But I need more details about him and you." An arrogant smile stretched thinly across his lips. It made her cringe, but she kept a straight face, hiding her dislike of him.

Anita wrapped her fingers around the wine glass, tempted to drink by a need to calm herself. After a gulp, she followed it with a sip of water. She needed to relax, but not here. Not now.

Mike leaned over closer and spoke into her ear. "I think we need to leave here and go to a private place where you're willing to talk about Jay. I can't help you if you don't tell me everything."

That made sense, but she didn't want to be alone with this guy. Being in public felt safer. "Based on my email, what do you think I'm asking you to do?"

He pushed back his barstool and examined her, tilting his head to the side. After a moment, he leaned in close again. "I'm guessing you want me to free Jay after we figure out who is holding him. He's your husband? Boyfriend? Do you know where he is?"

That was exactly what she needed, and it sounded like he was offering to help. Apparently, he believed someone was holding him. As she weighed her reply, she looked at the bartender, who was rattling a cocktail shaker in front of three empty martini glasses lined up. Telling Mike her story was a risk she had to take.

"He disappeared near D.C., so I'm assuming he's there. I was warned to hide. I can pay you, but I need to lay low. I don't want to go back to D.C. right now."

A hint of a smile showed on Mike's face, like he'd tricked her into admitting something she shouldn't have. Her stomach muscles clenched together. This was wrong. Her gut told her. Reaching into her pocketbook, she pulled out a pair of twenty-dollar bills and placed them on the bar.

"Never mind." She pushed back her barstool and snatched her jacket.

Before she could leave, Mike grabbed her wrist and she winced. It hurt enough that she worried he would break it and she stifled a cry. He pulled her toward him as he rose, gripping her arm with both his hands as he spoke into her ear.

"You aren't about to cause a scene or yell for the cops," he muttered. "You and I need to go to my place. We have things to discuss."

Anita clung to her jacket as he roughly escorted her out the door. He was right. She couldn't draw any attention or alert the police. She'd basically told him as much herself.

Stupid me.

Her legs shook as they stumbled onto the sidewalk. When

she spotted Paul walking in their direction on the other side of the road, she considered screaming for him, but feared what Mike would do if he didn't respond. Paul looked her way so she hung back, hoping he would recognize she was in trouble. Mike needed to yank her arm to move her. Paul turned abruptly into the parking garage where he had left his car.

Please don't leave, Anita thought desperately, her heart pounding.

"Don't make it worse for yourself." Mike twisted her wrist enough to make her yelp. "I will drag you down the street if I have to, bitch."

She shuffled beside him until Paul's car appeared leaving the garage, turning onto the one-way street, and passing them. At the sound of his brakes behind her, she twisted her head and watched him fly out of the car with a tire iron, leaving the driver's side door open. He whacked the back of Mike's legs, causing him to stumble forward. As he fell, Anita slipped from his grasp and raced behind Paul to the car. Glancing back, she saw Mike catch himself on one knee. Paul was already in the driver's seat as Anita jumped in, accelerating before she shut her door. She spun around in time to witness Mike holding up his phone like he was taking a photo of their car. Paul tore down Newbury Street, but Anita feared it was already too late—if Mike took a photo, he would have Paul's license plate and be able to find them.

CHAPTER SEVEN

QUESTIONS

"**Y**OU WANT TO tell me what's going on here?" Paul shouted as they merged onto the interstate. "I just assaulted a guy in the middle of Newbury Street. Who the hell are you and what just happened?"

Anita's heart was pounding, and she shivered, the shock hitting her. She pulled her jacket up around her shoulders. *If Paul hadn't come along . . .* Images flashed through her head from assault to murder, to being handed over to the same people who held Julian.

"Well?" Paul's face flushed as his voice boomed.

"I'm sorry. Sorry I got you into this. This guy I was meeting was a stranger. I thought he was going to help me."

"Help you with what? Who are you running from? It's obvious you left home in one damn hurry." He alternated between checking his rearview mirror and glancing over at her.

"Can I trust you?"

"Whoa. Can *you* trust *me*? You have some explaining to do, and I want the truth. Otherwise, get out of this car right now!"

"Okay, okay." She had to take her chances with Paul—he was clearly a better choice than Mike at this point. If she could convince him to help her . . . After all, his work had been in green technology. Surely they shared similar values. She explained as briefly as possible about Julian's protest, arrest, disappearance and her fleeing.

When she was done, Paul nodded. "That's scary. What a gutsy guy."

Something loosened in Anita at this. "I guess so. I think he wanted to rally people in this country who care about the planet's future. We can't keep pretending . . ." Her voice cracked as she spoke, wondering if this had motivated Julian, why he'd risked everything without telling her. She turned toward the window so Paul wouldn't see her tears. Leaning her head against the glass, she jumped when Paul's hand touched her shoulder.

"Sorry." He pulled away. "I didn't mean to startle you. I just want you to know I completely agree with him."

Her eyes closed and she took a deep breath, grateful he understood.

"So why were you meeting this guy? How was he going to help you?"

She winced a little before answering. "My husband gave me a list of email addresses before the protest and told me to use them if anything happened to him. That guy, Mike, responded to one. I thought maybe he could find Julian. Rescue him." She studied him as he stayed focused on the road. "Why did you help me?"

He gave her a sideways glance. "My sister had an abusive boyfriend, and I—I wasn't there to help her. I've always regretted it."

"Thank you." Knowing Paul was a man with a conscience reinforced her sense of safety.

"You're welcome. Where was he taking you?"

"His place, he claimed. Said we needed to talk. Called me a bitch and threatened to drag me down the street." She took a moment to think, then blurted, "Why would he be on this list?"

"Well, maybe he's just a hired gun. Wouldn't someone like that be sleazy?"

Realizing he might be right was distressing. She rubbed her temples with the thumb and forefinger of one hand as she thought. Mike might be the sort of person she'd be stuck dealing with to locate Julian.

"If he's a slimeball, he probably has my license plate now. And he's pissed." Paul let out a deep sigh. "Hopefully this doesn't come back to bite me."

"I certainly hope not." Guilt washed over Anita for putting him at risk. "At least he doesn't know who I am or who I'm looking for. I gave him a fake name." As she said it, she realized Paul still only had her fake name. She cleared her throat. "My real name is Anita."

"Anita. Okay." His eyes narrowed as he stared straight ahead at the road. "What else did you lie about?" His face began to flush again, while heat rose in her own cheeks.

"I'm trying to protect myself. I don't know who's safe and who isn't." If Mike had proved anything, it was that she was probably being smart by being so careful.

A sign ahead indicated the exit for I-95 South, which would take them back to Newport, but Paul drove past it.

She stiffened. "Missed the turn for Newport."

"No. I didn't."

The next question scared her. "Where are we going?"

His face softened, and he no longer appeared angry. "If you're right about Mike, going back to Newport probably isn't safe. He can find my address from the license plate. A better place for you to hide is in Vermont."

Relief washed over her. "What's in Vermont?"

"My daughter. She's a climate activist, too."

⁂

A few hours later, Mike Rossi pulled over in front of the Howard Street Bed and Breakfast in Newport. Only one car was in the driveway, and it had no visible plate from the road. He stepped out of his BMW, took a picture of the house, and threw his backpack over his shoulder. At the front door, he rang the bell several times.

When no one answered, he walked around to the side of the building and up the driveway, first stopping at the car, where he leaned behind it and took a picture of the Pennsylvania license plate.

The back door had a window looking into an unoccupied kitchen. If they weren't here by now, he figured they weren't likely to return. They'd left Boston hours before he did.

Reaching into his backpack, Mike pulled out a tension wrench and rake, inserted them into the lock and worked it until he felt the pins shift. With a twist, he entered.

To the right of the kitchen were stairs leading to the

basement, where he started his search for information about Paul Tanner. If he could locate this so-called "Janice" and figure out who her husband was, there may be money in it for him. He suspected whom she was hiding from, and if it was true, he could cash in on capturing her. Since Paul Tanner was helping her, finding him would find her.

She'd emailed a climate activist's account that Mike had hacked. By turning over that guy, he'd collected a nice bounty, and "Janice" would probably pay off too. Snatching these eco-freaks was easy money. With any luck, Paul Tanner would have interesting skeletons as well, but neither of them had shown up in his client's database.

At the bottom of the basement stairs, Mike stepped into a small room on the left. It looked like a cross between an office and a collection of junk for maintaining a house. On the desk was a computer—his favorite place to investigate. His computer science major was endlessly useful for working as a private investigator.

After inserting a thumb drive into the computer's USB port, he rebooted the machine, overriding the login security. He plugged a portable hard drive from his backpack into another USB port and copied the computer's hard drive. While it uploaded, he dug through the shelves and rifled through the desk drawers, finding nothing but folders filled with details of home improvements.

Once he finished with the basement, he stashed his hard drive in his backpack and walked up to the first floor. In the hallway was an antique credenza topped with tourist brochures and restaurant menus. He was about to walk away when he spotted two business card holders sitting side by side – one set of cards for the Howard Street Bed and Breakfast, the other for the Deer Run Inn in Stowe, Vermont. He picked up one of each and slid them into his pocket.

The second floor went quickly since none of the rooms were occupied. When he reached the bedroom on the third floor, the only room containing personal belongings, he assumed it must be Paul's.

He combed through the places where people typically hide stuff: shoes, underwear drawer, jacket pockets, beneath the dresser. Reaching between the mattress and the box spring, he worked his way around the bed until he hit a hard plastic rectangular object. When he pulled out a black hard drive, a rush of excitement made him a little high.

"Fucking amateur." He fist-pumped the air. Hidden hard drives often held profitable files, usually financial accounts for him to hack.

Along with the hard drive, Mike found checkbooks, but the entries were boring and the balance pitiful. He took a photo of the bank account numbers, throwing them on top of the bed for Paul Tanner to find when he returned. That fucker screwed up his day. No one was going to smack him with a tire iron and get away with it. Not anymore.

His hamstrings still stung but not as bad as when he was a kid. Not like when his father pulled out the belt.

CHAPTER EIGHT

ANSWERS

THE DRIVE ON Route 100 in Vermont wound through several ski towns and along scenic vistas. A few weeks earlier, the trees would have been glorious with red and gold leaves. Now any leaves still clinging to the branches were brown, but most had blown off.

Anita had been to Killington a few times when she, Julian, and Steven had skied together over winter vacations. The familiar storefronts around Ludlow and the views of Echo Lake caused Anita's chest to grow heavy—those happy times were gone forever. She longed for a return to the empty numbness defining her recent life, where she was able to shut off the pain of losing Steven by suppressing all her emotions. The shock of losing Julian and fleeing her home had ripped those wounds open again.

"What's on your mind?" Paul asked after a long quiet stretch.

Anita straightened up in her seat, glad to drag herself out of the past. "Just memories. Nothing worth discussing. Tell me about you. Are you divorced? Widowed?"

Paul laughed. "Neither. Although it's a little like both."

Anita nodded. This described her relationship with Julian before his disappearance.

"Nope. I'm still married. But my wife stayed in Philadelphia when I moved to Newport. She's got a big job at a law firm she loves. Does pro bono work defending homeless people, too. I mean, how can she leave all that to live in a bed and breakfast, washing sheets, and recommending restaurants? I understand. I wouldn't have left my work either if it hadn't left me."

"Do you see each other?"

"More at the beginning. Occasionally now. It's weird when I go visit her. I hardly know her anymore. And she seems perfectly happy." He glanced over at Anita, seemingly chagrined, a blush working its way up his face.

"Sounds a lot like my marriage, only we still live in the same house . . . lived."

Paul raised his eyebrows. "I used to be just like my wife at work. I couldn't wait to dig into my research. In fact, a lot of times I forgot to leave. When they closed us down, I was . . . angry."

"I don't blame you. My job ended much better. I sold my business and ended up with a nice retirement nest egg. I thought we were set for life."

She took a deep breath before continuing. No matter how many times she said this, each time was a collapse into hell. "Then our son was killed in a wildfire in California."

As Paul turned to look at her, his car drifted across the

divider. A pickup rounded the corner in the opposite lane, swerving away as it laid on the horn. Anita braced her hand against the dashboard and shrieked. Paul jerked the car back into his own lane. Once the vehicle was under control, he peeked in her direction again.

"Damn. Sorry about that."

Anita let go of the dashboard and exhaled. "I'll be careful not to distract you again."

"I'm sorry. You made me think of my daughter. I can't even imagine this." He slowly shook his head.

"No. You can't. I certainly never did." She resumed gazing out the window and their conversation ceased.

When they reached the center of Stowe village, Paul turned toward Mount Mansfield, driving uphill through a valley flanked by ski lodges and restaurants. After a few miles, he took a winding side road through the woods, until he turned into a driveway. A wooden sign marked the property. Deer Run Inn was embossed in black lettering over a painting of a deer leaping through a forest.

Three other cars were parked in the driveway of the white, two-story, rambling farmhouse. It had a long porch across the front. Four Adirondack chairs draped with plaid blankets faced the valley. As Paul stepped out of the car, a pale young woman in a flannel shirt and jeans burst from the front door and ran along the porch and down the steps.

"Dad. What a surprise."

Once she was in his arms, they hugged for a long moment. When they parted, she leaned over to look in the window at Anita, then stood again and turned to her father with her head cocked.

Paul beckoned for Anita to join them. Her face flushed with embarrassment. *I hope she doesn't think I'm someone he's seeing.* Stepping out of the car, she forced a smile.

"Caitlin, I want you to meet Anita. She needs our help. She's a climate defender and she's in trouble."

Caitlin frowned and gave him a questioning look. "Let's go inside and you can tell me about it."

Inside the house, they took seats together at a large pine table while Caitlin filled three mugs with coffee.

"It's fresh. I made a new pot for the guests who should be returning from hiking soon." She placed the mugs on the table and sat. "So. What's going on?"

Anita described the events leading up to her landing at Paul's B&B. Then Paul recounted their interaction with Mike.

"What if he went to your house?" Caitlin asked after he'd mentioned the man probably took a photo of his plate.

Paul stiffened. "He's after Anita, not me. That's why I brought her here, where she'd be safe."

"You're not worried he may retaliate against you for hitting him?"

He sighed. "I guess it's a risk."

The front door opened, and a woman around Caitlin's age entered, followed by two couples, all carrying walking sticks, their cheeks flushed from the outdoors. The woman leading was tall with straight, dark hair, light brown skin, and high cheekbones. She approached Paul and gave him a kiss on the cheek.

"Hi, Dad," she said.

"Hi, dear," he replied. Her gaze turned to Anita and Caitlin spoke up.

"Odina, this is Dad's friend, Anita. She's a climate activist whose husband disappeared after being arrested at a demonstration in Washington, D.C. Dad brought her here because some creep in Boston is after her."

Turning to Anita, she continued. "Anita, this is my wife, Odina. We run the inn together and she's also a guide for hiking and backcountry ski trips. No one knows these mountains like she does."

Odina grinned and leaned over to shake Anita's hand. "Nice to meet you, Anita. We honor you and your husband for defending our planet and causing good trouble. Our inn is a sanctuary for free speech and all those who respect the spirits of the natural world. They can lock me up for saying it, but I won't shut up."

Anita's head tilted as she wondered what she was talking about. Lock her up? Why would someone lock her up for what she was saying?

The two couples standing behind her smiled and nodded. One of the women gave a thumbs up and said, "You tell 'em, Odina."

"Easy for you Canadians to say," Caitlin said. "Actually, can you guys excuse us awhile, until we sort this out?"

"Sure. Let us know if we can help." They left the great room.

Odina took a seat and explained. "Our inn attracts visitors from Montreal who go back and forth to Stowe for skiing and hiking. That's been a useful cover over the last three years for the other work we do. Since Canada has largely abstained from this anti-climate nonsense, it's a safe haven for American activists and climate scientists at risk of being detained. Those people you just met are our Canadian colleagues. They bring us fake passports so we can smuggle people into Canada. We all have a little fun together while they're here."

"I don't understand," Anita said. "What do you mean by detained? Arrested? Imprisoned?"

Odina frowned. "You don't know? I thought you knew because of your husband."

Anita's heartbeat sped up. "All I know is he's missing. Someone has his phone, and I was warned to hide. I have no idea what happened to him. Do you?"

Caitlin sat down next to Odina who raised an eyebrow at her while Caitlin's eyes narrowed. After a moment, Odina crossed her arms and leaned back in her chair.

"Leaders of demonstrations and some climate scientists have been disappearing. Not everyone who gets arrested, but some of the organizers, especially outspoken ones. Just a few people here and there, but enough to damage the momentum. It sounds like this is what happened to your husband. If so, he's locked up somewhere with others like him."

Anita's breathing grew shallow. "Where? How do I get him out?"

"I hate to tell you this, but you don't. We aren't exactly sure where they keep them. It's not public knowledge. When someone's on the shutdown list, we try to sneak them out of the country if they come to us. Into Canada. So, if you need to hide from them, we can help you."

Anita's mouth fell open as she tried to digest this news that her husband was locked up somewhere because of protesting. And she had no way of getting him out.

"What's the shutdown list? Who created it?"

Odina shook her head. "We've only heard about it, so we have no idea who's on it, or who's behind it. But apparently, if you're on it, they hunt you down and lock you away. You find out you're on it when they come after you."

Anita's mind was spinning. Was she on this list? If so, Julian must be responsible. She wondered what else he'd been up to besides waving a flag. That didn't seem like enough to label him as a leader.

Odina leaned forward, putting her elbows on the table. "I'd guess you're on it. We can get you into Canada under a new name. We do it all the time."

Anita was struck by this generous offer. "Except I need to find my husband and I don't know if I can from Canada."

Anita explained how Mike was an email contact she'd been given by her husband. "I don't understand why he was on this list of people who might help me."

"We're pretty sure he got Dad's license plate, so he may have searched the inn," Caitlin said.

"Even if he did, I doubt he'd find my hard drive," Paul said. "That's the only important property I own. If he robs me, I have insurance for everything else."

"What's on it?" Odina asked.

"All Dad's research from the lab," Caitlin said.

Paul cleared his throat and folded his hands on the table, looking across at Caitlin. "That's not quite all."

She glared at him. "What else?"

He sat back in his chair and shoved his hands in his pockets. "I downloaded all the relevant data from the cloud at the lab two weeks before they closed us up. I saw this coming. I got all the specs, test results, blueprints, everything about the prototype we were developing. We were so close. I had to preserve it."

Anita became light-headed imagining the implications of something so important on a hard drive in his house. In her experience, you backed up important data multiple times across multiple platforms. Why was this the only version?

Caitlin's eyes widened, and she lunged forward in her chair. "Are you shitting me? How could you be so careless?" Jumping up, she pushed her chair back and paced across the room. Odina's eyes followed her as she squeezed her lips together and shook her head.

"Give me one good reason you didn't leave something so important with me when you *knew* the risk if someone came looking for it?"

Paul crossed his arms over his chest. "I didn't want to endanger you. Plus, I'm a nobody. They weren't interested in me. You should have seen them. They burst in and said the government owned all our research since they funded it, and they were taking what they paid for. Computers, servers, you name it. Even a couple of our IT security guys. But they never looked twice at me."

Anita was aware the government had defunded climate research, but she didn't know they were confiscating it.

Paul continued. "Anyhow, I figured I can wait until this blows over. As long as I have all the data, I can start the whole process up again. This administration won't last after the next election."

Caitlin stopped pacing and returned to the table, where she leaned over to her father, her voice raw with anger. "No one will be left by then. Do you have any idea how many people have disappeared? Where do you think your former team members are? Have you kept in touch with any of them?"

Paul looked at the floor.

All this new information was overwhelming to Anita. Her mind was spinning with questions and possibilities as she wondered how Julian and his disappearance were connected to this. Not just a disappearance, but he was detained by someone—for being a protest leader. This must be what he was keeping from her. All those meetings at American University with friends were for organizing. That didn't explain why he didn't share that with her. She wouldn't have objected. She might have joined him. Crossing her arms, she ran her hands up and down her biceps to comfort herself, glad to finally have some answers, but frustrated that they offered no help.

Paul's solution to replace fossil fuels went so much farther than simply protesting, however. This might be the change they needed. She'd had no idea she'd walked into a situation that was this serious. If this technology replaced fossil fuels, storms, drought, extreme heat, melting ice caps, even wildfires would decrease. Maybe another mother wouldn't lose her son in a senseless disaster.

The silence was broken when Anita's phone rang, and she jumped.

"It must be Mike. He's the only one who has this number. I think I had better answer it, but don't let him hear any of you."

They nodded in agreement. She turned on speaker phone for everyone to listen.

"Hello, Anita Forester. Your buddy Mike here. Tell that fuck-head Paul Tanner I have the hard drive he thought he hid so well under his mattress."

Caitlyn's hand shot up to cover her mouth as her eyes grew wide. Paul grimaced and dropped his eyes to the floor. Anita forgot to breathe for a beat before she forced herself to sound composed. "You know my name now."

"I do. There's a bounty on your head to deliver you to an interested party. Same party who already has your husband, Julian Forester. Jay Eff, right? What's it worth to you that I don't?"

Anita's heart thumped. Her fears were confirmed. Julian was a captive and they wanted her, too.

"If you know who's holding my husband, I can pay you to rescue him. More than they'll pay for my bounty." Anita's company had sold for a lot of money, but she didn't want to publicize how much.

"Sorry. They're my best client."

Pain wrapped around Anita's head like a tourniquet. Not only did this man have Paul's priceless data, but he knew where her husband was—did business with his captors. Her mind raced as she attempted to think of an option to both keep her safe and retrieve the device.

She forced a deep breath.

"I assume you haven't told your client about me yet? I'll pay you to keep my freedom. What will it cost to forget you met me?"

"You're right. Not yet. I'll ignore the bounty if you pay me a hundred-thousand U.S. dollars in cash by 10:30 Wednesday morning. After that, all bets are off."

A little less than three days. She'd have to make this work. The timing would be tight. She'd need help and her idea would have to work perfectly. "Throw in Paul's hard drive and you have yourself a deal."

Paul's eyebrows raised in surprise.

"Why do you want Paul's hard drive?" Mike asked.

"I don't. But he needs it and I owe him one."

The phone was silent for a beat. Then he spoke.

"Fine. Deal."

Caitlyn grinned and Odina gave her a squeeze.

"Meet me in Boston in front of Corey's Bar and Grill," he said.

Boston was four hours further from Stowe, and the Canadian Border she would need to cross. That added a lot of time she didn't have.

"Can you meet me in the parking lot of the Green Mountain Inn in Stowe, Vermont instead? Wednesday morning at 10:30?"

Everyone in the room was silent, hardly breathing until he spoke.

"Ok. Don't be late for our second date, sweetheart. A man doesn't like to be kept waiting. And don't bring Paul or he'll really be fucked when I'm done with him."

He disconnected.

The others stared at Anita.

"It's all my fault for dragging Paul into this. His data is too important to leave in the hands of that thug. I can buy my freedom and retrieve his hard drive, but I need to fly to Switzerland. Can you help me?"

"Bet your ass we can," Odina said. "But you'll need a different identity. Otherwise, your data will feed back to U.S. databases when you use your passport. You'll need to travel as a Canadian."

CHAPTER NINE

SWITZERLAND

ANITA HELD HER breath as she waited in line for the customs kiosk at the Geneva airport. Her red-eye from Montreal had been turbulent from the remnants of the storm over the northeast, and she'd struggled to sleep. She was haunted by a variety of possible bad endings if she was arrested for traveling with a forged passport. Now the two cups of Air Canada coffee she'd had gave her the jitters.

In her hand she held the forgery—a Canadian passport identifying her as Meghan Beckly, one of the Canadian women who'd been at the inn in Stowe yesterday with her husband Noah. They were the Canadian colleagues who brought Caitlyn and Odina passports. After crossing the border into Canada in the trunk of Noah's car, Noah replaced Meghan's photo with Anita's, without damaging the hologram or special ink. He coached Anita to memorize her new information: birth date, place of birth, full name. Then his colleague provided a replacement RFID chip. The only problem was, Anita needed to look forty-two, like Meghan.

"Buy some big jewelry at the airport to distract from your face," Noah had instructed her. "When you return, we'll work on getting you a forged passport you can keep. Meghan will need hers."

Anita fingered the multi-strand necklace hanging over her sweater and blew her new bangs out of her eyes. Caitlyn had given her long bangs to make her look younger, but they annoyed her. They did look good though, sort of rock-star looking, with her curly hair.

When she reached the customs and immigration kiosk, she scanned her passport, and the machine took Anita's photo. After a long minute, a message crossed the screen and spit out a printed paper: Proceed to the window with your notice.

She glanced around at the other travelers who were mostly leaving the kiosks and heading for the exit, instead of the window where her notice told her to go. Her breath sped up. *Stay calm*, she instructed herself. *Look the agent in the eye and do not blink.* Blinking signaled you were lying, she'd read. Breathing hard was probably a bad sign as well.

While she stood at the white line waiting for the next agent, Anita counted the length of her breaths to avoid pan-icking: *one, two, three in; one, two, three, four, five out.* A man in a blue uniform behind a glass partition waved her forward. Anita handed him the passport and her notice as she forced a smile, light-headed from the caffeine and anxiety. His face invoked the image of a poker player. He examined the passport under a light, scanned it and frowned at the results. Anita thought she might throw up. His fingers clicked across the keyboard, then he stared at the screen and waited. Nearly two minutes passed. Finally, he laid it open on the counter.

"Where are you going in Switzerland?" the official asked.

"Vevey. I have business there."

"How long will you be here?"

"I hope to conclude my business today and return to Canada later tonight."

He stamped the passport and handed it back to her. "You may go."

Anita barely breathed as she stuffed the passport into her handbag and headed to the exit.

❧

The last time Anita had ridden the train to Vevey, she'd been on her way to sell her company to Schrenger Holten, the Swiss billionaire owner of Holten Holding, who was interested in building up his U.S. tech holdings. Julian had sat across from her on the train, and she'd thought how handsome he looked with his graying hair and blue eyes, the laugh lines around his mouth accenting his dimples.

"Who was the jokester who said money can't buy happiness?" he'd asked her.

Anita had laughed. "I suspect we have a whole lot of happy coming our way once this deal closes. I don't want to jinx it though. You don't think anything will go wrong, do you?"

"Nothing will go wrong. You earned this. I've always known you had a brilliant mind." He'd made a little air kiss in her direction.

"When we return, I want to buy a condo near Steven's house. That way, we can visit without intruding on him.

And"—she'd winked at him—"when we have grandchildren, we can see them as often as we want."

What a difference three years made. Her heart hurt in so many ways, she wondered if she would ever experience joy again.

The electric train moved quietly through the countryside. Through damp eyes, Anita gazed at the grapevines on the terraced hillsides held back by stone walls emblazoned with the winegrowers' names. Along the lake, she spotted two white ferry boats crossing over from France. The mountain tops were almost bare on this too-warm November day. The sky was a deep blue and the sun glistened off the water. Spectacular weather, but it should be foggy and raining here in November, with distant mist from falling snow obscuring nearby mountains. Good for the Swiss wine industry—bad for skiers and the fish dying in the lake from the heat. Anita had read they'd had to move some species to colder lakes higher up in the mountains to keep them alive.

The announcement for Vevey station came over the speaker. She and Julian had spent two months here that summer. They'd stayed in a second-floor apartment along the waterfront, where they'd watched other vacationers and locals wander the flower-lined promenade. Some evenings they stopped at a lakeside bar for a glass of wine or an Aperol cocktail. Anita knew she'd been happy then, but she no longer remembered how that felt.

From Vevey station, Anita followed the flow of pedestrians across Avenue de la Gare, passed a Starbucks, and entered a busy intersection to where her bank was located. It held her anonymous safety deposit box containing Swiss francs and U.S. dollars— recommended by her asset manager as a hedge against unexpected turmoil.

Anita had chosen to have the bank securely store her key, rather than taking it home—an advantageous decision.

Once inside the vault with her box open, she pulled out packs of hundred-dollar bills secured in ten thousand dollar increments and placed fifteen of them in her suitcase.

Next, she stopped at the receptionist's desk.

"Bonjour, madame. Je suis ici pour voir Monsieur Christian Rochat, s'il vous plaît. Je m'appelle Anita Forester," Anita said, using the few French phrases she remembered from last time.

"Une minute, s'il vous plait," the receptionist replied, picking up the phone.

A few minutes later, a trim, middle-aged man dressed in a dark suit arrived, and they exchanged smiles of recognition.

"Madame Forester." He reached out to shake her hand. "It is good to see you. Please, come to my office."

As part of the sale to Schrenger Holten, he'd transferred a significant portion of her proceeds into a numbered Swiss bank account, which provided privacy from prying eyes. She still had to report the taxable income in the U.S., but the bank wasn't required to share her account information. As a result, no one could track her by the financial transactions from this account, a benefit she hadn't imagined needing when the account was established. At home, she had enough money for day-to-day expenses, but now she didn't dare touch it. The rest was left in Switzerland under Monsieur Rochat's management and in her safety deposit box—well, a portion of it in her suitcase now.

Rochat became her asset manager that summer three years ago. Walking along the path to his office invoked memories of when they'd worked through the details of how he would manage her finances. The familiarity caused a lump to form in her throat as she recalled the excitement she'd had for her future. She swallowed it down and focused on her current business instead.

"I have three matters I need help with this morning. The first is, I want to open an account to invest in crypto-currency and move two hundred thousand Swiss francs into it," Anita told him as soon as they sat down. If she was going to have to hire questionable accomplices to rescue Julian, she'd need a hidden way to pay them. What other expenses would arise from living evasively remained to be seen.

Rochat simply nodded and typed on his computer, then handed her a device to enter the code word for her numbered account. After she electronically signed several documents, a message appeared confirming the transfer was complete.

"Would you like me to purchase the coins I recommend for you?"

"Yes. Buy coins that are easy to sell on the peer-to-peer exchanges."

"Of course. I'll schedule buys this morning."

After more typing, Monsieur Rochat turned his computer screen toward her. She read her remaining balance. It had grown over the last few years she'd been ignoring it. To her relief, she had much more money than she'd made on her sale.

"Merci, Monsieur Rochat. I appreciate your continued attention to my account. The second matter involves the contents of my safe deposit box I store in your bank. As you recommended, I am keeping cash as a hedge here. I now need to take some U.S. dollars to Canada with me immediately, but for personal reasons, I do not want to transport them. Can you arrange transport by an onboard air carrier for me and produce the proper documentation for both countries?"

"I can arrange that. For the documentation, you need to tell me what the money will be used for."

"I am purchasing a collectible automobile from a private owner. A 1989 Ferrari Testarossa. If I don't provide him with the cash by tomorrow, he has another buyer lined up who's unwilling to wait."

"Nice choice." He revealed a sliver of a smile. "I will take care of that for you. And the third matter?"

"Can you issue a debit card to me?" It was complicated to navigate life without plastic, but a debit card from this account would be difficult, if not impossible, to trace to her in the U.S. She could move about freely.

⚜

Anita rolled her carry-on back across the street to the train station. An express train to Geneva was going to arrive in fifteen minutes, so she stopped at a café to purchase a coffee and a cheese sandwich, before proceeding to the platform.

Once on the train, she searched for the next flight to Montreal on the phone she'd purchased in Canada, after disposing of the one she'd used with Mike. A business class seat appeared on the Air Canada flight at 2:48 PM. *Perfect.* She booked it with her new debit card, then called Noah.

"I have what I came for. I'll bring Meghan's document back tomorrow. Will you have the one I need ready so I can return to Stowe? I can pay."

"Don't worry. I'm fairly certain I will have it by tomorrow and I can take you back to Stowe afterwards."

"You're a lifesaver. I can't thank you two enough for what you've done."

Relieved, she checked her Proton Mail account and found a new response from a different email address on Julian's list. The sender had included a Canadian phone number and asked her to call. Doubt crept into her mind as her stomach muscles tightened. She'd been focused on getting the money to pay off Mike's blackmail to let her go free and retrieve the hard drive, but finding Julian remained critical. Trusting these email contacts was risky, but they were her only leads for help. Desperate, she dialed and held her breath.

"Allo?" a man's voice answered in a French accent.

"You replied to my email about Jay Eff," she said, resurrecting her boss persona to sound stronger than she felt. "Tell me what you know."

"We are talking about Julian Forester, no?"

Anita broke into a cold sweat, her blood pulsing in her ears. Staring out at the lake, she fought back nausea as she cupped her hand over the phone to keep her words private. She nearly whimpered her next phrase. "Please tell me he is alive."

"He is alive, and I know where he is." There was a pause before he spoke again. "Anita, this is François. It has been a long time."

CHAPTER TEN

PLANS

DOUG STEPPED OUT of the shower and slipped into his plush hotel bathrobe. He took a sip of coffee and brushed his hair to one side, splashing Hermes aftershave on his face. From the top drawer of the vanity, where his personal items were stored, he selected a prescription bottle and swallowed a blue pill, washing it down with more coffee.

Out in the living room, he sprawled across the couch and picked up the weekend edition of *The Wall Street Journal* left by his butler.

"Fossil Fuel's Big Win," the headline read as it went on to describe the vote in Congress on Friday revising clean air laws, and what that will mean to various industries, consumers, and the economy. They ended with a quote from the President:

"Americans deserve this. The hard-working people of this country built our automotive industry, and they should not be dictated to about what they are allowed to build or buy. I will sign this bill as soon as it comes across my desk."

Doug's head buzzed with self-congratulations over engineering this political coup. He'd used his money and connections to ensure financing to help this man get elected, as well as the supporting congressmen to turn around decades of anti-oil legislation. Now his personal net worth was skyrocketing, not to mention his conglomerate of fossil fuel companies. Those in power recognized he was the one who held the purse strings, and they would do whatever he wanted to stay in his circle.

A knock on the door interrupted his thoughts, and he answered it.

"Martina!" He held his arms open for the voluptuous young woman in a fitted white dress.

"Come in, sweetheart." He kissed her on the lips. "I hope you brought what I need."

She pinched his check and winked as she pushed by him into the room, then rummaged through her Chanel handbag. "All the photos you asked for," she said, handing him a phone.

"Wonderful. Come sit next to me on the couch. Let's take a look, shall we?"

His bathrobe slipped open as he sat. Martina curled up on the sofa next to him, and he reached his arm around her and pulled her close. Her long, dark hair fell over his bare chest. Together, they scrolled through the photos of Senator Colton and Secretary Bernard in a private room at the nightclub where Martina had led them earlier that morning. During their two previous trips, Doug had provided them with seclusion from other people, gaining the men's trust until they believed they were invincible. Doug had left Martina with an open tab and strict instructions to spare no cost. On anything.

"I like this one." Doug laughed, pointing to a picture of a young naked woman, her hands tied behind her back, kneeling between the senator's legs. A rush of energy hit him like he used to get years ago snorting coke. Only this was better. This was the rush he got when he led powerful men to their own demise. Now he owned them. He gazed at Martina as her lips curled into a tiny smile.

"Damn, woman, you are worth every dime. You'll be rich as long as I'm around." He rested the phone on the side table and pulled her into his lap, ready to show off his power.

⁓

A few hours later, Doug, the senator and the Secretary of the Interior sat around the dining room table in Doug's suite, feasting on brunch. They each drank a Bloody Mary to take the edge off their hangovers. No one discussed the prior night's events.

"As I mentioned on the plane, we have a problem." Doug tapped his drink stirrer on his plate. "Getting these climate leaders shut down has been working well for us. Activism and press coverage has shrunk to almost nil since we started. But a couple have escaped. So far, no one important. But we can't have that. Voters can't find out that people are being held without trial in the U.S. If our President isn't reelected, we'll lose control."

The two men nodded as they chewed.

The senator took a gulp of coffee before speaking. "I have another idea."

He paused while Doug and the secretary stopped eating to listen. "Gitmo. Only forty-five people are there now. The place can hold several hundred. No one ever escapes and if we do it right, no one will ever know they're there."

Doug leaned back into his chair and grinned. "Brilliant."

The secretary frowned. "How do we transport them? We can't load them on a military transport without it being documented."

Doug thought about this while he tapped the stirrer faster, then stopped and sat up straight. "Easy. We put them on private jets to Haiti. Call them aid workers and include a big donation for our friends on the island. Then they take a Haitian boat to Cuba." Doug brushed his hands together as though brushing off dirt.

The secretary frowned. "I don't know. These are all Americans. I mean, getting them out of the way for a while is not the same as Guantanamo Bay. That's for terrorists."

"Well, they're like terrorists, aren't they?" the senator said. "Trying to destroy American businesses with their bullshit over fossil fuels?"

"I agree. They need to go." Doug threw the stirrer on his plate. "We're getting our way at last. If one of these mouthpieces escapes, we're screwed."

"I'll meet with the President as soon as I can get on his schedule," the senator said. "I'll let you know once he gives us the okay. He can call the commander and ensure we're all on the same page. If he's not, he'll appoint a new commander."

The secretary rubbed his forehead. "I don't see any role for me in this."

Doug's eyes narrowed. "Suit yourself."

The secretary put down his drink and glanced at the floor as all three were silent.

After a beat, the senator stood and refilled their Bloody Mary glasses, raising his for a toast. "To ridding us of the troublemakers."

Doug raised his glass to the senator's. "We need this done quickly."

The secretary tipped his glass and took a small sip before setting it back on the table.

CHAPTER ELEVEN

REUNION

Anita awoke to the sound of the airline attendant's voice announcing they would be landing in Montreal soon. She fished around for the button to raise her seat, then asked for coffee. Eight hours had passed, but the local time was only two hours later than when she left Switzerland, thanks to the time gained by flying west.

The shock had worn off at hearing François' name, his voice again, this man who had broken her heart. Thinking about him now pulled her into the past and caused a sting in her chest.

Thirty-five years ago, while still in college, she and Stacey had met François and Julian, best friends, both graduate students at American University, in a crowded bar in D.C. François' French-Canadian accent and conspicuous good looks drew her to him, but it was the fiery way he spoke about his ideals that sparked her deeper interest. She'd hoped Stacey and

Julian would also pair off, but Stacey found Julian too quiet and reserved. Instead, Julian often joined in with Anita and François during their activities.

Unlike most men she had dated, François did not hold back his emotions. Never had she felt so loved, so *in* love, as she did with this man who exuded passion in every part of his being. Despite that, she'd feared their relationship would end. François was going to save the world—at least from the corporate interests that were ruining it—while Anita was already planning how to be part of those corporations, to take advantage of the growing opportunities. Being with him meant one of them compromising their goals.

A few nights before graduation, she'd told him about her job offer. They were sitting in his bed, leaning on his pillows against the wall, the sheets rumpled from their lovemaking. He was smiling at her, his whole face radiating adoration. That smile burned heat into her body each time she saw it.

"You have no idea how beautiful you are, my dear." He'd reached out to caress a strand of her hair. "I will love you always."

The words she needed to tell him froze in her throat. When she pinched her lips together, he lowered one eyebrow.

"What is it?"

Reluctantly, she told him the news. "I received a job offer today. SysTech is filling positions on a new contract they have with Martin Marietta."

"Martin Marietta?" François recoiled. "You told them no, right? Or are you going to help make missiles that get fired at women and children?"

Anita's face burned in embarrassment. "It's a stepping

stone. It's not easy to find entry-level programming jobs right now. And I won't be working for Martin Marietta, but for SysTech. Once I have experience, I'll move on to a different contract."

François stepped out of bed and put on his clothes. As he was zipping his jeans, he spoke. "I am going back to Montreal after graduation. I was hoping you would go with me—was hoping you shared my vision of a better world."

A flight announcement startled Anita out of her memories. "We are on our final descent into Montreal. Seat backs up and tray tables must be placed in their upright and locked positions."

She finished her coffee and handed the attendant the cup as he came by.

At 4:30 in the afternoon, the sun had already set in this northern city. Anita's body clock was all confused, but at least she'd finally slept. Surprising after the phone call with François.

As she waited to deplane, she turned airplane mode off her phone, and several texts from Noah appeared.

All set with getting your new doc, the first text read.

Need the money up front. Can we meet tomorrow?

Might take 2 days, read the last.

Her jaw clenched shut. Two days from tomorrow would be Thursday—too late.

She texted back:

No! Can we meet tonight? I need it by Wednesday morning early!!!

Worried over this development, she joined the crowd heading to customs and repeated the check-in process at the kiosk. After a breathless moment, the kiosk spit out a confirmation slip to proceed to the exit. In her mind, she did a celebration jig.

Anita rode in her Uber to the Renaissance Montreal Hotel, repeatedly checking her phone for a reply from Noah, and a notification from her onboard courier, who would be bringing her money to her hotel. Tension ratcheted up in her head. Her thoughts flipped between getting the passport in time, having her air courier show up, and meeting François tonight.

When she was nearly at her hotel, a text update arrived that her courier had cleared customs and would be at the hotel within the hour. She checked her watch and noted the time. Noah still hadn't replied. Maybe extra cash would speed up the process with him once they connected.

In the meantime, she would meet with François tonight to discuss how to help Julian. *What a small world*, she thought, considering François was partially responsible for her marrying him. When François broke up with her, Julian had eagerly offered to step into the void, and before long, Anita had realized how easy he was to be with. Julian supported her decisions and took her out to celebrate her new job after she started. François left town without saying goodbye to either of them, and Anita had buried her pain by focusing on Julian and her work.

Anita had googled François a few times over the years. He ran a foundation that provided legal aid and support to climate activists, and initiated lawsuits against polluters. No images of him ever popped up in the searches, nor was he on social media. His foundation had a LinkedIn account, but he didn't. No photos were there either.

He's probably paunchy, bald, and married. With six grandchildren.

Once in her hotel room, she had a couple of hours to herself before their meeting. She set the small suitcase she'd been rolling with her since Pennsylvania on the luggage table beside the television and pulled out her real passport, to use as an ID for the courier. The luggage now contained only dirty underwear and tops, a pair of pajamas she'd worn at the bed-and-breakfast, a second pair of jeans, a bag of makeup, and duck boots with dried-on mud. Fortunately, she was only two blocks from Hudson's Bay department store.

Before long, the courier showed up with the package and she signed for it, returning to her room. Since she'd used couriers at her company, she trusted their reliability, but her life depended on this shipment. She tore it open and counted out the contents, then exhaled with relief: It was all there.

There was still no reply from Noah, so Anita locked the cash in her room safe and went shopping.

❧

From behind a black podium, the maître d' of Chez-Michel addressed her. "*Bonsoir, madame. Puis-je vous aider?* Welcome, madame. May I help you?" he asked as though it were a single sentence, as many did in this bilingual city.

"I'm looking for the bar." This is where François had asked her to meet him.

The maître d' held his hand out to the right and gave a little nod. "Enjoy your evening, madame."

Combing her fingers through her hair after her windy walk, Anita passed tables set with linen and candles. The bar area came into view behind a shoulder-high black partition, the long black marble bar accented by tall gray bar stools standing on shiny chrome legs. Behind the bar were shelves of bottles of brown, white, and yellow liquor backlit by bright white lights. The bartenders appeared almost like silhouettes against the backdrop. Jazz music played quietly enough to still allow for conversation.

Anita scanned the couple of dozen people in the dim light, then spotted a man sitting alone on a stool facing her. Tall, with a trim build and dark, longish hair streaked in gray, he wore a tweed sports jacket over jeans, a scarf draped around his neck. Anita stared, trying to match her memory with the thin straight nose and large dark eyes of this strikingly handsome man. Suddenly he smiled at her, and immediately she recognized him. She felt his eyes on her as she walked toward him in her new silk dress that fell over her knee-high leather boots. Thirty-three years disappeared as her heart pounded and her breath turned shallow. She was tempted to turn and run out the door rather than risk dredging up old feelings, but didn't. When she reached him, he stood.

"Anita. It is wonderful to see you. I am sorry it has to be under these circumstances. What would you like to drink?"

He extended his hand to offer her his seat, as no others were empty. When she brushed by him to the barstool, all her nerves zinged at the touch of his arm against hers. Like an awkward teenager, she tried to avoid contact with him again.

"I would love a glass of red wine." That's what he was drinking. "Whatever you suggest is fine."

François ordered one for her and another for himself, resting his foot on the rung of her barstool, close enough that she smelled his musky cologne. She avoided looking directly into his eyes as he gazed down at her.

"You look exactly the same. Just as beautiful now as then." He turned away, drinking his remaining wine. The heat of a blush spread up her neck. It had been years since anyone called her beautiful.

"Don't be silly. I've aged and I know it." She took a breath before adding, "But thank you."

The bartender delivered two glasses of wine, and François motioned with his head toward a high-top table across from the bar. "Let us move over there where we can talk."

The table butted up against a black tin-covered partition that separated the bar from the dining room. A pink glass pendant light hanging from a long chrome pole cast a rosy hue between them. Anita took a long swig of her wine, admiring its smooth, rich flavor. François had good taste. When she finally looked him in the eye, her stomach fluttered. Torn between wanting to catch up and needing to know how he would help find Julian, she decided on a topic that might do both.

"I didn't know you and Julian were still in touch. He left me your email on a list right before the protest."

François nodded. "He called me a couple of weeks ago at my foundation and told me he expected to be arrested for protesting the climate crisis. He wanted me to help you if you contacted me. You did not know?"

"I didn't." Embarrassment and anger burned up her neck while wondering what else Julian had told others and not her. "Where is he now? How did you find him?"

François crossed one leg over the other and began shaking his left foot as he replied. "He is in the U.S., in a detention center where they are keeping climate activists. It is not a normal jail or an actual arrest. The police have no records of it. I have a source who has access to their database. We believe he got himself captured on purpose, to look for someone." Pausing, he looked at her, his eyes narrowing slightly. "Did he ever mention anyone to you?"

Anita slowly shook her head. She stared into the glazed black table, wanting to dive into it and avoid this discussion. Instead, she took a deep breath and explained. "We didn't talk. About anything. Ever. Not since our son, Steven, died in a wildfire in California two years ago." Her voice cracked as she finished her sentence, avoiding his eyes, ashamed to admit the state of her marriage.

He reached out and gently touched her other hand that rested on the table. "I am so very sorry, Anita, for your pain."

Tears formed and she pinched her lips to hold them back. Neither spoke as Anita dabbed her eyes with her finger. He shifted around in his chair and drank more wine before leaning toward her. "Listen. I think I can smuggle Julian out and into Canada."

His closeness distracted her, but she was buoyed by this statement.

"I have done it before. But he is not on the radar of my regular contributors, so I am not getting donations. I am going to need money for the operation. Please understand, even if he was not your husband and my long-ago friend, I would still try to free him. I am passionate about saving climate activists, and I am good at it. We will free Julian."

He grabbed her hand and squeezed it tightly between both of his. His strong grip reinforced his sincerity. For the first time since Julian disappeared, Anita believed he would be saved, that she finally had someone to trust and rely on.

"Thank you."

She placed her other hand over both of his. Warmth spread up her arms and into her chest like a bolt of energy. This man whose hands she once knew well now belonged to a stranger— but something inside her remembered and trusted him.

"You always did follow your principles. Once upon a time, I resented your idealism, but I can see that was my mistake." *He's become the man he promised he would be back when he left me. Perhaps leaving was for the best.*

François blushed and pulled away. "Would you like another wine?"

"Absolutely."

CHAPTER TWELVE

NOVICE

Anita's handbag sat on the sofa in her hotel room, but it might as well have been a mile away. Nausea churned in her stomach, while a spinning sensation attacked her when she moved. The handbag contained Advil and she needed them. Tums, too. No other potential hangover cures came to mind. It had been years since she carried them around, but right now, she wanted them.

Instead, she called room service and ordered coffee, orange juice, and dry toast. At least she'd been coherent enough to plug in her phone last night. Or was it this morning? What time had she come in?

She tried to sit but broke out in a cold sweat and lay down again. Last night was like a dream, a fuzzy memory. François had hailed a cab when the restaurant closed and ridden with her, to make sure she got back to her hotel. Apparently, she'd made it to her room okay. That was a blur as well, but she was aware she'd been alone.

Her phone buzzed, notifying her she had a text message. It was from Noah. Finally.

Can't drive you to VT. Rent a car in Meghan's name and use her document. Sorry.

"Shit!" Anita sprang upright, briefly clear-headed as adrenaline shot through her. If she drove across the U.S. border with Meghan's altered passport, she feared U.S. Border Patrol would detect the modified photo or RFID chip, which was in questionable shape. She needed a new one, not one that said she was forty-two years old.

After gulping down water on her nightstand, Anita staggered over to her handbag and carried it back to bed. Inside, she found the passport and examined it. A tiny gap showed on the edge of the cover where the modified RFID chip had been inserted. It wasn't there yesterday. All the handling during her travels, including checking into the hotel, must have stressed the glue holding the cover together. No way could she use this to cross into the U.S.

She called Noah. No answer.

Shit, shit, shit!

The only other person able to help her was François. He answered after two rings.

"Good morning, my dear."

The warmth of his greeting startled her. "Good morning to you too. Except it's not a good morning. I'm in trouble and I need your advice."

"We should speak in person. I do not like to discuss trouble on the phone. I will call you a cab."

The prospect of seeing François again gave her a lift. "I need a little time to pull myself together. An hour?"

&

Green painted wooden steps led up the front of François' gray granite two-story building. Anita gripped the handrail to steady herself as she searched for the last name *Gerard*, then pushed the buzzer. Breakfast had helped her hangover, but she still hadn't recovered. A moment later, the green door swung open, and François ushered her into the hall, then his apartment.

Just as handsome as last night, she thought. It wasn't fair. She hadn't even put on makeup, and probably looked like a train wreck.

His apartment was sparsely furnished, with a small sitting area containing a brown upholstered couch on wooden legs and a well-used leather recliner facing a television on the wall. Between the two was a wooden table with water marks and wine stains. Two high-top chairs at a counter divided the room from a tiny kitchen. The entire area looked one step above where he lived in college.

"Please sit."

The couch was as stiff as an airline seat in coach. "How long have you lived here?"

"About a year. I move around a lot. It comes with the work. Tell me about your trouble."

After their intimate conversation last night, his business-like tone put Anita off balance. *Focus. It doesn't matter.* She was here to obtain advice on crossing the border by tomorrow morning.

"I'm traveling on an altered passport." She laid out what was going on with Noah and the lack of a new identity, then handed him the well-used book and pointed out the flaw.

After examination, he nodded. "You are right. You should not use this. If you are caught, you will be arrested immediately. The Americans are a suspicious lot. Did this man say why he cannot go?"

She shook her head. "It was a text. I tried calling but he didn't answer."

François frowned. "He is likely being watched. Avoid him."

Anita's heart rate rose. "Where else can I get a new passport? I need to be back in Vermont tomorrow morning at 10:30 with the money. Otherwise, this thug's going to continue to hunt me, and that hard drive I told you about will be sold on the black market—or destroyed."

He slumped back in his chair. "All this is not good. Maybe I can find you another passport. It is so little time. You will also need a matching driver's license."

Another wave of nausea rushed through her body as worry took over. She'd forgotten about needing a driver's license, too. The room seemed to spin as she closed her eyes. "I think I'm going to be sick."

François rushed forward, slipped his arm around her waist, lifted her from the chair and ran her to the bathroom. As she knelt over the toilet, he held her hair while she vomited a couple of times, then dry heaved. In between, she leaned back against him. As she recovered, she sat back on her own and grabbed toilet paper to clean her face.

"Thank you." She tried to catch her breath. "I'm so

embarrassed. I hardly drink anymore, and last night . . . Do you have any mouthwash? I think I'm okay now."

"Yes. Can you stand? I will get you a glass for the mouthwash."

He gently lifted her into a standing position, and she held on to the sink until she was steady. After she cleansed her mouth, he led her back to the living room and sat her in the recliner.

A few minutes later, he placed a cup of ginger tea next to her along with a few biscuits on a plate and they resumed their conversation.

"I'm a total novice here. I don't know who I can trust, and what's safe and what isn't. It's too easy to make a mistake and land in jail—or worse." She thought of Mike and whatever he had been planning when he tried to take her away on her own.

"It is. But you are smart. You will learn. Do you believe going back to Vermont is safe?"

Anita stared at the floor for a minute as though she were examining the Persian rug. "I have no idea. But it's my fault the hard drive was stolen. If I hadn't asked Paul to drive me to Boston, it wouldn't have happened."

They locked eyes together. "What if this technology can truly solve much of the climate crisis?"

His frown softened. "Then the value is priceless."

Anita nodded. "That's why I have to go. And I will also make sure Mike doesn't come after me again." The tea settled her stomach, but François stroked his chin, lost in thought.

Suddenly, he stood and faced her. "Do you think the stolen hard drive is a lie? What they say is on it, I mean. Might this be a setup to rob you?"

Despite finally calming down, Anita's pulse started sending alarms again.

"Did the man who drove you to Vermont realize you had money?"

Frowning, she strained to remember her discussions with Paul before meeting Mike. "No. I hadn't told him my real name. He couldn't have. Besides, the look on his face when he found out his hard drive was stolen—it's like they'd kidnaped his baby."

"Just be cautious."

That's what Julian told me. She finished her tea, trying to relax, stressing over the new dangers and roadblocks coming at her from all directions.

"We need to visit my passport connection. Are you well enough to go out?"

❧

The walk to the metro station improved Anita's head. Warmth and sunshine suggested Montreal had forgotten it was November. François moved quickly while Anita struggled to keep up.

"Is this man a friend of yours?"

"Not a friend. Occasional business associate. Works for anyone who pays. He may or may not be a supporter of our agenda, but he is useful."

At the metro station, they ran down the escalator in time to catch an arriving train moving quietly on rubber wheels.

After disembarking at the Laurier stop in Mont-Royal, they walked a block along Berri Street. François stopped at a brick building with a twisting iron staircase that led to a second-floor balcony. Three doors stood side by side. As Anita followed, François jogged up the steps, knocking on the closest door. When no one answered, he carefully turned the door handle—it wasn't locked. Gesturing for Anita to stand back, François tapped the door open and crept inside.

"*Tabarnak!*" François cursed. Anita crossed the threshold into a vacant room while he checked the others. "Empty. This is where my contact lived two months ago. He must be spooked, like your Noah."

She leaned against the bare wall, slid her hands into her jacket pockets and looked at the floor. "I'll never reach Stowe by tomorrow morning."

François' mouth was set in a firm line. "My contact said he had competition in the neighborhood. Maybe we can find them. Or they will find us."

They walked outside onto the iron staircase in view of the street and left the door open.

François pulled out his phone. "Stand here where everyone can see you. We will look at our phones like we are searching for something."

After about ten minutes, a black door framed by crumbling concrete opened in an old building across the street. A short man with graying hair and light-brown skin stepped out, dressed head to toe in black.

"Do you know him?"

The man stretched out his hand into a thumbs-up gesture.

"No, but he might be who we are looking for." François reached over to Anita and slipped a metal tube into her jacket pocket. "It is pepper spray. Do not be afraid to use it if this does not go well. Do you feel the lever you turn with your thumb? When it slips into the open slot, you can fire. Shoot at his face and clothes. It will seal his eyes shut for a few minutes. Make sure you cover your face so you do not breathe it in."

Anita slid the thumb lever back and forth to make sure she understood how to move it. "Ok. Ready."

François gave the thumbs-up gesture back and they joined the man across the road.

"You are looking for Pierre?" the man asked in French.

François nodded. "Can you speak English? My friend here speaks only English."

"Of course," he replied in English. "Pierre is now gone but I can help you."

"When did he leave?"

"Yesterday afternoon."

Anita wondered if Noah was in trouble, too. She would have to destroy her connection to him by shredding Meghan's passport.

"Are you an artist like he was?" François asked.

The man smiled and held out his arm toward his door. "A better artist. Come into my studio and look."

"After you." François held back until the man entered first.

Anita flipped the pepper spray to the open position and followed them through the dilapidated door. Her pulse increased as she scanned the room for anyone else but was dazzled by her surroundings. Instead of the shabby furnishings she was expecting, the living room was decorated in colorful anodized aluminum and glass tables, polished wood floors, a spotless white sofa, and large abstract paintings. François' face showed the same surprise she was experiencing.

"My art is as flawless as my surroundings. I am a

perfectionist. I am paid well for my art—and my silence. Do you think you can afford me?"

François glanced at Anita, then answered first. "What should I call you, Monsieur Artist?"

"Saeed. You can find me here when you need me. For what are you looking? Perhaps the specialty of your friend?"

François nodded. "Correct. Do you have samples we can view of your work?"

Saeed nodded and motioned for François and Anita to sit on the white sofa and left the room. Anita sat stiffly, afraid to move, lest she make a mark on the upholstery.

"What do you think?"

"I think he's your only option. We should make sure his product looks good." On his phone François typed into his notes app, then showed it to Anita.

Say nothing about passports in case the room is bugged. He will do the same if legit. In case we are wired.

Anita raised her eyebrows and nodded her head. There was a staggering amount of new information she needed to learn to stay safe.

François deleted the note before placing his phone on the table.

A few minutes later, Saeed returned with a leather portfolio. He opened it and slid it across the glass coffee table. Inside were several passports with Saeed's face but different names and countries, including Canada, the UK, Israel, and Saudi Arabia. He handed François an ultraviolet light. As he held it above the passport samples, holographic images jumped out. Saeed pointed out various drivers' licenses, medical ID cards, and even press IDs from international news services. Additionally, he had FBI and RCMP badges. Anita was impressed, but she wondered how dangerous this man might be. She kept her thumb glued to the pepper spray.

"Your wish is my command." Saeed smiled. "Technology does complicate it of course. You must expect that cost. I handle it all."

François typed onto his phone and showed it to Saeed.

Canadian passport for her with U.S. border entry and return. Matching driver's license.

Saeed pulled his phone out of his pocket and typed:

C$25,000. Bitcoin only.

Anita was relieved he wanted crypto. It would prevent anyone from tracking her. She nodded.

"Today?" François asked out loud.

Saeed retyped and held out the phone.

Tomorrow morning early. Half now. Half at pick up.

François looked to Anita for confirmation. The timing would be close, but she had no other option. She nodded again, grateful for a solution.

"Thank you, my friend." François leaned over and shook hands with Saeed. Anita followed suit. Saeed held his phone toward her.

"Don't smile," he said, taking her picture.

CHAPTER THIRTEEN

GUIDE

MIKE ROSSI SAT at the black and chrome dining room table of his sublet Beacon Street condo, cursing the external hard drive he'd plugged into his laptop. Valuable information must be stored on it since Anita included it along with the cost of her bounty. And Paul hid it, so he thought it important. Perhaps it was financial data, brokerage accounts, or secret information that he could sell or use to blackmail someone. After trying every decryption tool he owned, Mike perused the dark web and bought two other tools that looked promising. But none of them were breaking the security. He'd seen proprietary encryption before on hard drives. Depending on how far it deviated from commercial encryption, some tools read it. Not this time. He needed the software engineer who created it, or at least someone who knew the sequence of access codes. That was Paul Tanner.

Anger and frustration pumped through Mike's body like a

caffeine overdose. He clenched both hands into fists, ready to slam them into his laptop. After spending a day and a half working on it, he forced himself to back away. Instead, he rolled his chair over to a different computer and plugged in the backup he'd copied from Paul's desktop computer in the basement.

This one hundred thousand dollar payout from Anita would be sweet, but he wondered about turning it into more. If he handed her over to his client and collected the bounty, it would only pay him fifty thousand, so he was doubling his money just by having Anita pay him instead.

But he had a hunch about this hard drive. The deep encryption along with Paul's effort to hide it, and Anita's interest in including it with her freedom pointed to it having some significant value. He'd have to try a different approach—digging into Paul's background to discover what he cared about.

One of the easiest ways to investigate someone was through their browser history. Paul had visited several websites frequently: ones on recent solar research and a process Mike hadn't heard of before—photoelectrochemical water splitting to create hydrogen fuel. Mike read the websites and deducted it wasn't viable in the market yet due to cost and stability. However, a couple of websites insinuated that once it became affordable and mass produced, it's potential was unlimited.

Next, Mike googled Paul's name and searched LinkedIn but found nothing. Maybe Paul had a résumé? Mike searched Paul's documents and found several versions. Paul's last job was ten years as a research scientist at a company called EnerGeLabs near Philadelphia. His end date for that job was two years ago, right after the government defunded climate science research. His job description opened with: "Responsible for research and development of proprietary processes and components for cutting edge green technology."

Mike rolled his chair over to the other computer and accessed his client's database, the Shutdown List, they called it. Beside individuals, they maintained a list of companies that interested them if former employees were located. Under the E's, he found EnerGeLabs with a note that read, "Company closed. Call for quote." That meant the capture of certain individuals may pay a bounty, others will not, depending on their role.

"Hot damn!"

Sparks of excitement shot through his torso. He leapt from his chair and began pacing around the room. This had to be what was on this hard drive—something to do with water splitting, something discovered by this company. But he couldn't prove it.

The drive was worthless without someone able to decrypt it. He needed Paul. More importantly, he knew exactly who would care about this, someone much more important than this client.

He pulled out the contents he'd been carrying in his pocket, spreading them across the table. A business card he'd only glanced at earlier caught his eye. *Deer Run Inn — Stowe, Vermont. Caitlyn Tanner — Innkeeper.* The same town where Anita asked to meet him tomorrow morning.

Looks like I'll be seeing Paul Tanner again. This time I'll enjoy it.

Wednesday morning at ten o'clock, Mike sat in the parking lot of the Green Mountain Inn in his BMW, where he and Anita had agreed to meet in half an hour. A ding announced a text.

Anita: *Running late. Have the money. Will arrive by 11:30.*

Past his deadline. No matter. She'd discover soon enough the plans had changed. Although he preferred to receive his money from her first, moving to the next step on his agenda was possible: finding Paul Tanner.

His backpack sat on the seat next to him with his usual tools, including handcuffs, rope, and a stun gun. If everything went the way he hoped, he'd soon have the respect he craved from the one man who never gave it to him. He shivered with anticipation. Then he started his car and set the GPS for directions to the Deer Run Inn.

✖

Paul, Caitlyn, and Odina sat at the dining room table of the inn, drinking coffee and glancing up at the clock. They were silent as they waited for Anita to return from her meeting with Mike, scheduled to take place in fifteen minutes. The last two days of waiting were agonizing to Paul as he worried what might go wrong. He wished she'd called with an update.

Paul picked up his cup and walked over to the window. Leaves they'd raked into the woods the day before were blowing across the parking area and onto the front porch. A BMW with Massachusetts plates drove in and parked next to his car.

"Somebody's here." The others looked over.

When the car door opened, he recognized the man stepping out, sending panic into his chest. "Shit! It's Mike. The guy who stole my drive."

Caitlyn jumped up and ran to bolt the front door.

Odina grabbed her guide backpack and their jackets from the hook by the entrance. "Run! Out the back now!"

The three of them bolted down the hall, past the guest rooms, and out the back door, Caitlyn pushing it shut to lock it behind them.

The cold wind struck Paul like a baseball bat, knocking the wind out of him. Odina ran, the jackets still in her arms as she headed for the cover of the forest. Caitlyn was on her heels, Paul struggling from behind, his breathing overpowered by the cold and his fear. A couple of times he looked back as he ran, the inn soon disappearing from his sight. His hands were like ice.

"Odina," he called out. "I need my jacket."

She let him catch up, before throwing him the jacket. Caitlyn glowered at him as he struggled to put it on.

"Listen, Dad," Odina said. "You aren't used to this, but we need to put a lot of space between him and us. He sounds like a professional thug, and we know he's dangerous. You can't outrun him if he spots you. Ready?"

Paul nodded and dug his hands into his pockets. It always warmed him when Odina called him Dad. As Odina had no relationship with her real father, Paul was honored that she considered him a substitute, and she was often kinder to him than his daughter Caitlyn was.

For the next couple of hours, Odina led the way—across a riverbed, stepping on stones to keep their feet dry; climbing over downed logs and bolting up a hill into an area of fir trees interspersed with brush. Caitlyn forged ahead, right behind Odina.

Paul fell behind again, breathing hard, and had a fleeting thought that hopefully Odina had a defibrillator in her pack. His heart pounded as he tackled the last fifty feet of the current incline, sweating now. Caitlin stopped at the top and glanced back, catching his eye before she turned away and continued.

He paused for a moment to catch his breath, miserable that Caitlin was still angry with him over losing the hard drive, at his foolishness in rejecting her proposal when she'd offered to keep it safe.

With another push, he reached level ground a few steps later. The women were almost beyond his sight. He channeled all the energy he could gather and jogged forward, breathing heavily, wondering if they would abandon him if he just collapsed.

Mike knocked on the door of the inn several times after finding it locked, but no one answered. Then he rounded the building in search of another entrance, which was also locked. Frustrated, he returned to his car and retrieved his backpack full of tools, then picked the lock.

Inside, he searched the guest rooms that were open, finding no one. He'd recognized Paul's car out front, so he knew the man must be nearby. Two other vehicles had Vermont plates. He guessed Anita would come here when she didn't find him in the village knowing Paul should be waiting.

Mike decided to commandeer room number one, where he would ambush whoever returned first. Laying out three pairs of handcuffs and his stun gun on the bed, he set the thermostat higher to sap the cold from the room. After propping both pillows against the headboard, he leaned back and rested his boot-covered feet on the white duvet cover. Then he passed the time by reading his phone, alert for any sound of movement.

CHAPTER FOURTEEN

DOORS

As she crossed over the U.S. border, Anita slid her new Canadian passport back into her handbag, relieved Saeed's work had gone undetected. Unfortunately, however, it made her late. It was ten o'clock and she wouldn't reach Stowe before 11:30, but at least the one hundred thousand U.S. dollars were packed into the lining of her suitcase in the trunk.

She texted Mike. Surely, he would wait another hour and wouldn't leave with all this cash on the way.

If only it could bring Steven back. That thought hit her like a hammer to her gut when she least expected it, always lurking in her subconscious. Shifting in her seat, she took deep breaths, pushing down painful thoughts that threatened to derail her. *Stay focused.* Facing Mike alone required a clear head. This was no time for melancholy. Last night she'd acted responsibly by dining in her hotel room instead of drinking with François again. As she sped toward Stowe, tension built in her head and tightened the muscles in her neck.

At 11:40, she pulled into the parking lot of the Green Mountain Inn and looked around for Mike. Seeing no one, she sent another text.

I'm here!! I have the money! Where are you?

A few minutes later, she called, but it rolled over to voice mail immediately. She waited another agonizing fifteen minutes, called again, and had the same result. The tension in her head made her want to scream. At an hour and a half past the time they were to meet, Anita resigned herself to Mike not showing up. He had warned her not to be late.

As she drove to the Deer Run Inn to deliver the bad news, she shrieked as loudly as possible, releasing her frustration, anger, and disappointment before breaking into tears.

She had failed. Despite all her best plans and efforts, she hadn't been able to buy back the hard drive or pay Mike off to ignore the bounty on her head. The risk that he would hunt her down and turn her in remained.

In the inn's parking lot, she recognized Paul's and Caitlyn's cars in the driveway next to Odina's Jeep. Alongside them was a BMW with Massachusetts plates. She stiffened, fearing it might belong to Mike, since he lived in Boston. With her suitcase and purse in hand, she fought back the anxiety creeping up her neck, shivering while her breath turned into mist. The cold had finally arrived.

Inside, the great room was empty. She rolled her suitcase behind the front desk where it sat hidden.

"Caitlyn? Odina?" No one answered. Odd, considering all their cars were outside. Clenching her teeth, she scanned the room. The long pine-wood table still had two partially filled coffee mugs on it and the chairs were at an angle, as though they'd left in a hurry.

"Hello?" Her breathing became shallow, and her headache was returning.

Still no answer. She set her handbag on the table and crossed the room toward the kitchen. A noise from her left made her jump.

Cuckoo . . . Cuckoo . . .

A little bird called out twelve o'clock from its Alpine cottage.

Silence otherwise. Where was everyone in the middle of the day? She walked into the hall with a row of guest rooms. Room 2 was the first on her left, its wide-open door revealing a pristine, untouched space.

To her right was Room 1. This door was shut and the surface was warm. Should she knock? Must be the BMW owner, she guessed. Before she backed away, the door flew open and Mike lunged at her. Her heart beat wildly as he twisted her arm behind her back and spun her away from him, slamming her face-first against the opposite wall as she yelped. Pain shot through her shoulder and jawbone, stunning her. A moment later, the cold metal of handcuffs tightened on her wrists, and she heard them click into place.

With a rough grip on her arms, Mike shoved Anita into his room. Reacting by instinct, she kicked him, but he caught her leg with his and tripped her onto the bed. He flipped her over to her back with her arms pinned beneath her and jumped on her legs. She screamed with a long explosion of air. Before her next breath, he jammed a pillow over her face and leaned on it.

Terror engulfed her as she struggled to inhale, the pillow getting sucked against her nostrils and into her mouth. *I'm going to suffocate!* She went limp, hoping he would remove the pillow if she didn't fight him. *I give up,* she wanted to cry. Her head grew fuzzy, and a whooshing sound grew louder in her ears as her chest began to cave in on itself. Struggling to move again, her body was held immobile by his, and she had no more strength to fight. As she surrendered to the outcome, the pressure on her face lessened, and a sliver of light appeared. She coughed, then hyperventilated as air reached her lungs. The pillow was still barely an inch from her face.

"Quiet . . . I'll be quiet." Anita choked and gasped.

Mike threw the pillow against the headboard and stood. Anita stayed frozen in place.

"I brought . . . the money." Her breaths came out erratically. "I'm late but . . . can we still do this?"

"Where's the money?"

"It's here. Do you have the hard drive?"

Mike let out a harsh laugh. "Look who thinks they're in a position to negotiate!" He moved closer to her and jammed his knee between her legs, forcing them apart, causing her to flinch. "What else you got to offer me sweetheart? Got anything to add to the deal?"

Nausea churned in her stomach. "I'm *old*. I've got nothing you want."

He hesitated, looking her over with a sneer. "Got that right." His knee moved away. "Tell me about the money."

"It's in my suitcase. Behind the front desk."

From his backpack, he pulled out a length of twisted brown rope. Tying one end of it around her ankle and double knotting it, he held onto the other end. "Let's go take a look. You lead the way."

Anita stood slowly, trying to regain her equilibrium.

"Move!" he shouted.

Shaking, she hobbled ahead while he wound the rope around his hand. His other hand gripped her by the handcuffs still locked behind her back, preventing her from either running away or kicking him.

When they reached the great room, he tied his end of the rope to a pole beam and looped it around her other foot and through her handcuffs, pulling it tight to force her into a squat. She groaned. Her knees did not like this position.

He found her suitcase behind the counter and laid it out on the sofa, unzipping it.

"Look in the lining. It's all there. One hundred thousand dollars, as we agreed."

Mike threw Anita's clothes on the floor and unzipped the lining. As he extracted packs of hundred-dollar bills, he nodded and smiled. After counting out the first bundle, he pulled out the other nine stacks and compared their size, then flipped through the bills in each, examining them.

"You're a good girl after all. I wasn't sure you'd come through."

Anita was still shaking, but her breathing had slowed. "I've satisfied my end of the deal. Where's the hard drive? Can we finish here and be on our way?"

"In my car. I thought it belonged to Paul Tanner. Where is he? His car is here."

Anita worried about Paul, Caitlyn and Odina. But the fact

that Mike hadn't seen Paul suggested he was safe—even hiding from him. Maybe he would come in and rescue her again.

"I just got here. Your guess is as good as mine. Was anyone else here when you arrived?"

"No one."

Anita breathed easier, knowing he hadn't harmed any of them. She squirmed as she struggled to move her legs. "Can you untie me now? This hurts. My legs are cramping. You have your money. Leave the handcuffs on if you want but at least let me stand."

He scooped the bundles into the suitcase and carried it out the front door.

"*Please?*" She shouted, fearing he would leave her in pain.

A couple of minutes later, he returned with a plain black hard drive. "You must know what's on here since you want it so bad. What's so important?"

She didn't like the sound of this. "Why does it matter to you? I paid for it so it's mine. Unless you're going to double-cross me."

"You paid for your freedom. The drive was an add-on. Can you read the data on here?"

"Yes." Anita was getting good at lying. "Do you have a laptop with you? We can boot it up and I'll show you."

Mike peered at her. "How would you know how to decrypt it? You didn't work with Paul. I checked you both out."

Her mind raced. "My company consulted for EnerGeLabs. That's our encryption. I reviewed and signed off on the specs. Tested it, too. Security was our business." This part was almost true. There was often a security component to their projects. Her oversight provided her with enough information to fake her knowledge.

"Ow. Leg cramp. Please untie me."

He walked over and pulled the rope out of the handcuffs but left it tied to her feet.

Anita moaned as she gradually straightened her legs, using her handcuffed hands to rachet herself up the pole.

"I'll fetch my laptop. Show me what's on here and we're done." He walked to the guest room and returned with his laptop. After he set it on the table, he attached the hard drive with a USB cord and turned it on.

"I can't decrypt it tied to this pole with my hands behind my back."

"Tell me what to type and I'll do it."

"I need to read the details and respond accordingly. It has multiple steps, and if you type something wrong, you'll need to wait an hour to try again. You already tried. You know how tricky it is."

He scowled, reached into his pocket for a key and unlocked her handcuffs. She rolled her shoulders in relief. Next, he untied her feet, leaving the rope on one foot and wrapped it around the table leg in a loop and tied it.

"I'm staying right here, not going anywhere," she assured him while inside her stomach was in knots. "We should be able to finish here and have both of us walk away with what we want, right?"

What she wanted was for Mike to say yes, that he intended to let her go, hand her the hard drive and leave with the money, like they'd agreed. But that was likely wishful thinking. If he planned on giving it to her, he wouldn't care about decrypting it. All she could do was stall him long enough until the others returned to help, or she could discover a way to escape.

"Start decrypting," he said, as his phone rang. Looking at the caller, he answered it.

"Hi. I'm glad you called."

Anita typed commands she remembered which spit back technical messages. Mike wasn't paying attention now. The call was distracting him.

"I have very interesting information about a climate science research laboratory they shut down two years ago. Something you care about. We need to talk in person."

His conversation suggested what she suspected—he was taking the drive to someone else. She began running a useless process to scan the drive, which displayed a progress bar across the screen. *10% done* it read. It might buy her some time if Mike wasn't reading over her shoulder.

Think! Think! Her mind was blank, and she probably didn't have long before he saw through her charade. As she ground her teeth together and stared at the screen, she shoved her hands absently into her jacket pockets. Her left hand hit a cold metal tube. François' pepper spray. Carefully, she slid the lever open with her thumb.

"Yes. Absolutely. Text me the address and I will bring it to you. Thank you. Thank you very much. I deeply appreciate it."

As Mike put the phone away and turned his attention back to the screen, Anita's hand flew from her pocket, spraying directly into his face.

He howled like a wounded animal, coughing and spitting as he staggered backwards and fell over a chair behind him. Using her jacket to cover her face, she lifted the corner of the table and slid out the rope. She yanked the hard drive off the cord and tossed it into her handbag that was still on the table where she'd left it, then rushed outside to her car.

She slammed it into reverse and swung around behind Mike's car. He hadn't come out of the house yet, so she leaped out, grabbed her suitcase with the money from the BMW and threw it into her front seat.

When she reached route 108, she turned right and drove north, instead of left toward the interstate. Since no snow had fallen yet, the gates were still open for the mountain pass through Smuggler's Notch. The road narrowed to where two cars could scarcely pass each other but she sped along the twisty turns in the gorge, high on adrenaline, basking in her triumph.

CHAPTER FIFTEEN

FALLOUT

Mike opened his eye a slit and tried to blink away the pain. A harsh odor was wafting from his jacket and shirt, causing him to violently cough. He yanked them off and threw them across the room as tires squealed out of the driveway. His face burned, as if scalding water had been thrown across it. With his fingers pinching his nostrils shut, he staggered to the kitchen.

At the sink, he flushed his eyes under the faucet, but his face continued to sting. He snatched a pump bottle of hand soap and squirted it over his burning skin. As he scrubbed, the pain gradually subsided. Grabbing the sink sprayer, he rinsed himself while water ran down his torso to his jeans. His hair was drenched. Puddles covered the counter, floor, and water soaked the towels hanging on the rack.

He shivered, dripping, as he ran to his room to dry off using the towels in the bathroom, relieved by the warmth.

"Stupid. You're so stupid!" he shouted at himself, hearing his father's voice. "You fucking, stupid idiot!" Anger ripped through him like wildfire. He yanked the glass-shaded lamp from its electrical socket on the end table and threw it across the room where it smashed into pieces against the wall. The end table was next. He smacked the legs against the wall, splintering them into pieces. Lastly, he shattered the entire tabletop against the headboard, leaving a deep gouge.

Breaking stuff helped diffuse his anger. Now he was able to think.

Grabbing a wet towel, Mike covered his nose and mouth, and stormed into the great room for his backpack. The lingering pepper spray still stung his eyes, causing him to squint. With his free hand, he stuffed the laptop into his backpack. When he flung open the front door, a blast of wind struck his bare chest. Three jackets still hung on the rack beside the door. He picked the biggest one, slipped his arms into the oversized sleeves, and ran to his car.

Through the back window of the BMW, he discovered Anita's suitcase with the money had vanished.

"*Bitch!*" he screamed. "You are dead, bitch. You are dead."

His anger had focus now. Throwing down his backpack, he returned to the kitchen and grabbed a chef's knife. Outside, he grunted as he jammed the knife deep into the first tire of Paul's car. A satisfying gush of air escaped when he removed it. By the time he'd punctured all the tires on all three vehicles, he felt in control again. Finished, he stabbed the knife into the ground behind Paul's car.

⌇

Paul, Odina, and Caitlyn stood on a boulder looking out through a clearing at the tops of trees below being tossed around by the wind. A few brown leaves clung to their otherwise bare branches. Paul gazed uphill at the trail ahead, exhausted.

"Can we go back now?" Paul asked Odina after wolfing down one of the protein bars she'd given each of them. "I don't think I can walk anymore. We still have to hike all the way down."

She checked her watch. "He definitely isn't following us. We would have seen him by now. The question is whether or not he's gone. What's the consensus?"

"I say we go regardless," Paul said. "I'm worried about Anita. She was supposed to meet him at 10:30."

Caitlyn brushed the crumbs from her hand and Odina offered her a box of apple juice from the pack. "Sorry, love. Didn't have time to fill the water bottles before we left. I only have these."

Caitlyn gave her a feeble smile. "Thank you. I'm grateful you're here to think for both of us. I panicked." She took the juice and hugged Odina.

"Do you have any more of those?" Paul asked.

Reaching into her pack again, Odina threw a box to Paul, who caught it. "I have to agree with Paul," she said to Caitlyn. "We should return and find out if he's still there. If he is, we may be able to catch him off guard."

They finished their juices and began their descent. An hour later, they spotted the inn through the trees. Odina halted and signaled for them to stop. "You two stay here. I'm going to cut through the woods to the parking lot. Check if his car is gone."

Caitlyn frowned. "I'm not letting you go by yourself. Two of us might be able to take him."

"No." Her hushed voice was stern. "Seriously. I'm stealthy in the woods, and I don't want to be worrying about you. I need to stay focused. Wait behind a tree. If I yell, then come."

"I'll come with her, too." Paul's legs shook from the climb, making his promise dubious.

Odina stepped off the trail and navigated through the brush to their right, then disappeared behind a stand of firs. As she promised, only a slight rustle of leaves sounded from the woods while the wind tossed their branches.

Paul leaned against a tree while Caitlyn stood behind another one across the trail.

"Honey," he said, "I know you're mad at me. I don't know how to make this right."

"You can't. What's done is done. Let's not talk about it."

Her words were like a gut punch. Paul hung his head. It was bad enough his wife thought so little of him, but now Caitlyn?

Odina shouted. "He's gone."

Paul dragged his jellylike legs the last few yards toward the inn as Caitlyn sprinted on ahead to the parking lot to join Odina. As he got near, he heard Caitlyn yelling. "God damn it! Damn it, damn it!"

He rounded the corner of the inn where the two women stared at flat tires on their vehicles. Then he realized his were also flat.

Wow. Mike was pissed. Sure glad he didn't catch us.

His eyes drifted to the knife standing upright, the blade half buried in the ground, and his heart rate rocketed.

"What the hell?"

They turned to him as he retrieved the knife.

Caitlyn's eyes widened. "It looks like that's meant for you. And he made sure we aren't going anywhere."

CHAPTER SIXTEEN

AUTHORITY

PAUL WAS THE first to reach the front door of the inn, carrying the chef's knife he'd pulled up in the parking lot. Caitlyn and Odina were right behind him.

"It's not locked," he said, recalling Caitlyn using the dead-bolt when they fled a few hours earlier. Dread crept up his spine as he stepped inside. A powerful chemical odor hit him, causing him to wheeze.

"What's that awful smell?" Caitlyn asked as she and Odina began coughing.

"Cover your face . . . open the windows." Odina gasped and pulled her jacket across her face. "It's pepper spray."

Odina dove out of the great room while Caitlyn and Paul rushed to the windows and shoved them open. Paul took a deep breath of the cold outside air. A couple of minutes later, Odina returned with two large fans they set up. Once they began to breathe normally, Caitlyn took her chef's knife from the windowsill where Paul left it and took it into the kitchen.

"What the hell happened here?" Caitlyn asked, her voice strained.

Paul and Odina joined Caitlyn and stepped onto the wet kitchen floor. The cabinets were streaked in water, the faucet sprayer was fully extended and hanging out of the sink, and soaked towels were hanging askew on the rack.

"I was pepper sprayed at a protest once. I can guess what happened," Odina said. "Whoever was pepper sprayed ran to the sink to rinse their eyes out and wash the spray off their face. That stuff burns like hell."

"So at least two people were here," Paul said. "One got sprayed by another. We know one was Mike, but who else? Anita?"

"There are clothes over on the floor." Caitlyn pointed at crumpled garments lying in the great room near the dinner table.

Paul grabbed them and held them at arm's length. He wheezed again as he ran for the door and tossed them outside. "Pepper spray on men's clothes," Paul said. "Looks like Mike got the worst of it."

Odina studied the floor and followed the water trail along the hallway to where the guest rooms were located. "Shit!"

Paul and Caitlyn joined her at room number one.

"Look at this! Was there a fight here?" Caitlyn asked.

Chunks of broken glass were strewn across the room and splintered pieces of table legs and broken furniture were lying about.

"I loved that glass lamp," Caitlyn said, her voice cracking.

"With all the people we've had here, nothing had ever actually been damaged, and now . . . The table's a goner. And look at the gouge in the headboard. It's trashed."

Odina put her arms around Caitlyn who started to cry, holding Caitlyn's head against her shoulder and murmuring. "It's okay, love. It's going to be okay. We'll get through this. We will."

Paul approached his daughter and tried to hug her.

"Don't touch me." Caitlyn nudged him away. "You brought this to us. This is all your fault. We aren't even safe in our own home now."

Paul stepped back and choked down his hurt. Glass crunched under his feet as he walked away. In the great room, the air was getting fresher, but was frigid with the windows still open and the fans running. He shivered and zipped his jacket.

Keep busy, he told himself, ignoring the wound growing in his heart. He stood up the chair lying on the floor, then straightened the other chairs around the table. As he carried the coffee mugs into the kitchen, he cursed himself for trying to help Anita. He should have minded his own business and told her to rent a car to go to Boston.

In the kitchen, he put the faucet sprayer back, found dry towels in the drawer, and wiped down the cabinets and countertops. In the broom closet, he found the mop and mopped the kitchen floor, then took all the wet towels and set them in the sink. Mindless work, like he did all the time now. He flushed at the realization. No wonder no one respected him.

At least Anita had showed an interest in his work. That must be why he felt compelled to help her. What he wouldn't give to be back at work, using his brain. He ached over how much he'd lost. But with his hard drive, he could finish his work one day. He could feel it. Everything he needed was on it. His muscles tightened as he resolved to find it.

Caitlyn and Odina reappeared in the kitchen, where Paul was replacing the mop.

"Thank you." Odina gazed around at the neat kitchen. "Come have a seat. We need to talk."

The three of them returned to the table, where a few short hours earlier, they'd sat together having coffee.

"We need a plan for when Mike returns," Caitlyn said to Paul. "The first part of our plan includes you being gone."

He was stunned, and hurt, that his own daughter would insist he leave when she was in danger. "I can't go. I have four flat tires." Heat crawled up his neck over the injustice of her demand. "Besides, I want to be here to protect you both if he comes back."

Caitlyn sighed. "Your being here is what's endangering us. If you're gone, he may leave. He doesn't know who we are. But he knows where to find you in Newport. He'll look for you. You need to hide out somewhere else. Not here."

He understood she was right but refused to admit it. "You should both leave for a couple of days, too, until you know he's not coming back. Do you have friends you can stay with?"

Odina nodded. "I'll feel safer sleeping somewhere else tonight."

The inn's phone rang. Odina and Caitlyn ignored it, letting it roll over to voice mail. Moments later, it rang again.

"Do you think it's him?" Paul asked.

They sat still until it stopped.

"I'll check for messages," Caitlyn said. "If it's a customer, I can call them back."

It rang again, and this time Caitlyn answered. "Deer Run Inn. How may I help you?" She paused. "Oh. Hi, Anita. We've been wondering what happened to you. Were you here today?"

Paul motioned for her to give him the phone.

She waved him away. "Oh, wow," she said after listening. "No, we're fine. He was gone when we returned, but we're still airing out the pepper spray. In addition to that, he slashed all our tires on the way out, so we're expecting him to come back."

Paul walked over to Caitlyn and stood beside her, trying to listen.

"Well, I'm glad you have the hard drive. We were worried about it." She looked at Paul and nodded. Paul let out a huge breath of relief.

"It's probably safer with you. That might be the best place for it now. Mike already stole it from Dad in Newport, and he knows where we are. No one knows where you are. Let's keep it that way."

Paul's mouth dropped open as he frantically shook his head "no." Caitlyn had no right to decide where it should be kept. It was his hard drive. He grabbed her hand to wrestle the phone away, but Odina jumped between them, glaring. He let go, not wanting to fight.

"Have to go," Caitlyn said and disconnected.

"Hold on a minute," Paul shouted. "Who gave you authority over my hard drive?"

"You did," Caitlyn shouted back. "You did when it was stolen from you. You did when you led that monster to our inn. That technology does not belong to you alone. Somebody can finish developing it. We need it. The planet needs it. Isn't that what we've been doing here for the last two years? Trying to make a difference in our collective future?"

Paul glowered at her as he burned with anger. "It wouldn't even exist without me. They destroyed everything when they came through our building. I had the foresight to save it. I'm the one who should start it up again. I'm like its parent."

"And parents need to understand when to let go of their children, when they're doing more harm to them than good. That's what's happening here."

Paul's self-control kept him frozen in place, despite the anger seething through him.

"It's time for you to go now," Odina said. "I'll give you the number of a garage in town. They can tow you and fix you up with tires. I'm sorry."

As Odina texted the number to Paul's phone, he channeled his anger into determination. He would get his hard drive back and prove his value. He swore it on his life.

CHAPTER SEVENTEEN

STOP

THE HERTZ RENTAL facility was three blocks from Anita's hotel in a neighborhood of high rises. The attendant examined her car while her eyes darted around the garage, wary of unsavory characters who may have followed her. A man sat in another car nearby. Was he staring at her?

"Madam?" The attendant's voice startled her to attention. He was holding out her receipt.

"Merci." She snatched it from him and stuffed it into her bag, then rolled her suitcase away.

Silly, she chastised herself as she tried to calm her jitters. *No one would be following me in Montreal.* Except maybe someone who knew she bought a fake passport. Or were hunting her for the bounty. She shivered.

On the walk to the hotel, she battled the fierce wind ripping between the skyscrapers, shielding her face as she dragged her suitcase. The blast cut through her lightweight jacket and stung her bare hands. A block from her hotel, she relinquished the fight and slid into a doorway to warm up. A man in a dark coat passed by her and glanced her way. She shuddered, hesitated a moment, then peeked around the edge to see where he'd gone. The street was clear. Her heart pounded as she imagined him waiting in a doorway to attack her.

Stop it, she scolded herself. *Just stop.*

After a few breaths, she mustered the courage to make one last sprint to her hotel.

Once in her room, Anita dumped her suitcase on the luggage stand next to the television. When she unzipped it, she discovered loose hundred-dollar bills scattered among the bundles. She scooped the money together and stacked it all in her room safe.

After she flopped onto the bed and kicked off her sneakers, she dialed room service and ordered a turkey sandwich and a glass of red wine—her body was screaming for food.

The elation from earlier in the afternoon had disappeared. Instead of relaxing, she felt restless. Muscle aches intermittently shot through her shoulders and back from the strain of having her arms pinned underneath her and driving for five hours. Slowly she moved her head around, trying to release the tension in her neck. Her thighs burned from being forced to squat in the great room. Finally, she jumped up and began pacing, agitation building in her core. The memory of the pillow over her face made her chest tight and her breathing shallow, as though struggling for air. She pressed both hands over her chest, flinching from a sharp pain stabbing her wrist. Upon examination, she discovered her skin was rubbed raw in one spot where the handcuffs had been. She wailed, breaking into tears.

Her body shook. She fell onto the bed and curled into a ball, sobbing as she wrapped her arms around herself and rocked. If only Julian were here to hold her, to tell her in his calm voice that she was fine. When she was stressed, he'd been a steady anchor in a storm. Where had *that* Julian gone? Long before someone dragged him away, that part of Julian was already missing, leaving her alone in her grief.

Although Julian had failed as a husband when she needed him after Steven's death, he'd always been a wonderful father. When she couldn't be around because her work pulled her away, he had been there. Reliable. She couldn't abandon him now. The memory of Steven compelled her to rescue him.

The tension in her body eased from crying and rocking herself. Sitting up, she grabbed a tissue from the side table and blew her nose.

A knock on the door unnerved her, causing another rise in her pulse, but it turned out just to be room service.

Before she ate a bite, Anita set her tray on the bed and gulped down half of her wine. She leaned against the headboard and relished the heat of the alcohol as it flowed through her head. Her jaw relaxed. After a few more breaths, she devoured her sandwich in silence. Now calm, she called François to tell him she'd made it back to Montreal.

"I am glad you called. I was very worried."

"You had good reason to be. I'll tell you about it later. When can we talk?"

"You must come to my apartment tonight. We have an

important meeting to plan. I will have dinner for us. Eight o'clock?"

Three hours. Enough time to shower, change, and ignore her guilt because of her excitement over seeing François again.

⁂

When François opened the door to his apartment, he raised one eyebrow and gave her a nod. "You look far nicer than last time you were here, my dear."

"Thank you," she replied, glad he noticed, touched by the term of endearment she recalled him using years ago. She'd blow-dried her hair and applied makeup, although she hadn't dressed up. Jeans and a new cozy red sweater were her attire for a quiet evening, along with knee-high boots.

"The meeting starts in five minutes," he said as he poured her a glass of red wine from an open bottle on the kitchen counter. "In my office. Follow me."

His musky cologne was the same scent he'd worn at the restaurant. Excitement stirred in her, but she brushed it aside.

The office was nicer than she'd expected after the living room. This must be where François spent most of his time. Dark gray walls were offset by white-trimmed baseboards and a polished wood floor. Track lighting hung from the ceiling over the black computer desk.

He took a seat in a rolling chair and motioned for Anita to sit beside him in a folding metal one. At the computer, he started a meeting and adjusted the webcam, then pulled her chair close so she appeared alongside him.

"I have a highly secured connection here. We can talk freely." Their shoulders touched.

Two other participants popped onto the screen and François began.

"How is the weather in Toronto today, Zack?" he asked. "It is finally like November here."

"Still warm here. Disturbing. Who's with you?"

"My guest is Anita Forester. Her husband is Julian Forester, our current rescue project. Anita is financing this operation, so she deserves to see how her money is spent. I also want you to all meet each other. We will be working together."

Anita was pleased he trusted her to meet with his team. The man and woman on the call greeted her and introduced themselves. Zack was a thin young man with black-rimmed glasses, pale skin and short brown hair—he looked like a banker to her. Erin was a lightly tanned young woman with blond hair streaked by the sun and blue eyes. She wore no makeup but looked like a model, Anita thought with a touch of jealousy.

"Zack, have you verified Julian Forester is still at the Coal Creek detention center?"

This was the first time Anita had heard the name of where Julian was held, a real place detectable on a map. Hope fluttered in her belly that they could rescue him.

"Yes. I've been doing research and I think to get him out will require an insider."

"This will not be easy. No one hates environmentalists more than coal miners, but everyone has their price. Erin, can you go there now and make contact with the locals, find someone who needs cash? That may be everyone in Appalachia. Getting them to trust you will be harder."

"I'll be fine. Coal country has always been on my bucket list." Erin chuckled. "You send me to the best places, François."

Zack laughed.

"Only the best for the best. Let Zack know what identity you are using and any supplies you may need. Once you cross the border, we will be out of touch. Burner phones only, okay?"

"You got it," Zack replied.

François muted the mic and turned to Anita. "Erin has done the preliminary work for our other rescues in the North Dakota and Nevada detention centers. Those went well. But we have never done one in West Virginia. I find it useful to have a beautiful woman work a town to charm the locals before I arrive." He winked and Anita forced a smile of approval as she wondered about his relationship with Erin.

Flipping the mic back on, François continued. "Zack, have you discovered anything new about this person in detention you said Julian wanted to find?

Anita bolted upright. Maybe this would explain why he put himself in such a risky position, like he wanted to be captured, an unanswered question that haunted her.

"Rumor has it he's located him."

Anita's eyes widened.

"Do we know who he is?" François asked, voicing Anita's thoughts.

"Sorry. That's all I got. It's getting harder to find information. The one source I had has gone dark. My other information is coming through Nevada from my guy who reads their database. All it has is Julian's name and date of arrival."

François frowned. "This is bad news. Without sources, how can we work? This complicates the operation. I want to have passports for both Julian and whoever the other person is. Otherwise, we will have to walk them across the border."

"Who are these people?" Anita was more confused than ever.

"We do not know who runs these places," François said. "They are all in previously abandoned buildings in remote areas. Any contacts with higher-ups are done by phone. No visuals. Based on our one remaining contact, the employees are all paid in cash, and they carry weapons."

"So even if we break Julian out, we have no idea who the enemy is."

"None." François slowly shook his head, dropping his eyes.

The four of them were silent. As Anita studied the other two onscreen, she recognized the same discouragement she felt.

Erin interrupted the silence. "I already have what I need. I can leave as soon as you have the passport and license tomorrow," she said. "I'll pose as a photographer on assignment."

"You need to be extra careful this time, Erin. I do not like what Zack is hearing. We will meet again tomorrow at the same time for an update."

"Ok, boss. If I'm not here, say a prayer for me. Nice to meet you, Anita. Next time I'll see you in person, somewhere in the danger zone. I'm pumped!" Erin threw them a double thumbs-up, blew a kiss, and exited the meeting.

"Catchya later." Zack disappeared from the screen.

François ended the call and rolled his chair back as he faced Anita. "That is my team. What do you think?" He folded his hands in his lap.

"They're knowledgeable. Erin seems fearless. But I thought there'd be more."

"Less is better. Not as dangerous. I trust these two completely. They are loyal and they do it for the right reasons."

Anita hesitated. Had Julian done what he did for the right reasons? She wished she understood. He'd never been much of an activist before Steven's death. Of course, neither had she, except to donate money and call her representatives. Now he was searching for someone being held in an off-the-books detention center—another activist, she imagined, since anyone else would be held somewhere more accessible. "What do you consider the right reasons?"

"To preserve life on our planet. To rescue those who are persecuted for speaking out or practicing science. To stop big oil from destroying our future for riches."

She stared into his eyes, and he glanced away, as though uncomfortable. Neither of them moved right away. Then he met her eyes again. "That is not why I am doing this one," François said finally. "I do this one for you."

Goosebumps shot up Anita's arms. Her eyes steered away from his gaze. She feared he would see her growing feelings for him, and she couldn't allow that. Julian was her husband and this—whatever it was—was wrong.

A loud buzz rang through the apartment, breaking the tension of the moment and making her jump.

"Dinner has arrived."

They sat at his kitchen counter sharing plates of Thai ginger vegetables over jasmine rice, and tofu with peanut sauce and fried spinach as Anita relayed the events of the day. She pushed up the sleeves of her sweater to show François the raw skin on her wrist.

He cradled her hand and inspected it. "It hurts me to think he did this to you. You were very brave and a quick thinker. I wish I could have been there to help."

"Thank you. Your pepper spray saved my life."

"Are you okay? It can be very upsetting when something like this happens."

"I'm trying not to think about it. Being here makes me feel safe."

"I am glad. Call me anytime you are afraid." He squeezed her hand before letting it go.

They continued eating and Anita finished her wine. The aroma of their meal filled the air between them. Setting down her chopsticks, she poured the rest of the bottle into her glass.

"Tell me what your life has been like," she said. "You know about my life, but I know nothing about yours. Were you ever married?"

He nodded and continued to eat. Anita stared at him, growing impatient and drinking more of her wine. "So? Aren't you going to tell me about it?"

Shrugging his shoulders, he rested his chopsticks on his plate. "Twice. Six years the first time. Two years the next time. No children. Women want a husband who is not married to his work." He took another bite of his dinner.

"Maybe you never found the right one," she said, trying to sound casual.

Without looking at her, François replied. "No. I found the right one. But she married my best friend."

For a moment Anita forgot to breathe. Her racing pulse throbbed in her ears and her mind exploded with "what ifs."

François gulped down the rest of his wine and walked into the kitchen, where he pulled another bottle from his rack and placed it on the counter.

"Am I confused?" she asked. "Because I seem to remember you left me. Left me to come back here and follow your dream."

He twisted a corkscrew into the bottle, gave it a pull, and refilled his glass before placing the bottle between them. The wine swirled around his glass as he held it up to the light, spinning it as though the results were critical. After taking a mouthful, he closed his eyes for a moment before he spoke. "You made your decision to take that job and never asked what I thought. I knew then I did not matter enough to you."

Anita's blood rose in her cheeks as she swallowed back tears, slowly shaking her head. "That wasn't it at all. I was just excited about getting a job offer. I wasn't even thinking . . ." She stopped when she realized what she was about to say. *I wasn't even thinking about you.* Stepping away from the counter, she turned away from him, knowing she had indeed taken him for granted all those years ago. After thirty-three years of believing he'd broken her heart to follow his dream, she now realized she'd broken his.

While she leaned against the counter and stared at the floor, she ruminated over those last days: François throwing her clothes in a paper bag and telling her they were wrong for each other, the calls he ignored, Julian rushing over to comfort her when she'd cried over François leaving.

Tears filled her eyes.

François walked around the counter and pulled her to him. "I am sorry, my dear. I did not mean to upset you. But it is the truth, no?"

She lay her head onto his shoulder and wept. "You never . . . even said goodbye." The pain she believed she'd conquered many years ago now felt fresh.

"I know. I could not bear it." He stroked her hair as he rubbed her back, letting out a deep sigh. "I never stopped loving you. It is why two marriages failed. Not because of my work. Because I never got over you."

Pulling back, Anita studied his face. The truth was in his eyes, in the longing and hurt reflected there. François bent forward and kissed her hesitantly. She kissed him back, tentative at first, then deeper. His mouth, his lips, the heat of him against her churned up old memories. A slow burn inched through her body as she was dragged back in time.

François stopped suddenly and backed away. "I think you must go." He reached for his phone. "I will call you a cab."

Why, her mind screamed, as she ached for him. But she knew why. She was married; they were going to rescue her husband, who was in a detention center in West Virginia, maybe being tortured because he was trying to do the right thing.

"You're right. Of course. I should go."

As she made her way out, François said, "Come back tomorrow at eight o'clock for the next meeting. Have dinner before you arrive."

CHAPTER EIGHTEEN

CHECKMATE

TIME TO PULL out the winter jacket, Paul thought as he stepped out of his car in Newport, shivering. The temperature had dropped thirty degrees from when he'd left with Anita three days earlier. His legs ached from the forced hike in Stowe earlier, and he was exhausted. At his back door, he turned the handle and it opened. At least Mike hadn't smashed a window to break in, but after the mess at his daughter's inn, his neck muscles tightened from anxiety over what he'd find inside. He could probably hide from Mike somewhere else for a few days, but what was the point? If Mike was coming for him, sooner or later he'd find Paul here. At least now he was ready for him.

The kitchen looked the same as he'd left it—breakfast dishes put away and ready for guests. He circled the rest of the first floor, starting with the dining room, where all eight chairs were pushed under the lace-covered table. In the adjacent living room, the large-screen television—the most expensive item in the house—still hung on the wall, untouched. Apparently, Mike wasn't a common thief looking to hawk Paul's belongings. A Newport photo book remained on the glass-topped coffee table and decorative pillows were still spaced neatly along the leather couch.

Paul remembered his computer and dashed to the basement office. It hadn't moved. The yellow Post-it note for Anita's guest account name and password was still stuck to the bottom of the monitor, but several folders were on the floor, their contents scattered. Inside the open desk drawers, envelopes, plastic bags, markers, and charging cords were strewn around.

Seeing his personal records spread about like trash made his stomach churn. He tried to remember if they contained anything important Mike might have taken. On top was a folder with papers sticking out. Paul shuffled through it, seeing invoices for carpeting, cash register receipts, and the floor diagram he'd drawn for the carpet installers. Shoving them back inside the folder, he dropped it on his desk in disgust.

Right now, he wanted to go upstairs and lie in his own bed. Catch a football game. He'd bought pepper spray at Walmart on the way home. If it worked for Anita, it could work for him. In the kitchen, he selected one of his cast iron frying pans from the rack over the sink and carried it with him to his room. There on his bed sat all his checkbooks.

"Aw shit," he muttered as he dropped the frying pan onto the bed. He'd forgotten he'd hid those under the mattress along with the hard drive. Mike must have found them but didn't bother stealing them. Perhaps Mike was taunting him, showing off how easily he'd found all Paul's hidden items.

He propped his pillows against the headboard, turned on

his reading light and shut off the ceiling light, then checked the bank balances on his phone. Both accounts were untouched, but he'd still have to close them out and open new ones. Slipping the pepper spray under his pillow, he threw his jacket over the frying pan on the bed.

A nearby thud startled him. He grabbed the pepper spray and flipped off the reading light, darkening the room. Two more thuds came quickly, followed by a swishing sound. Snatching the frying pan, he flung himself onto the floor behind the bed where he was hidden from sight, suppressing a groan because of his throbbing leg muscles. His heart jumped as something moved to his side. Staring wide-eyed in that direction, he slowly realized it was shadows caused by outdoor lights flickering through the gaps in the window blind. The wind howled. He crawled over to the window and peeked out, watching tree branches whack the side of the house. Disgusted by his panic, Paul climbed back onto the bed, dragging the iron pan along with him but leaving the light off this time.

When he checked his email on his phone, it contained a lot of junk: a bunch of ads hawking pre-holiday gift shopping and requests for donations. Basketball was on television. Not his favorite. Besides, he couldn't hear other sounds with the TV playing, so he shut it off and scrolled through social media.

When he grew bored, he flipped to his phone app and stared at his favorites, focusing on his wife's number, but not calling. When was the last time they'd talked? Scrolling through his recent calls, an unfamiliar Pennsylvania number caught his attention. Anita had used his phone that day to call her friend. A jolt of excitement shot through him, hoping the friend would know how to reach Anita. He tapped the number. A recording answered, identifying the owner as Stacey and asking him to leave a message.

"Hello. I'm Paul, a friend of Anita's. She called you on my phone a few days ago. Now she's in Canada and needs help, but I don't have her new number. Can you give me a call?"

Whatever it took, he needed his hard drive back.

Mike took a slow drive past the Deer Run Inn to check for Paul's car. Floodlights lit the parking area. Gone. The other two vehicles were still there, but he didn't care. The hard drive was what mattered, and he needed Paul to unlock the data on it. Slamming on his brakes, he pounded the steering wheel. *Shit! Shit! Shit!* A vision of walking into his father's hotel room and admitting he'd failed gnawed away at his chest. This was supposed to be his chance to prove his worth, and instead, he was proving the opposite. He drove south to the interstate, grinding his teeth. What was he going to do about this meeting? If he admitted a woman got the better of him, his father would call him a loser. There had to be some way to fix this.

His thoughts raged. Back in the schoolyard, bullies called him names because they didn't believe he had a father. He'd given them black eyes more than once. Showed them he was tough. Defended his mother's honor. But he wasn't some street thug. He was smart and proved it to all of them—proved it to his father too, when he got his computer science degree. His father hadn't seemed impressed, but he would be now, if only he could crack the encryption on the drive. If only he still had it. Clenching the steering wheel, anger tightened the muscles in his hands, arms and neck, demanding action.

Newport. That had to be where Paul went. Mike cranked up the speed on his BMW and checked his police and traffic tracking app. Cars on his right became a blur as he passed. Driving fast quelled his anger and made him feel in control. The faster the better.

❧

When Mike arrived in Newport, it had been dark for several hours. After parking up the street from the Howard Street Bed and Breakfast, he removed a new gas mask from his Home Depot bag, inserted a filter, and slipped it into his backpack. No need to alarm the neighbors by wearing it on the street. Paul's car was in the driveway as he had hoped, next to Anita's, which was still covered in leaves. The porch lights were on, along with the interior first floor lights, so he walked along the driveway to the back.

The floodlight switched on as he approached the back door. Locked again, but that wouldn't stop him. He'd have to work fast to break in before anyone spotted him.

Once inside, he ducked into the cellar stairway and set down his backpack. He retrieved a set of handcuffs and slipped them into his pocket, then fastened the gas mask across his face. No way was he getting pepper-sprayed again. He positioned a stun gun in his right hand.

The house was quiet. Careful to avoid the windows in the well-lit rooms, where a neighbor might report a man in a gas mask walking around, he hid in the hallway, peering around the corner into the dining room, then the living room. At the stairs, he bolted up two floors over oriental carpet runners toward Paul's room, stopping dead when a stair creaked near the stoop. A Tiffany style lamp lit the third-floor landing. Through the railings, he saw Paul's door was shut. Slowly raising his foot, the next stair creaked as he put it down. Mike gritted his teeth and listened. No sound from the bedroom. He inhaled and prepared to ambush. As he exhaled, he charged through the door of the bedroom and found . . . no Paul.

He silently panned the room. The bedcovers were rumpled, and pillows sat against the headboard. Paul had to be here. He jerked the bedroom door toward him—nothing. At a rustling sound from behind, he swung around. Something hard and heavy hit his gas mask, knocking it sideways. Mike shoved the mask back into position and grabbed Paul's arm mid-swing on his next attack, bending it backwards. Paul yowled and dropped a cast-iron pan as Mike jabbed the stun gun into Paul's side and hit the trigger. Paul fell backwards onto the bed and didn't move, his eyes staring into space. Mike grabbed the handcuffs from his pocket, threw one on Paul's wrist, and dragged him to the wrought-iron headboard. He pulled the handcuffs through the rungs before fastening the other cuff on him.

Paul began to stir. He blinked twice and his eyes widened.

"Checkmate," Mike said.

Yanking at his handcuffs, Paul twisted his body in vain, as Mike stood above him still in the gas mask.

"Don't kill me, please don't kill me. Please."

Mike tossed the gas mask on the bed. "Stop whining like a little girl. It's embarrassing. I'm not going to kill you."

"Then why am I handcuffed to my own bed?" Paul shouted.

"Because you tried to hit me with a frying pan. And I need you to listen. I'm not sure you will without the handcuffs."

Paul's eyes narrowed. "Okay. I'm listening." He leaned on his elbow and moaned as he pulled up his legs into a half-sitting position.

"Sorry about the stun gun. Those hurt."

"Ya think?" Paul groaned.

"Here's the deal. I was supposed to be paid a hundred thousand dollars by Anita to overlook her bounty with your hard drive thrown in. Anita agreed to that. Instead, she took off with the money *and* the hard drive. You and me both got screwed. The way I see it, we have a common enemy. Anita Forester." Mike sat on the edge of the bed, hoping Paul would agree.

Paul frowned. "If you hadn't robbed me to begin with, I would still have the hard drive and Anita wouldn't be my problem."

Mike smirked. "Here's the part you're forgetting. You robbed me of Anita. With the bounty on her, I would have collected it if you hadn't decided to play hero. The hard drive was my way of making up for my loss. But apparently, I stumbled onto something far more valuable than her bounty. Plus, I can help you get it back."

Paul's face contorted as he shifted around as much as the handcuffs allowed. Finally, he sighed and sat still. "Why would you do that?"

"Because we can both benefit from this in a big way. But I need you to do so. And you can benefit much more than you probably think, which is why you need me."

"Okay. You've got my interest. Now take these handcuffs off so we can go downstairs and discuss this."

❧

The next morning, at the Four Seasons Hotel One Dalton Street in Boston, Mike gave the valet his car and entered the stunning curved triangular high-rise, using the keycard his father left him at the reception desk to reach the fifteenth floor. Along the way, he rehearsed how he would present his proposal.

Inside the room, his father sat in an oversized light-gray chair with a pillow tucked under his arm. Beyond him was a curved floor-to-ceiling window overlooking the massive dome of the Christian Science church.

"Good to see you, Mike," his father said. "It's been a while. You doing well?"

Mike's father had aged since the last time he'd seen him three years ago. His hair was no longer dark with white strands, but gray. More wrinkles in his face as well, and he'd put on a few pounds.

"Yes, sir," Mike replied. "Very well. Got a new Bimmer this summer and a brownstone on Beacon Street."

"Good for you. Glad to see you're making something of yourself. I always knew you had it in you."

Mike flushed. He wasn't sure he believed his father always knew he had it in him, but he hoped a change was coming with this meeting. His arms tingled as he tried to control his anxiety.

"Please sit." His father motioned toward the plush dark gray couch across from him.

Mike settled into the middle.

"Tell me, what did you find out about that hard drive?"

"It's exactly what I thought," Mike replied. "A blueprint for creating hydrogen fuel through photoelectrochemical water splitting using solar power. Apparently, using this equipment they developed, they can do it affordably."

'Well! That is interesting," his father said as he sat forward in his chair. "We can't have that, can we?"

"I knew you'd want to know. I also found the scientist who created the hard drive, and is the only person who can decrypt it."

"This is getting better by the minute. Is he nearby?" His fingers tapped on the chair's arm.

"In my condo right now. I think you should meet him. His ideas can make you money."

"Well, Mike, I think this may be the best conversation we've ever had. Why don't you bring him around tonight and we'll talk. I'll order dinner, a few drinks, see what the man has to say." At this he stood, and Mike followed. Placing his hand on Mike's shoulder, he gave it a squeeze. "Great work, son."

Mike stomach fluttered. This was even better than he'd hoped. He almost never called him "son."

"Bring him at six. We'll have cocktails first. You haven't mentioned my name to him, have you?"

"No, sir."

Douglas T. Hayes smiled. "Good. Let's keep it that way."

CHAPTER NINETEEN

BOSTON

AFTER SPENDING THE night in Mike's condo, Paul sat in the passenger's seat of Mike's BMW, still dubious about this development. Last night, he'd been shocked to discover Mike lived in a brownstone condo in the Back Bay, one of Boston's priciest old neighborhoods. Wherever Mike was getting his money, Paul guessed it was illegal. No matter what the man said, Paul kept returning to the knife in the ground behind his car and the trashed room at the inn, wondering if he was making a mistake. He stretched his head in circles to loosen the tension in his neck.

What mattered now was this man whom Mike was taking him to meet. If he was as wealthy as Mike suggested, this might be a breakthrough for developing this product.

"Don't give him any details about how Anita got the hard drive, okay?" Mike said, as he drove to the hotel. "All he needs to know is she has it, and only you can decrypt it. He's interested in clean fuel. You'll like him.

"I understand," Paul said, opening the window to let in fresh air as his chest tightened. He didn't understand at all, but if this is what it took to bring his data back, he was eager to explore the possibility.

At the hotel room, Mike knocked. A bartender dressed in a white shirt and black tie opened the door.

"Come in," Doug called out from the couch. "We're mixing martinis. Mine's dry with blue cheese olives. How do you like yours?"

Paul wasn't a martini guy. In fact, he hardly ever drank, but he did like blue cheese olives. Rather than offend his host by refusing one, he replied, "Same for me."

"Me too," said Mike.

The bartender went to work as Paul surveyed the tony hotel suite and the city lights shining below through the wall-sized window.

"John, I would like you to meet Paul Tanner, scientist extraordinaire." Mike addressed Doug. "Paul, this is John St. Claire, a man who can make things happen."

Paul leaned over and shook Doug's hand while the bartender stabbed two olives onto each cocktail pick and set them into the glasses on the black marble tabletops.

"Have a seat, my friend," Doug said. "I'm looking forward to getting to know you. We're going to have cocktails first. They'll be bringing dinner around 7:30. Hope you're hungry." Doug smiled.

Paul sat on the sofa across from Doug while Mike sat in a matching chair as their glasses were filled.

"Thank you," Doug said to the bartender. "Leave me a shaker with some refills and come back at seven o'clock for a refresh." With a nod, the man mixed another shaker and placed it on the table in front of Doug, then silently exited the room. "Now then, Paul. I understand you have developed a fascinating new clean fuel product. Why don't you tell me about it?"

Paul pulled his collar away from his neck, trying to cool off. He was uncomfortable about how much to say, since clean fuel development was frowned upon by the current administration. It wasn't exactly illegal, but no companies he knew of were still in business.

"I'm not sure what Mike told you already. I want you to understand this was all done before the current administration discouraged this type of research. When our funding was cut, we closed like everyone else.

"Of course. I'm not here to accuse you. Just interested in learning about this. You might call me an investor."

Investor. Paul nearly trembled at the word. He gripped his hands together to avoid betraying his excitement. With an investor, government funding wouldn't be required, so maybe he could proceed with his work without interference.

Doug held up his glass as a toast. "To learning about the future."

Paul took care to hold it steady as he raised his glass in return and took a drink. Maybe the martini would calm his nerves. After a few more sips, he returned it to the table.

"I'm glad you're interested," Paul said. "Sooner or later clean fuel is going to replace all fossil fuels. The electric car market is well entrenched, but what about trucks? Ships? Jets?

Hydrogen fuel goes way beyond what batteries can produce. Hydrogen-powered airplanes already exist. They're just working out the design issues. The problem is, hydrogen is expensive to create and transport. Right now, hydrogen is produced by splitting water molecules using electricity. We don't. With our technology, we can produce it using concentrated solar, powered directly by the sun, onsite where it will be used. Imagine what that does to the cost. No other fuel could compete."

"I like the way you think, Paul," Doug replied. "Explain to me how you envision this will make money."

Paul took another swig of his martini. "Well, the company I worked for never received patent approval. Others are researching this, but no one else is this far yet. And we don't need any fossil fuels or mined minerals to create it. It creates no carbon emissions or polluting byproducts. Nothing. It's the perfect clean fuel."

"Interesting." Doug shifted forward in his seat.

Paul continued. "For a person like you, if you wanted to finance this and be the owner, the company would apply for and hold the patents, as well as manufacture the equipment. Anyone else who wants to use the technology would have to pay you. At least in this country. Internationally, too, if you hold the patents globally.

"Brilliant," Doug said.

Paul ate his olives and drank more martini. He liked it better than he realized. Maybe this would be his new drink.

Doug picked up the shaker and shook it a few times, then refilled Paul's glass. "Where is all this information other than in your head?"

"It's on a hard drive. I used proprietary encryption so no

one else could read it. Only me and a small group who worked with me, and I don't even know where those people are anymore. A woman is keeping it safe for me. The only problem is, I've lost touch with her."

"What's her name?" Doug asked.

"Anita Forester. Last I knew she was in Montreal. Mike said you might be able to find her. Is that true?"

Doug smiled. "Absolutely. I have a lot of contacts, and I'm sure I can find her and reclaim your hard drive. With your knowledge, I think you are exactly the kind of person I would want to lead a company like this. Who else has this data besides you?"

Lead a company like this. Paul tried to suppress a smile. This was better than he had expected. He swallowed more of his martini, enjoying how smooth it was, how it wasn't as strong as he'd first imagined. "What was that again?" he asked, realizing he'd missed what Doug said after the part about leading the company.

Doug smiled. "Who else has this data?"

Paul nodded a few times.

"Just me. I had the foresight to download it from the cloud before the government came through and confiscated all our research. As far as I know, my hard drive is the only remaining source." Paul was smiling ear to ear now as he leaned his elbow on the sofa to prop up his head. At last someone recognized the importance of what he'd done. He gazed around for snacks, feeling a little drunk. A snack would hit the spot.

"This has been a very productive meeting," Doug said. "I'm glad I had a chance to meet you. I'm sure we can work together in the future. Create a company and have those patents approved. With your knowledge, you'll make a fine leader to pull this all together."

Paul couldn't believe his good luck at finding an investor eager and able to finance the development without government funding. He was warm all over, practically glowing in his confidence. Regardless of all he'd lost getting here, he had finally arrived.

"Now where's that bartender? I'm ready for a refill. Anyone else?" Doug asked.

Paul grinned and pointed to his glass. "Another for me."

In the morning, Doug sat at the hotel desk reviewing the information Mike had given him about Anita from her license plate. Having a private investigator for a son was useful. He'd underestimated him. The phones Elena had given them were a terrific idea. Now they were able to work together on this without risking any surveillance.

On his regular phone, he searched for the mobile number of the U.S Deputy Attorney General. DAG in his contacts list.

"Hey there, buddy," he greeted him when he answered. "Is this a good time to talk?

"It's always a good time to talk with you. What's on your mind?"

"How's this crazy November weather treating you? Ready for another getaway down to the southern hemisphere? It's sunny and warm, and golf is calling."

"A break would be excellent," the deputy attorney general replied. "I can sneak away for a few days next month."

"Fantastic! Have yours call mine and we'll schedule it.

Listen. I need a favor. Nothing big but I need it quickly. There's this woman. Name Anita Forester. I have her basic info. I want to know everything about her. I've been told she's in Canada. Hopefully that's helpful."

"Text it to me. I'll see what we have on her and put trackers on her moves. If you find her, you'll let us have her when you're done, okay? If you think she'd be useful to us?"

"Absolutely. And if she turns up on your radar, I need to speak with her off the record."

"Understood. I'll be in touch."

CHAPTER TWENTY

CHANGES

ANITA KEY-CARDED INTO her hotel room and dumped her shopping bags on the bed—four new bras in pastel shades with matching lace trimmed panties replaced the underwear she'd lost when Mike emptied her suitcase at the inn. Additionally: two turtleneck sweaters for the colder weather—one in pale green to match her eyes, and another in rose pink—and new jeans she'd bought because they had a flattering fit. She'd been thrilled to find a store that sold clothes made from responsible cotton, wool and recycled plastic bottles.

When she opened her drawer to put the items away, the photo of Steven stared up at her; she'd put it away to avoid dwelling on her pain. Instantly, her mouth began to tremble, but she placed her clothes on top of it and slammed the drawer shut as tears threatened to fall. Instead, she forced herself to think about what to wear tonight, and took a few slow breaths.

Pink. She would wear pink. Pink sweater, pink bra, pink panties. Pink was a good color on her.

Two hours were left until the meeting at François' place.
Anita had to keep busy. Flopping onto the bed, she pulled out
her phone and checked her Proton Mail account.

An email from a new address that she didn't recognize
appeared:

"It's me, BFF who you used to call a brat (just so you know
it's me). I have a Proton Mail account now too, so we can email
safely. A friend of yours called. Said his name was Paul. Claims
you have something important of his and he is worried about
you. Can you call him? Here's his number. And if you can, call
me. I have been wondering if you are okay. I have a new phone
number, too. Memorize it. I'm keeping the old one for work,
but don't call me there. This one's a pre-pay. Not traceable."

"Stacey the brat," Anita used to call her in their college
days, because Stacey would always say exactly what she was
thinking, which sometimes got her into trouble. No one but
Stacey knew that.

"Hello?" Stacey answered. "Is this who I think it is?"

"It certainly is. Oh my God. How wonderful to talk. I have
so much to tell you, but nothing I can tell you."

"I understand. Thank goodness you're safe. I've been worried. That Paul guy says you're up north. Is it true?"

"Yes, but not for long, I'm afraid. I'm safe here, but when
I leave . . . I can't explain, but I'm scared. How did we all miss
the signs of what was happening?"

"I don't know. One day we're just pissed off about bad
leadership, and the next, we're on burner phones, afraid of

who's listening. Let's not discuss it. What's the deal with this guy who contacted me? Friend or foe?"

"Friend. He helped me a lot and I caused him problems. What he said is true—I have something of his. I can keep it safe here for now. Can you tell him? I shouldn't call him."

"Sure. Now tell me, how are you doing?"

"It's been difficult, but I'm managing. I keep thinking about my son and all those photos and emails on my Google account. I wish I could see them again. From his first day of school to college graduation. Remember when we all went to Cape May and you took the picture of him holding a starfish?" Anita's voice began to crack.

"Mm-hmm," Stacey murmured.

"That time when you helped him make a chocolate cake for my birthday? What if I never see those again? They've robbed me of my memories. What right do they have? What damn right?" Anita exploded into tears.

"I wish I could throw my arms around you right now and hold you tight." Stacey paused while Anita gulped down her tears and sniffled.

"Now tell me something good that has happened. One little experience that brought you joy."

Anita stood with the phone, then walked over to the window and peeked out at the city. "Actually, there is." She paused. "You'll never in a million years guess who I've seen."

"Not the one we aren't mentioning?" Stacey asked. They both knew using names might trigger a deeper look at their phone call if bulk calls were being captured and scanned for specific identities.

"Not him," Anita replied. "Remember the best friend from college? A certain Frenchman?"

"No!"

"Yes! He's here. And helping me. It's strange seeing him again." She sat on one foot in the chair by the window.

"Oh, do tell. How does he look? Old and decrepit?"

"Not even a little. Hot, sweet, and dangerous." Anita gazed at the rug as heat spread along her neck, embarrassed by her confession.

"Sounds like lava cake. Be careful you don't have your heart broken."

"Well, I'm still married so it doesn't matter."

"Married or not, you need to do what's right for you. You need a chance at happiness again. Just don't get played."

Anita was warmed by Stacey's words. For a moment, she could almost imagine a chance, but like the blink of a firefly, it disappeared into blackness.

"One day. Right now, I know what I have to do. Even though I don't want to. Even though I'm terrified. My husband doesn't deserve this, no matter how much of a shit he's been."

"Please be careful. I'm always here if you need me," Stacey said.

Anita closed her eyes as she reflected on how little she'd done for Stacey lately. Her stomach ached. "Thank you. I hope I can be there for you again one day, too. I haven't lately."

"You got me through the breakup with Malcolm. Don't ever think you owe me. By the way, I haven't seen anything suspicious around my house or at school, so I think I'm safe."

"Thank you for that. I better go. Goodbye for now," Anita said. "Kisses to you."

"Kisses to you too."

Stacey hung up.

For a few moments, Anita had forgotten how alone in the world she was since Julian had shut her out for years, Steven was lost forever, and she couldn't go home. Speaking with Stacey made life normal for a few minutes. François was back in her life but had pushed her away at the end of last night. With Stacey no longer connected, Anita's strength was draining away.

⌘

The cab dropped Anita at François' building at 7:55 PM. As she climbed the stairs to the entryway, a door opened below the stairs, and a man stepped out of the shadows. Anita jumped and threw herself against François' door, pushing the buzzer frantically. The man glanced her way before walking up the street. François yanked the door open, dragged her in by the arm, and slammed the door behind her.

"What is wrong?" His eyebrows were drawn together.

Unable to answer because she was hyperventilating, he gently pulled her farther inside his apartment where she stood shaking.

"A man. Scared me to death. I guess he's your downstairs neighbor. I hadn't noticed the door before."

François wrapped his arms around her and stroked her back. "This can happen. Your mind has not recovered from the trauma of being captured. It might take a long time. Each time it happens, you need to remind yourself you are safe and breathe calmly. Will you try?"

Nodding, she forced a few deeper breaths.

"I am sorry, but the meeting needs to start. Come to the office."

She followed him and sat again in the metal folding chair. This time only Zack appeared on the screen, and he looked panicked.

"Sorry we are late, Zack. What is wrong?"

"We have a problem," Zack said. "This came from my source at the Nevada detention center about an hour ago. They're preparing to move everyone out of the center, but no one knows where they're taking them. It's going on at the other detention sites, too, and he thinks it's going to be soon. They're throwing stuff out and filling box trucks with supplies from the storage rooms."

"This is bad," François said. "Erin left for West Virginia this afternoon and I have no way to reach her. She should be there by tomorrow morning."

The two men stared at each other silently. François turned to Anita.

"We have to go now. We cannot wait for word from Erin. I have the passports for Julian and me, and you have yours. We do not know what they might do with him. We may lose any chance of rescue."

Anita was stunned. She wasn't ready. This was too soon. But if they were moving the detainees, they must be moving them somewhere more secure, maybe high security where they wouldn't be able to break Julian out. Or worse. "Do you think they might kill him?"

François wrinkled his brow and turned back to Zack.

"Final plans now. I will take three burner phones and I want you to have three as well. When we need to, we throw out one and move to the next number. Never leave a message. We should have another call at four AM and exchange the burner phone numbers. Meanwhile, I want you to search for information. If Erin contacts you, call me. After we cross the border, I will rent a car and leave the Canadian car in Vermont until we return."

"Gotcha," Zack replied. "When are you leaving?"

"I want to beat the traffic out of the city and across the border, so we'll be leaving around five AM. We could reach Coal Creek by tomorrow night or early the next day."

"Okay, boss. Talk later." Zack disconnected.

Overwhelmed by the speed and her fear of what was taking place, Anita was light-headed and couldn't think clearly. "What do you want me to do? I have money in my hotel safe. I can't carry it around. But maybe we'll need it?"

"Take a cab back to your hotel and pay for the driver to wait. Pack everything, check out, then bring it all here where it is safe. We will bring some money and leave at 5:00 AM."

CHAPTER TWENTY-ONE

LIES

"Come in here," François called from down the hall when Anita arrived back at his apartment. "Bring everything with you."

She followed his voice to the last room at the end, François' bedroom. A small open suitcase lay on one side of the bed on top of a white, gray, and black plaid duvet. It was partially packed, but other items were still on the bed—deodorant, toothpaste, and a handgun. Dread washed over her as she fixated on the weapon, glancing up at François as he dug through his black and chrome dresser. The reality of their journey hit her in the gut.

"You can lay your stuff out on that side. Pack only what you need. Leave the rest here. I made room in a drawer."

Placing her suitcase on the bed, she unzipped it, revealing all the money inside. "I didn't picture you as a gun owner."

"Neither did I. I only take it with me when I travel to your

'Wild West' south of the border. Since I do not have a license to match my passport, I will not be declaring it."

"What happens if you're caught?" Her pulse accelerated.

"As long as no dogs are sniffing cars, I will not be caught. That is why we are using a quiet border crossing."

This news didn't make her heart rate slow at all. "Do you expect to need it?"

François stopped what he was doing and scrutinized her, cocking his head to the side as he swept his hair away from his face. "We are dealing with people who make other people disappear. We are dealing with people who have their own police and operate as though they are untouchable. I have no intention of dying while I do this or seeing anyone with me die. If I must use it, I will."

As Anita stared at her belongings, trying to decide what to bring, a high-pitched ringing started in her ears and her knees began to buckle. Shallow breaths came faster and faster, giving her just enough time to shove her suitcase to the floor and flop onto the bed. A cold sweat engulfed her. "I can't . . .," she said, gasping, covering her face with her hands and rocking. "I'm . . . terrified."

François walked around the bed and lay behind her, spooning her. The warmth of his arms wrapped her in a safe cocoon. She took long, deep breaths until she stopped shaking and her heartbeat slowed, laying her hands over his.

The smell of him distracted Anita as his face rested against her neck. A jolt of excitement ran down her arms to her hands, triggered by the touch of his skin. Slowly she raised one of his hands to her face and kissed it tenderly. A deep longing for him pulsed through her body.

His lips grazed her neck, and a moment later the heat of his breath filled her ear. With a deep exhale, she turned around to face him. Their lips found each other, coming together in a dance to which their memories knew the steps.

When her hands glided under his sweater, he trembled. François smoothed the hair back from her face and stroked her cheek, then slid his hand under her sweater, where he unlatched her bra. Sitting up, Anita let him pull her sweater over her head; then he removed his own clothes. He unzipped her jeans and slipped them off along with her pink-lace panties, kissing her belly before slowly exploring the rest of her nakedness. Desire consumed her, quivering at his touch.

When their mouths again connected, his breath became her own and they melted into one another.

The alarm woke Anita at 4:00 AM. François and his suitcase were gone, but the aroma of coffee floated in from the kitchen, hinting at his location. The soft sheets were begging her to stay and snuggle underneath, instead of facing the day ahead.

Leaning over the side of the bed, she found her belongings still on the floor—the suitcase right where she'd dumped it last night, the clothes scattered. But the bundles of cash were gone. *No worries. François put them somewhere safe.* She rose out of bed, slipped on her sweater, and headed to the bathroom. François' voice came from the office, conversing with Zack. In the shower, she used his soap, loving the luxury of rubbing it all over herself where he had touched her last night. It had been far too long since she'd been touched like a lover. The steamy air filled her lungs and warmed her.

When she was finished, she rubbed her hair dry and wrapped herself in a towel, returning to the bedroom. As she lifted her suitcase onto the bed, a hand touched her waist. Before she could think, her arms spasmed from adrenaline and she dropped the suitcase, spinning around to François' startled face. He backed away.

Anita was shaking. "You scared me. Don't sneak up on me like that."

"I am sorry. I forgot you are nervous. One hug?"

She put her arms around him, and he kissed her, but she couldn't relax. Her stomach churned from guilt over last night, and fear of today.

What am I doing?

"You need to pack. We leave here in forty minutes. I stored your money inside my box spring. I have a hidden compartment there. Even your Mike would not find it. I kept out ten thousand dollars for expenses and bribes."

From his top drawer, François pulled two bundles of her bills and tossed them onto the bed. "Bring clothes for warm weather. Zack says it is unseasonably hot in West Virginia. And there's a tropical storm developing to the south. Are you okay now?" His raised eyebrows questioned her as he stroked her arm.

"Yes. Better."

"Can I bring you coffee?"

"I'd love coffee. Thank you."

He reached over to her and pulled her towel away, then stood, gazing at her with his sexy smile.

Her body tingled in arousal, wishing they didn't have to leave.

"I'll hang this up for you, my dear."

Anita dug through her clothes and pulled out her duck boots. She hadn't shopped for shorts in Montreal because it was November, so she didn't have hot weather clothes. They probably wouldn't be gone long—she hoped.

When they came back, Julian would be with her if they were successful. Then what? Would she bring him here to collect all her belongings from François' dresser? She had no idea what her future looked like, and she didn't dare let herself imagine it. Because if she did, she might imagine a life with François instead of Julian.

No. She put that thought out of her head right away. They would be successful. They would rescue Julian and bring him safely to Canada.

✧

They reached the border at 6:50 AM on a quiet road which passed into Vermont. Orange cones shuttled traffic into one lane. A huge stop sign hung over double bays, but only one was open. Two cars waited in line ahead of them. When Anita reached into her oversized purse for her Canadian passport, she discovered the hard drive lying on the bottom and cursed to herself. In the rush, she had forgotten to stash it. Bringing it to Coal Creek was too risky, but she didn't have a choice now.

"Look happy and laugh a little, like we are having a fun conversation about our trip." François forced a smile. "It will help you relax. Plus, I think the cameras are already on us, looking for any suspicious activity."

Anita chuckled and reached over to run her fingers

through his hair. "You mean we are just two lovers having an adventure?"

"We are." He smiled back at her, took her hand, and kissed it. "And I am pleased I have not seen any dogs. Keep smiling. Our turn."

François drove to the booth and rolled down the window.

"Passports, please," the agent said. He opened the first one and addressed François. "Your full name, address, date and place of birth, please."

François replied effortlessly. At Anita's turn, she did the same. They'd practiced on the way, to make sure they had it right, including other data not on the passport: What country are you a citizen of? What is your occupation?

"What is your purpose for traveling to the United States today?"

"We are going to view rental properties around Jay Peak and Stowe for skiing this winter," François said.

"How long will you be here?"

"Four days."

"Where are you staying?"

"The Green Mountain Inn in Stowe," he lied.

"Are you bringing any weapons, plants, fruit, drugs, or alcohol into the country?"

"No." François lied again. His gun was buried in the trunk under a pile of rope.

The agent turned to his computer and scanned the passports. Anita barely breathed, but she forced herself to look happy. If only this story were true. She imagined skiing with François this winter. They'd race each other down the trails, drink hot cocoa at lunch, and soak in the hot tub before making love in their room.

The agent handed the passports back to François and wished them a good trip.

"Saeed does impressive work," François said as Anita watched the border crossing disappear in her visor mirror. "I had planned on having him make us badges for the Coal Creek Detention Center, once Erin lifted one off somebody, but no time now."

"You're very good at lying to border agents," Anita said, smiling.

"It is easier every time. The trick is to believe it. Forget real life and believe the imagination. I tell him because I believe we are going to Vermont together to plan our winter with each other. Do you still ski? You were good back in college."

We're both pretending what we wish were true. "I haven't for a few years, but I would love to again. I wish ski season didn't keep getting shorter. There's too much rain and not enough snow in the Northeast now."

As they drove by a gas station, Anita shook her head. "The price of gas has dropped fifty cents a gallon since I left on Sunday. It must be because oil companies got their way on changing the laws. I thought the prices were being manipulated to make people mad."

François nodded in agreement. "A common tactic. Scare people in the wallet and they support anything to stop hurting. They forget it makes worse pain later."

"Where do you plan on renting a car?" Anita asked.

"Can you find me something between here and Stowe? I am hoping we can hide at the Deer Run Inn on the way back if we need to. I like to have a safe house near the border. We should stop and ask them."

And I can give Caitlyn the hard drive for Paul instead of carrying it around.

Anita pulled out her phone and checked for rental cars. "Found one in Morrisville. It doesn't open until nine, but we drive right through there."

"Okay. We will drive to Morrisville and stop for a proper breakfast. How does that sound?"

"Perfect." Anita shifted around in her seat and stared out at the gray mountains, her stomach smoldering from coffee, hunger, and worry. Everything was almost too perfect.

CHAPTER TWENTY-TWO

PREPARATIONS

DOUG SAT IN his private office on his Virginia estate, in a building not in the direct sightline of his house. His family never interrupted him there, so his personal guests came and went without being observed.

He'd flown back from Boston earlier that day, after calling the deputy attorney general. The man called him back on his cell phone while he was reviewing this week's financial reports.

"Hey," Doug said. "Thanks for getting back to me so soon. Are you calling with news about Anita Forester?"

"Sure am," the deputy attorney general said. "I'll give you the highlights, but you should read the full report. Where can I send it?"

"Print it off and fax it, old school." Doug prided himself on maintaining privacy by sidestepping certain technological advances. One way was by using a stand-alone fax on his own dedicated landline. He aspired to be the richest man on the planet untraceable on the internet.

"Here's what we have on her." The deputy attorney general gave Doug a rundown of her and Julian's background, his arrest and release at the Capitol followed by his clandestine detention, the death of their son, and her disappearance when they tried to trace her.

"She used to own a technology consulting firm which did work for us and a few other agencies. I'm guessing she understands our abilities, which is worrisome. Three years ago, she sold it to a Swiss conglomerate, but her accounts don't reflect assets from a large sale. However, her tax returns referenced a numbered account in Switzerland. We think that's where she's going."

"Can you track the account?" Doug tapped the desk with his coffee spoon.

"We'd need a court order to demonstrate fraud on her part. We'd have to show clear evidence. The Swiss are sticklers about it. We won't get one."

"Where's the husband?" Tap, tap, tap.

"His name was on the shutdown list. He's an agitator. We've got him in a detention center in Coal Creek, West Virginia. One of those planned for evacuation to Guantanamo Bay. We also have his phone. Bunch of family pictures on it. Husband, wife, and the dead son, apparently. I'll send the contents over to you."

"Thanks. If I had to guess, I'd say she's not going to Switzerland without the husband. I've got a private investigator I can send down to Coal Creek. Give him a couple of days to check it out. No point in your people getting involved and having to write up all those reports. Just keep an eye on the airports and borders."

"We're already on it. Her name's on the list now, too, so someone may pick her up. Heads up on Coal Creek. It's not the sort of place where it's easy to blend in. They don't trust outsiders. Tell your PI to bring a stash with him to bribe low-lifes. Money has a way of building trust, too."

Doug grinned, dropped the spoon on his desk and clicked on his computer calendar. "Well, thank you for the advice. I will pass it along. I appreciate your immediate attention to this matter. Meanwhile, how does the twelfth of December look for busting out of Dodge and heading south?

The GPS on Mike's phone kept cutting out as he rounded the bends through the West Virginia mountains, getting farther from the interstate. The roadside was sprinkled with abandoned barns collapsing on themselves, small houses with peeling paint and tarpaper roofs, and empty gas stations with grass growing through the pavement.

Beside him on the front seat of the older model Mitsubishi Mirage Mike had rented, he had a stack of flyers he'd printed with his phone number and Anita's photo from her LinkedIn account. She looked like someone the bank would send to foreclose on your house.

His BMW with Massachusetts license plates was the wrong image in coal country, so he'd rented the cheapest car they had at Enterprise. It was one of those they used as loners when your car was in an accident and the insurance company was only paying twenty dollars a day. It attracted no attention, especially with its Ohio plates.

His BMW was left at his father's estate in Virginia, a place he'd never been until yesterday. Damn. The man was even richer than he'd realized, and Mike wanted his share. Although he wasn't allowed near the house, he was invited into his father's private office, which was even better. Apparently, his half-brother, Doug Jr., never went there.

Mike didn't like thinking about Junior, but he couldn't help it. He imagined him as a pudgy boy who sat behind a desk, licking a silver spoon and growing softer. Not like Mike. Mike was tough. Smart. Strong. His chest swelled when he imagined his place in the family hierarchy on the rise.

The odometer hit forty-eight miles from the highway exit as Mike descended into a valley. Coal Creek should be a right-hand turn soon. The river he'd been following alongside was moving slower. The water was a muddy orange red and gave off a pungent odor which penetrated the air despite the air conditioning running.

Minutes later, Mike flew by a small road on the right and slammed on his brakes. The mileage indicated he'd reached Coal Creek. Shifting into reverse, he sped backwards to his missed turn, then crossed some railroad tracks and a level bridge over the river into what might be called a town. Two abandoned houses appeared first. He turned left, continuing on the only paved road through an area of similarly styled homes, some surrounded by mowed lawns, nicely maintained with decorations on their doors, others with sagging roofs and vehicles on blocks.

The road ended where a rusty chain-link fence, overgrown

with brush and weeds, surrounded a two-story brick building. A metal guard shack stood at the end of the fence, with two red cones blocking the entryway to a parking lot. A sign read: PRIVATE. NO TRESPASSING. STOP FOR INSPECTION. Mike stopped to survey the area.

"Coal Creek School" was carved in concrete over the front entryway, but unless they put bars on schools here, he guessed he'd found the detention center. The building was decades old, from better days, when the town probably needed its own school.

Mike rolled down the window and crinkled his nose, disgusted with the stench from the river he'd crossed on his way into town. At the guard shack, he stopped. A young man dressed in an olive-drab camo jacket and pants like a Vietnam-era army soldier stepped from the shack into the driveway and faced Mike. His arm rested on a military-style semi-automatic draped over his shoulder and pointed at the ground. He looked like a teenager.

Mike held up both his hands to show they were empty. "I have a photo I want to give you of a woman who's coming here."

"Out of the car. Hands up!" the guard shouted as he lifted the barrel of the weapon.

Mike grabbed one of the flyers as he stepped from the car, waving it. "See. I have a photo," he said, sucking in his cheeks to keep from laughing at the kid.

The guard continued shouting despite Mike standing a few feet away. "Hands on your head. Spread your legs."

Mike let the flyer float to the ground and obeyed.

The guard reached up, grabbed Mike's hands and patted

him down. Mike knew he could flip this kid onto his back, if he needed to.

"Okay," the guard said. "You ain't on my list. What's the photo?" He pointed the weapon back to the ground as Mike retrieved the flyer.

"This woman is on her way here to break out her husband," Mike said. "I'm guessing she'll be pretending to be someone she isn't. Maybe disguised. We want her when she shows up. There's a reward. Five thousand dollars."

The guard's eyes widened as he examined the flyer.

"You capture her and call this number, the money is yours." Mike pointed to his phone number on the flyer to make sure the guard saw it. "No questions asked. Cash on delivery."

"Okay, sir." The guard gripped the flyer. "I'll be lookin' out for her. She ain't gettin' by me."

"I'm sure she won't," Mike replied. "Thank you. When's your shift over?"

"Six. The other guy's on nights."

"Here's a hundred dollars to make sure you give this other photo to him too. I'll check on him tomorrow, so I'll know if you don't."

The guard gaped at his hand as Mike put five twenty-dollar bills in it along with two more flyers.

Okay, sir. Need anythin' else, I'm the guy. You a Fed?"

"Naw. I don't like cops and I'm not here to snoop into anyone's business. I just need to find this woman. Don't hurt her, okay?" He paused for a beat. "That's my job."

CHAPTER TWENTY-THREE

MENDING

FRANÇOIS AND ANITA drove to the Deer Run Inn in a Chevy Malibu with Maine license plates they'd rented from Enterprise in Morrisville, where they left their Canadian rental. Anita was relieved to see only Caitlyn's and Odina's vehicles in the driveway.

When she walked toward the inn, her pulse ratcheted up and her legs trembled. Her memory replayed from two days earlier, when Mike had attacked her, and she noticed her knees still hurt and one wrist was tender. On the porch, she stopped and beckoned François, who sprinted to her side. The door handle was locked. She rapped the deer head knocker three times. No one answered. Anita's anxiety rose into her stomach, where breakfast sat like a rock. Last time the inn was empty, Mike lay in wait for her. Logic told her this wasn't happening again, but her breathing accelerated. No footsteps sounded from inside when she knocked one more time.

With an exhale, she crept across the porch. Sunlight reflected off the window, preventing her from seeing inside. She shaded her eyes and leaned against the glass to peer into the great room. Caitlyn appeared from the shadows, standing two feet away, her arms crossed as she glared back. Anita recoiled and let out a sharp breath.

"What is wrong?" François asked as he joined her at the window.

Caitlyn stood a bit longer before unfolding her arms and coming to the door. "What are you doing here?" She stood in the doorway, blocking it. "Is my father with you?"

Anita was taken aback by her cold greeting, but relieved that Caitlyn was there, and not Mike.

"No, he's not. I hope I'm not intruding. This is my friend François. We're on our way to try to rescue my husband in West Virginia."

Caitlyn nodded and stood aside. "Come in. I thought my father was with you. That's why I didn't answer. It's been a rough week around here."

Anita entered the inn and tried to ignore the anxiety crawling over her skin as she gazed around at the familiar surroundings she hadn't seen since her attack. Caitlyn locked the door behind them.

"Did you two have a fight?" Anita asked. "I hope it wasn't my fault."

"Never mind about my father," Caitlyn said as her voice rose. "What about Mike? That monster came into our inn. We had to run up the mountain to escape." She gestured with both hands, pointing around the room as she continued. "He destroyed our guest room, wrecked the kitchen, and has jeopardized the work we're doing here. You've ruined every-thing. Why did you lead him here?"

Anita's mouth dropped open. "I didn't. I swear. All I told him was the Green Mountain Inn in town. I have no idea how he found your place. He was already hiding here when I arrived, and he ambushed me. I was terrified he'd kill me. I'm still shaking. Thank God I had pepper spray, or I'd be dead."

Odina appeared from the hallway. "What's all the yelling about? Can you two talk without screaming? How about we all take a seat and calm down?"

Caitlyn frowned but pulled out a chair as she gestured to the other two chairs near Anita and François. The four of them sat facing each other. Anita filled Odina in about their trip to rescue Julian.

"I'm glad Mike didn't hurt you," Caitlyn said in a calmer voice. "We ran when he arrived and came back to the damage later. He slashed our tires—not an expense we can afford this time of year. And I've been worried he'll come back. I always left the front door unlocked when we were here. Now I'm afraid to go to sleep at night."

Anita's cheeks burned. "You're right. This was my fault. If I hadn't asked your father to drive me to Boston, none of this would have happened. I hope this doesn't offend you, but I want to pay for the damage. I'll send you more when we get back to Canada. You were kind to me, and you don't deserve what you suffered."

She pulled several hundred-dollar bills from her pocket-book and placed them on the table in front of Caitlyn, who took the money and thanked her.

"What happened between you and your father?" Anita asked.

"I told him to get out of my life and stay away." She heaved a deep sigh. "This has been a long time coming. All this drama he brought with him because he wouldn't trust me to keep the hard drive safe. I asked him about it two years ago."

Caitlyn rose and paced in front of the table. "I knew what was best, but he refused to believe how evil this administration is, how much control they've amassed. As though all this corruption will just vanish. Poof." She blew imaginary dust from her hand and shrugged her shoulders.

"I guess he's a better scientist than a political analyst," Anita said.

"That's the truth. When it comes to judging character, definitely. He's easily duped. I'm lucky my mother taught me a thing or two. He drove her nuts, too."

Odina rose and put her arm around Caitlyn's shoulders, who stopped pacing. "But I can't deal with him in my life anymore. I've had it. At least you have the hard drive now, so if Mike comes back, at least it's safe."

Damn, Anita thought. *What am I going to do with this hard drive? Leaving it here isn't an option.*

François stood. "We have to go. It's a long ride to West Virginia, but Anita wanted to make sure you were both okay after the incident."

"We appreciate it," Odina replied. "Remember, I'm a backcountry guide for this whole region of Vermont, should you need one. I've walked people over the border before. Not my favorite, but I can do it if I have to. This is a brave mission you're on."

"Can we hide here if we need to when we return? I do not want to mislead you. It will be dangerous," François said. "We plan to have Julian with us, and they will be looking for him and us. I will work hard to not lead them here, but I want you to understand in case something goes wrong."

"We're tough." Odina squeezed Caitlyn's shoulders. "As long as you're doing the right thing, we'll try to help."

Caitlyn nodded and held on to Odina's other hand. "She's right. We are tough, despite all my complaining. You can count on us to help."

Anita hugged them both. "Wish us luck," she said as they headed out the door, wondering if she'd live to see them both again.

CHAPTER TWENTY-FOUR

MIRROR

"**D**O YOU THINK we'll make it to West Virginia tonight?" Anita had asked as they drove south.

"I do not think so. Neither of us will be able to drive that long. We will have to take a break somewhere and sleep. Maybe around the Pennsylvania-Maryland border."

"What if we make it to Gettysburg? Stay at Stacey's? I'd love to see her, and she always liked you. I think it would be safe. I talked to her yesterday, and no one's been snooping around."

"Okay. Plan on it."

Anita drove in the dark as François slept in the passenger's seat. At Gettysburg, she turned off the highway, a growing ache in her chest, desperately wishing she could drive by her house. She resisted the temptation, but the familiar roads were painful reminders of her old life.

François' sleeping face was illuminated by streetlights. What a gift to have him back in her life—a gift she didn't deserve. He'd suffered because of her, even though she hadn't intentionally caused him pain. Her throat tightened. Here he was, risking his life to help her and Julian, the two people who hurt him years ago by getting together, guaranteeing her relationship with François was over forever. How she wished he'd explained at the time, instead of simply leaving. She'd hurt too. A lot.

Stacey's road forked right. At the second long driveway, Anita turned, pulling up to the ranch house hidden from the road by many large trees. The floodlight came on as she parked next to the garage, out of view of the street.

"We're here," she said, gently shaking François awake. "Did you have a good rest?"

François stretched out, sat up straight and blinked, taking in his surroundings.

"Nice spot. Stacey did well."

"It hasn't been easy for her. For either of us. I wonder if moving here with our husbands when they were both hired at the college was the right thing to do."

At the patio door, Anita knocked hard on the glass. The blinds were closed, but lights were on inside. A shadow of a figure appeared, and the door swung open.

Stacey let out a howl. "Oh wow! You're here! I'm so glad you're safe." Stepping outside, she threw her arms around her friend, burying her face in her hair as Anita hugged her back. The two of them rocked back and forth like they were comforting a newborn.

Stacey stopped suddenly and pulled away, staring at François. "Wow. Look at you. Didn't you turn into one hunk of a man."

François blushed as he smiled and shook his head. "You always did say exactly what you think. I guess you are still very bold."

Stacey laughed. "Bold? Is that what I am? I always loved the cute way you talk. Me? I just speak the truth. If people don't like it, they can kiss my ass." Stacey reached over and hugged him too, giving him a kiss on the lips. "It's wonderful seeing you again. Come into my humble abode."

They followed Stacey into the living room where plants filled her windows, and an overstuffed couch and matching loveseat invited them to relax. Anita cuddled into the corner of the couch, while François sat in the opposite corner. Stacey retrieved three long-stemmed wineglasses and a corkscrew from her hutch and set them on the coffee table. After pulling a bottle of red wine from the rack, she held it out to show François.

"This is what Anita drinks. You?"

"Perfect."

Pulling the cork, she filled all three glasses generously, and handed them their wine. "What brings you here?"

"Well, I wanted to visit you, of course. We're on our way to West Virginia where Julian is held. We're going to break him out." Anita spoke more confidently than she felt.

Stacey's eyes grew wide. "Oh wow. How will you do that?"

"François won't tell me. In case we get caught, he's keeping me in the dark. Safer, he claims."

François nodded to show she was right.

"You better not get caught. After everything you've been through. You deserve to have something go your way for once."

Stacey raised her glass in a toast as the others joined her. "To your success, and your safety."

They all leaned in, clinked glasses, then drank.

"I will make sure she is safe," François said. "Not knowing is one way, but I have other ways to make sure as well."

Stacey squeezed her lips together and raised her eyebrows. "Ok. I won't ask." She paused a beat. "How long can you stay?"

"Can we sleep here tonight?" Anita asked. "We should reach West Virginia around noon tomorrow."

"Absolutely. You can use my guest room. Can I make you something to eat? I can throw a frozen lasagna in the oven, and we can eat in an hour or so."

"I would love that," François said. "It is very thoughtful of you. I will fetch our bags from the car."

When he was gone, Stacey gave Anita a conspiratorial wink. "Mm-hmm. Lava cake all right. Once you break Julian out, you should ditch that husband of yours and go live your life. You owe him nothing more after the way he's treated you. Remember that."

Anita gave Stacey a half-smile. *How easy she makes it sound.*

"I'm living one day at a time right now. That's as much as I can handle."

François reappeared at the back door with two rolling bags and a backpack, and Stacey led them to her guest room down the hall, where no one objected to the one king-sized bed.

⌁

After dinner, the three recollected the old days over more wine. This time Anita was careful not to drink too much. She wanted to relish her time with her friend. There was no telling when she would see her again—or if she would see her again.

"Remember the time you tried to fix me up with the lawyer who'd just won his first case for a big D.C. firm?" Stacey chuckled between gulps of wine. "He was a hot looking guy, but too conservative for me. We were all doing shots, and he was saying God likes him to keep his body pure." She raised her hands in the air, looked at the ceiling and wiggled her fingers like she was getting a message from heaven.

"Oh yeah, I remember him," Anita said. "We kept telling him, 'Stacey needs you to save her, she wants to repent;' meanwhile you were downing those shots like it was Armageddon."

The three of them laughed. "Yeah. Why did you all think I needed to be saved? I was having a hell of a time."

"No, no," François said to Stacey. "He needed you to teach him how to have fun. You were the expert."

"Damn. I sure was, wasn't I? I guess that's how I ended up marrying a cheating partier who dragged me here. All fun and games until it wasn't. I should have stayed single. Anyhow, I got rid of him, didn't I?" Stacey looked at Anita who nodded.

"You did indeed," Anita said.

"Well, I'm going to turn in and let you two reminisce in my guest room. I'm at the other end of the house so you won't keep me awake." Stacey stood. "See you in the morning."

Anita had slept in the guest room before—when Julian made her furious and she couldn't stay in her house another minute, or when the pain of seeing Steven in every square inch of her home haunted her nights. Stacey let her show up any time of the day or night, but usually at night was when pain and anger overwhelmed her.

She pushed those thoughts away. Tonight would be different.

Tonight, she would not look beyond this room or beyond this night. Tonight, she wouldn't worry if she had a tomorrow.

"I'm going to jump in the shower, my dear." François reached out his hand. "Join me?"

His request sent a fluttering of anticipation through her. "I will."

Once in the shower, the water flowed over them, around them, between them, as though baptizing them, making them reborn. They made love without hesitation. Anita wanted him more than she'd ever wanted a man, and as their bodies merged, she abandoned any reality beyond this night.

➊

Around 4:00 AM, Anita couldn't sleep. This was the day they would reach Coal Creek and try to free Julian. Her world would be pulled apart regardless of the outcome. If they were successful, what would become of her and François? She imagined him disappearing from her life again, leaving a crater-sized hole in her heart. Or worse. A vision gripped her: the moment a shot fired into François, then Julian, each dropping to the ground; then screaming until the next bullet came for her. Her breath seemed to catch in her lungs as she stared into the darkened room.

There was no point in tossing and turning. She rose and pulled on the bathrobe Stacey had left for her. Slipping the hard drive out of her pocketbook, she tiptoed from the bedroom, silently shutting the door behind her. The house was quiet. The wood floor was cold against her bare feet as she walked to Stacey's office, where a computer sat on a desk that faced a bay window. The curtains were open, but only blackness showed outside. When she flipped on the recessed lighting, a face appeared in the window. She gasped and threw her arms across her chest. The image in the window mirrored her. The tension sunk from her body.

She gazed around the room for a place to hide the hard drive. If Stacey didn't know Anita hid it here, Stacey would be safe. No one would come here looking for it. Across the side wall were built-in bookcases, four shelves high above wooden cabinets. Anita opened one of the cabinets and pulled out a folded step stool, using it to climb up to stand in front of the shelves. There, she removed two volumes of Shakespeare, slid the hard drive behind them, and lined up the front of the other books until they were all level.

After replacing the stool, she scooted over to the computer. Paul's in Newport was the last one she'd touched. The familiar leather chair she'd sat in many other times called to her as if they were old friends, inviting her to have a seat. With a click of the mouse, the computer awoke, begging her to travel to places she feared to go.

It will all be over tomorrow anyhow.

Her heart pounded wildly as she opened her Google account and logged in. *Only a few minutes. Hopefully, it won't trigger any alerts. Long enough to see his photos and read his email one last time. Long enough to say goodbye.*

She opened Gmail and found lots of unread messages. Skipping these, she scrolled to the folder labeled STEVEN and opened the last email he'd written to her.

Hi Mom. I'll try to call you over the weekend, but lots going on so don't worry if I don't reach you. I've been working with an impressive company I can't wait to tell you about. You'll be proud. XOXO love Steven.

Tears dribbled down her face. *Never a day went by when I wasn't proud of you, Steven.* She remembered waiting for his call that never came, thinking how young people are busy with their lives, forgetting their moms. She forgave him. He'd call when he had a chance. But the call never came because the fire did.

The tears turned to sobs that shook her body.

Google Photos contained none from the last two years. Before that were the photos of Steven. At his new house in California on the deck, Steven with his arm around her—Julian had taken that one. They were smiling and she recognized how much he looked like her—same curly brown hair, same green eyes. But the smile was Julian's. Zooming in on it, she touched her finger to his cheek, the cold screen reminding her he was gone.

With a gulp, she flipped to the next photo of Julian with Steven—Julian not looking at the camera because he was smiling at their son. Oh yes. Those smiles were almost identical. Anita smiled through her tears at their happy faces, the joy spilling out of the photos. The last was one Steven took with a selfie stick of the three of them. Julian was in the middle with one arm around Steven and the other around her. Her head was on his shoulder, and she looked like she'd been laughing. They were the faces of a family. The faces of people with history between them but who also had a bright future.

Anita logged out and shut off the computer. Staring at her reflection in the black window, she wondered who this lost person was looking back at her.

CHAPTER TWENTY-FIVE

RUMORS

ERIN SAT AT the Formica counter of Ben's Café in Marlin, West Virginia, on a wooden stool with no back. As she drank her Coke, Ben assembled a lettuce and tomato sandwich on toast and dropped her fries in the fryer basket into the sizzling oil.

A man sitting two stools away was eating a sandwich while he glanced at Erin in between bites. *Dennen Correctional Facility* was on the shoulder patch of his pale blue shirt tucked into black pants, where a gun was clipped into a holster around his waist. She'd intentionally driven by the facility a mile away, looking for the closest lunch counter. Although she was twenty miles from the detention center in Coal Creek where Julian was being held, she hoped the guards working at this prison might be familiar with the place.

Ben wiped his hands on a towel hanging from his apron, then set her lunch in front of her. "Ketchup, mustard, relish are all here," he said, sliding the jars of condiments along the counter to her.

"Thank you, sir."

"Never seen you around before. I'd remember a pretty girl like you. Where're you from?" He leaned against the wall and folded his arms across his chest.

"Ottawa." Internally, she cringed over the pretty girl comment, but she wanted him to talk to her, so she smiled. "I'm a photographer. Here for several days to do a photo shoot of coal country towns and the people who live here." She flipped her blond hair behind her shoulders.

"I'm pretty sure folks don't wanna get their picture taken," Ben replied, "but there's plenty of history in these parts if you wanna know about coal."

The uniformed man laughed. "Honey, I'll pose for you. I'll even take my clothes off for no extra charge."

Ben stomped his foot. "Damn, Virgil. She don't wanna see you naked. This here's a lady, and she's our guest, so treat her like one."

"Sorry, miss," Virgil said. "Didn't mean no disrespect. Welcome to Marlin. What's your name?"

"Erin. I see you work at the Correctional Facility. Are they a big employer around here?" Erin spread ketchup on her fries, mustard on her toasted sandwich, and took her first bite.

"Yeah. The best these days. It's steady work and good benefits. And you can't be a drug addict, which reduces the competition."

"A lot of drugs here, eh?" Erin asked before munching on a fry.

Ben snickered and Virgil said, "Too many."

"That place in Coal Creek don't care," Ben said. "No piss test either."

"What place is that?" Erin asked.

"Trash works there. Stay away from 'em. Rumor's they've got a bunch of terrorists locked up," Virgil said. "None of our guards worked there."

"My cousin's nephew applied for a job the other day, and they're not hiring anymore. Thinks they're closing. Said there's box trucks loading up, taking stuff out, not in," Ben said.

Erin kept her face neutral. With no way to call François directly, she would have to contact Zack to pass along this critical information. Meanwhile, she'd need to monitor their activity.

"How come there's two prisons this close together?" she asked.

Virgil sneered. "I wouldn't call that dump a prison. Whatever it is, we don't want no terrorists mixing with our inmates. No one I know working there."

"People do what they gotta do," Ben said. "Not too many choices in these parts."

"What are you taking pictures of around here?" Virgil asked. "Not much to see but vacant buildings."

"Sometimes vacant buildings have stories to tell. The camera sees what people don't say. Are the mines still operating here?"

Virgil put down his sandwich. "My daddy, three uncles, and two grandfathers all worked the mines. Those used to be good jobs before the companies ran the unions out. Nowadays, it's mostly all mountain top removal, so they hardly need any workers. They got machines tearing up the place, turning it into the moon. When they mined underground, it didn't destroy everything around it. Now the creek's no good for fishing and the towns get flooded when it rains. Sucks what they're doing. There won't be anything left of these mountains when they're done."

"It's all the government's fault," Ben said. "But, they just changed the law about restricting oil. Maybe they're waking up up there. I heard coal's included. It'll pick up here again soon."

"It's not going to help us. They'll just tear off another mountain top with all their machines. Pretty soon we're going to be living in the flatlands," said Virgil.

Erin was saddened by hearing Virgil describe the destructive mining practices.

"You ever go four wheeling?" Ben asked. "It's the best way to get around in the mountains here."

Erin nodded. "I have. I grew up west of Montreal and we rode through the Laurentian Mountains in the summer."

"Well, girl, this is your kinda place," Ben said. "We got hundreds of miles of trails. The most trails in the world. You want to take pictures, go for a ride." He leaned forward, resting his arms on the counter. "My cousin Billy rents them out. Not much business this time of year so I'm sure he's got some. He's over south of Coal Creek. Tell him Ben sent you and I said to give you a good deal."

The door dinged and Erin turned to see a man holding flyers.

"Can I help you?" Ben asked.

"I hope so," the man said as he held up a flyer. "I'm looking for this woman. I know she's in this area. There's a five-thousand-dollar reward if you find her and turn her over to me. My phone number is on here."

"Damn," Ben said as he, Virgil, and Erin each took a flyer. "Five thousand dollars! What'd she do? Rob a bank?"

Erin suppressed a gasp as she recognized Anita on the flyer, but her pulse leapt into overdrive. Who was this man, and how did he learn Anita was coming here? *Call Mike*, it said on the flyer next to the phone number. She folded it and put it in her pocket.

Mike sat on the empty stool next to her and smiled. She gave a quick smile in return while committing his image to memory: hazel eyes; olive skin; dark, wavy hair. Older than her but not by much. Had an odd accent, too. British almost, but not British.

"Can I get you something?" Ben asked.

"Sure," Mike said. "This is the first place I've seen to eat. I'm starving."

"Gotta run," Virgil said as he rose and put money on the counter. "Tomorrow."

Ben nodded, then turned back to Mike.

"I'll have a cheeseburger and fries."

Ben went to work cooking and Mike turned to face Erin.

"A nice . . . juicy . . . burger." He gave her a big grin.

Erin tensed at his remark, the way he made it sound obscene by drawing out the words. It made her stomach lurch.

"Not a meat eater, I see. What brings you here?" he asked. "You are much too pretty to be a local."

"I'm a photographer, shooting coal country," she answered, struggling to sound calm.

"Really? Where are you from? Is that your car out front with the Ontario plates?" Leaning on his elbow and facing her, his stare made her uneasy. Rather than backing off, she gaped at him like a challenge.

"Where are *you* from? You have an unusual accent."

"I asked first." He held her gaze.

"Ottawa."

"Our liberal neighbors to the north. Funny to run into a Canadian here in West Virginia. You are a long way from home, sweetheart. What have you taken pictures of so far?"

Glancing away, she let him win the stare down. "I just arrived today. In fact, I need to move along while the light is still good." She pivoted toward the window at the front of the café, pulled money from her handbag, and placed it on the counter.

"Want company?" Mike asked. "I'm hanging around until this woman shows up. It might not be safe for someone as pretty as you to go wandering around by yourself."

Was that a threat? Or a come-on? Either option upset her.

"I do this all the time. I can't have people distracting me. Thank you for the offer though." Erin turned and casually walked to the door, praying he did not follow her.

CHAPTER TWENTY-SIX

LUCKY

Erin drove her rental car into the parking lot of what appeared to be a grocery store to make a phone call. A cloth sign hung off the store's overhang: County Assistance Food Pantry. She hadn't seen another grocery store and Ben's Café was the only restaurant she'd found on her drive through the area. Considering the limited options he served, it almost didn't count. Where did people eat and shop for food?

Next to where she parked was a small strip mall, but most of the windows had plywood over them. A pile of junk sat behind the unit closest to her.

She used the first of her burner phones to call Zack. While she waited for him to answer, a dented car drove into the parking lot with a loud muffler and a broken window taped with plastic. A woman younger than Erin, with vacant eyes and unbrushed hair, stepped out and dragged two small children from the back seat dressed in ill-fitting clothes. *Drugs?* she wondered. *Or poverty? Or both? The mom is a kid herself.*

"Hey," Zack answered, pulling her attention away from the woman. "I'm glad you called. A lot has changed."

"Here too. This is important. You must tell François a man is here passing Anita's photo around. He's offering a five-thousand-dollar reward to turn her over to him. Take down this description. Five foot nine, wavy dark hair, hazel eyes, white, probably of Mediterranean descent. His name is Mike, and he has a weird British accent."

"Whoa. That sucks because Anita and François should be arriving anytime now. I'll call him as soon as we hang up. And I got a tip. They're moving all the prisoners from every detention center soon. This came from my contact in Nevada who works for them. He's not clear when or where, so François and Anita left for Coal Creek the morning after you."

"I heard about the move, too. I'm going to rent an ATV to check the place out and explore the area for escape routes through the woods. Coal Creek has no cell service, so he won't be able to call me."

"Okay. I'll call François and inform him. Be careful."

"Over and out."

A few miles past Coal Creek, Erin saw a large sign for Billy's ATV Resort and Rentals. Turning left, she crossed the railroad tracks and the creek, then followed a winding road uphill to the resort.

Had she turned a few minutes later, she would have seen an oncoming Chevy Malibu with Maine license plates driven by François with Anita in the passenger's seat, on its way to Coal Creek.

❧

"We need to discuss what to do when we arrive," François said, as they passed a sign for Billy's ATV Resort and Rentals.

"I'm glad you finally decided to share this with me. I was wondering when you'd let me in on the plan." Anita had a growing headache from the anxiety building all morning. Her nerves were frayed, and she was losing patience.

"Some of this I do not know until we arrive. Usually, I plan with Erin after she makes contacts and investigates the area, but I have not heard from Zack. She must not have checked in. I am worried about her."

"You mean you don't have a plan? Is that what you're telling me?" Heat traveled from Anita's chest into her throbbing head. She shouted at him, riddled with fear and anger. "You dragged me here with no plan knowing our lives are in danger?"

"What else could I do?" François shouted back. "We know they are moving him. Maybe today. Maybe tomorrow. Where? Is he gone forever? Do they kill him?"

"Damn! Damn! Damn!" Anita screamed and stomped her foot. "Why did he do this? Why am I even here?" She turned away from François, gritted her teeth, and glared out the window, oblivious to the scenery.

They drove in silence until he turned at a sign reading *Coal Creek* with an arrow pointing right. After the railroad tracks and the bridge, he stopped on the side of the empty road and spoke quietly.

"You are here because it is the right thing to do."

Spinning around, she faced him. "I stopped doing what was right the moment I saw you."

By saying it out loud, she let loose all the shame and guilt she'd been burying since François came back into her life. Now, she almost sensed Julian's presence nearby and dropped her eyes to her lap. The reality of his suffering in this wretched place tainted her rekindled love for François.

"Look at me," he said softly. "You must listen."

Shifting her gaze to his face, Anita felt his eyes seemed to reach right into her soul.

"You let your heart lead you. Now your heart leads you here. You can never live with yourself unless you do this. It is who you are. Remember. I know you. You are strong and you are good. It is why I love you."

Anita choked back the wails rising in her throat. "I'm not. I'm not any of those things. I'm a coward! I'm weak! I'm terrified of doing this!"

"You are the strongest woman I know. You can do this."

She took a deep breath, wanting to be this person François believed her to be. Julian certainly didn't deserve to be locked away in this horrible place or taken to somewhere worse. She had to do this, regardless of her fear, knowing François would keep her safe.

"Okay. Tell me what to do."

"This is going to sound scary, but it will work. Erin and I have used this before. I am going to let most of the air out of one tire. You are going to drive to the facility and ask to use their phone to call the garage because you have a flat. You must act helpless. Our cell phones do not work here," he said, showing her his phone with the No Service message. "They know that. Of course, rental cars do not have spare tires or give you kits."

"So we're stuck here until the truck arrives. And what the hell is that smell? These people have to live with that?"

"Maybe it is better when it rains."

Anita shook her head ruefully. "What do you know about this place already?"

"I have seen the entire town on Google satellite. Unfortunately, no street views. Only one road goes in and out. This one. The facility must be in the old school at the end of this road. It is the only large building. What I do not know is how heavily it is guarded or how sophisticated the security is. Judging by the area, it may be basic. If you can get inside, you can see, and we can plan how to do this."

Anita nodded her head. This was making sense to her now. "What am I looking for?"

"How many guards? What kind of locks? Keyholes or electronic? Do they use a pass to enter? Anything you can see from wherever the phone is. Ask to use their restroom and get all the information you can. Be friendly and chat with them. It will take a while for someone to come from a garage. After they change the tire, you drive away, and I will meet you on the other side of this bridge. I will be watching for you and this road the entire time."

"Damn. Okay." Anita stepped out of the passenger's seat and watched François depress the pin in the tire's valve stem with a stick. Air whooshed out. The tire shrank beneath the car's weight, but he stopped before it was completely flat.

"Pop the trunk," he said. "I am going to hide my suitcase behind that deserted house across the street. They must not know anyone is with you. You can leave yours in the car. There is nothing important in it?"

"No. The money is in my handbag, along with my phone and passport."

"Leave your handbag with me but take some money and the pepper spray. And remember, you are Janice Knowles." He paused and smiled at her. "Good luck, Janice."

Anita slid the pepper spray into the pocket of her jacket, shoved several hundred-dollar bills and her fake driver's license into her duck boot and handed over her handbag.

Her teeth chattered as she started the car and hobbled along the road. In the rearview mirror, her eyes followed François as he disappeared behind a stand of trees dragging his suitcase. How she wished he were in the seat next to her, giving her courage.

At the end of the street, she reached a two-story brick building surrounded by a rusting chain link fence. A guard shack sat at the entrance. "Action," she said to herself, pretending this was a scene from a movie set. A young man walked out of the shack. He pointed a semi-automatic weapon at her, while a huge grin grew on his face.

"Put your hands where I can see 'em and get out of the car," he shouted like a drill sergeant.

Her body shook as she followed his order. "I have a flat—" she started to say, but he moved forward and jammed the gun barrel into her chest.

"I been waiting for you, Anita. Today is my lucky day."

REUNITED

ERIN ARRIVED AT the ATV resort and parked in a dirt lot by the edge of the road. Several wood cabins sat on two sides of a dirt path, each with a little porch. A sign reading Office hung by the door of a modest two-story farmhouse next to a large, flat-roofed garage.

She removed her camera pack from the trunk and walked toward the office. An engine revved to a roar, and one of the garage doors flew open. A plume of black smoke trailed from inside, stinking of burning oil. A middle-aged man wearing dirty work clothes walked out coughing while the engine sputtered and stalled. He spotted Erin and smiled.

"Hello," she said. "Are you Billy?"

"Sure am, miss," he said. "How can I help you?

"Your cousin Ben said this is the place to rent an ATV." She didn't mention getting a good deal, since the rescue budget would cover it.

"It sure is. Although I'm only renting side-by-sides right now. They're the ones that seat four and have a roof over them. They're more stable when the trails are muddy. Where're you from?"

"Ottawa. I'm a photographer, doing a photo shoot of the towns and scenic areas in coal country. Someone recommended renting an ATV to catch the views. I rode with my family in the mountains north of Montreal and loved it. A side-by-side will work fine for me, too."

"You'll have a treat. It's warmer this year, so there's still some pretty leaves on the trees. Seems like the season's longer every year. It's great for riding the trails though, and you won't freeze your butt off either."

"It was late in Ontario, too. It just got cold a few days ago. Does it worry you?"

"Worry me? Hell no. Makes business better. Why would it worry me?" Wiping the sweat from his brow with his dirty arm, he left a dark streak on his cheek.

Erin was disappointed that Billy didn't recognize the damage from the warming climate, but the man had to make a living, which was difficult in these parts. Guilt gnawed at her stomach for renting a gas-powered side-by-side, the way it always did when she had to compromise her values to accomplish these rescues.

"I want to rent for two days. Maybe longer."

"Are you alone? I don't recommend riding alone. It's better to take two vehicles in case there's an accident or one of you gets stuck."

"I understand, but you'd be surprised at what I can handle by myself. In my profession, working solo's the only way to go. I've done trailside repairs half my life."

Billy frowned. "Okay, young lady. I'll let you go out today if you promise me to be back an hour before sunset, you hear me? The rangers patrol out here, so you can't be out after dark. It's against the law."

"I promise."

"Follow me." Billy turned toward the garage. "I'll outfit you and show you the ropes."

Inside the garage, Billy led her to a wall covered in trail maps. "We're here," he said, pointing to a red X on one of the maps. "When you leave, you're going to take this trail at the end of my property out to the main trail over here."

Blue arrows ran onto a trail that connected with lots of others, winding around altitude rings with switchbacks. "Once you're here, you can go either way. These are mostly easy trails and they run into the other towns nearby like Coal Creek and Three Forks."

Billy pulled four maps from separate cubicles, then drew circles and red Xs through some spots.

"These areas are closed for logging or mining," he said. "Never go on a trail marked closed. They might be dynamiting."

Nearly an hour later, Erin was finally ready. She packed her camera bag into the cooler behind the seat, inserted the padlock she'd been given, slipped the visor down on her helmet and waved goodbye. Recalling the left forks on the map, she followed the trails to a marked turnoff for Coal Creek.

One way Erin thought they might rescue Julian was to drive him through the mountains on these trails to a parked car on the other side. Later she would study the maps for the best route, but first she needed to check the facility.

When she arrived in Coal Creek, she rode down the

main road until the building she'd identified on Google maps appeared. Much of the building was obscured by a chain-link fence overgrown with climbing vines, but the bars across the windows confirmed her suspicions that this was the place. A car with Maine license plates and a flat tire sat next to a guard shack. It reminded her of the trick she and François did back in Nevada, and she wondered if he and Anita might already be here. Before she reached the guard shack, she turned away, determined to find a different access point for a close-up view.

Instead of heading back to the trail, Erin stayed on the road to where it crossed the railroad tracks and stopped. If she followed the railroad bed on foot, she guessed she would come out behind the building.

Just then, she spotted a man in her rearview mirror walking by. She leaped from the machine, raised her visor, and shouted to him. "François!"

He pivoted and ran to the passenger side of the vehicle. "Erin. Thank God you are here." He jumped in next to her. "They have taken Anita. I have no idea what went wrong."

"Didn't Zack call you?,"

"I have not heard from Zack. Or you. We came down here and I had Anita do the flat-tire trick to get inside."

"Oh no. Not good."

François' face crumpled with concern. Reaching into her pocket for the flyer, Erin handed it to him. "They were waiting for her. A man's been passing these flyers around to everyone."

He read the paper and slapped his forehead. "*Mon Dieu!* I should have gone instead of her. I convinced her it was safe when she did not want to go. This is my fault." His eyes shifted around like he was a caged animal looking for an escape.

"Is she still inside?" Erin asked. "We'll break them both out."

"I have been watching for cars, but none so far. She must still be inside. What have I done?"

She had never seen him look so desperate. François, who was always in control, had bluffed his way through worse situations than this. Now his sad, drooping eyes and lack of focus were alarming to her.

"It's going to be dark soon," Erin said. "I'll park behind that abandoned house across the road. Then we'll walk near the edge of the tracks and hide until it's dark. We should be able to look inside then."

Since it was illegal to be on the trail after dark, Erin hoped they wouldn't run into any rangers later—and that Billy wouldn't realize what time she returned.

"What's that bag you're carrying?" she asked.

"Her handbag. Anita left it with me when she went inside. It has her passport and phone, so I didn't want to leave it sitting around."

"That's your car by the guard shack, right?"

"Yes. Her suitcase is in it; mine is behind the house across the road. They think she is alone."

Erin hopped off the side-by-side and unlocked the cooler in back. "Let's lock her handbag in here with my camera bag."

Erin felt strange giving directions to François, who was always the one in charge. He made the decisions when they planned together. She might have ideas, but he said yes or no. Decisions needed to be made fast, and his abdication of power worried her.

She steered the machine across the street, and he pulled aside overgrown brambles to hide it from the road. Then they sidled through the shadows along the railroad bed. Once the old school building was in sight, they perched on a broken-down brick wall and waited.

"What did this man look like?" François asked, as though his mind had just tripped over a clue. "The man with the flyers."

"Thirtysomething. Wavy, dark hair. Hazel eyes. Well-built, about five foot nine. Could be handsome if he wasn't so creepy. Said his name was Mike."

François closed his eyes. When he opened them, they glistened in the pale light. "I have destroyed her. He will turn her in for a bounty and they will torture her to find the hard drive. Perhaps they will trade me for her. I am probably worth more to these people."

"Oh no. Absolutely not. You know that doesn't work. They'll keep you both."

François remained silent.

"Tell me you won't do that."

Silence.

"Tell me!" Erin wanted to shout, but the best she could do under the circumstances was a harsh whisper.

The silence was broken by a helicopter flying into the valley toward the detention center. They dashed toward the building and stopped where they were hidden by overgrown brush but had a view. It landed in the parking lot between the guard shack and the front door. The passenger door swung open, but no one stepped out. Moments later, Anita stumbled out of the building, shoved forward by Mike, who controlled her by the handcuffs fastened behind her back. François drew his pistol and pointed it through the fence.

"No!" Erin said, as François cocked the trigger. "If you miss, you might kill her. And if you hit him, they might kill us both. They have automatic weapons. Then, who will save her?"

François let go of the trigger as his eyes followed Mike. He watched Mike force her into the helicopter and climb in after, shutting the door behind him.

Erin listened with alarm to François breathing as though he were suffocating, until she realized he was gulping down sobs.

CHAPTER TWENTY-EIGHT

MISUNDERSTANDING

Anita's heartbeat was flying, despite the helicopter not yet moving. Mike locked her handcuffs behind her seat and buckled her in, then slipped a blindfold over her head and pulled the elastic straps tight.

"No. Please. Uncover my eyes. I get motion sickness. I'll vomit." Terror coursed through her body, making her arm and leg muscles ridged and her stomach queasy. "Oh God, I might be sick right now."

"Barf bags are behind my seat," said the pilot. "I don't want to clean up a mess. Take care of her. It's going to be dark soon anyhow, so she won't know where we're going."

Mike ripped off her mask. Anita yelped as it pulled a clump of hair with it. The helicopter rose rapidly, spun in another direction, and took off. She heaved into the barf bag as Mike held it to her mouth. Little came out, but moments later, he detached the handcuffs and handed her the bag before settling into his seat.

Taking deep breaths, she chanted to herself. *You're okay. You're okay.* The tension in her muscles loosened a few notches and she rubbed her freed wrists. She'd outwitted Mike in Stowe, she reminded herself. She could do it again. Unfortunately, they'd taken her pepper spray when they'd captured her, but her boots still contained money and her driver's license. If she escaped, she could rent a car, maybe pay a stranger to drive her to safety. Keeping alert and clear-headed was the only way to stay alive. Gradually, her stomach stabilized.

The light was fading over the horizon. Oddly shaped stretches of gray were gouged out of the green mountains below, as though massive bombs had randomly exploded across large portions of the landscape. It hurt to witness the lifeless, gaping craters—lifeless except for the small number of trucks and giant machinery plopped around them like a toddler's sandbox mining for coal.

And they locked up my husband for protesting, she thought. Was there any hope? When these men, whoever they were, were able to pluck anyone from a remote location, put them in a helicopter, and send them to . . . wherever she was going.

Mike was strapped in the front seat next to the pilot, wearing wireless earbuds, smiling as he slapped his hands on the tops of his legs and bobbed his head in time to whatever he was listening to.

François worried her, stranded in Coal Creek with no car. *But he has a gun*, she remembered. *He can protect himself.* They thought she was alone, so they wouldn't be looking for him.

An aching numbness was overtaking her, filling her bones, her brain, her heart. It was a mistake to let herself love

François again. He was one more person for her to lose and she couldn't stand losing anyone else. If she got out of this alive, she would go somewhere far away and live alone—a hillside in Switzerland overlooking the lake. A small house surrounded by a vineyard. She would forget the life she once had, the people she loved who had vanished, and she'd just be alone and drink wine until she vanished too.

Gazing over the valley below, she wondered how it would feel to jump from the helicopter. Her pain would be over. She'd join Steven.

Not yet, she thought, sitting up straighter. *I still need to do what's right first.*

⌘

The lights of Washington, D.C. glowed on the horizon when they landed on a helipad in the middle of an estate. Out one window was a huge mansion, and out the other, a horse barn and riding paddocks under floodlights. A couple of other buildings closer to the helipad matched the house—all white sided with black shutters and accented by decorative lighting.

The pilot shut off the engine. Mike opened the door and jumped out, motioning for Anita to follow. She thought it odd that they weren't handcuffing her again. Although from the air, the estate looked massive, so perhaps they weren't worried about her escaping. A man appeared from the closest building and walked toward them.

Anita was stunned when she recognized him, relieved to discover a friendly face. "Paul?" Anita said. "What are you doing here?" Walking up to him, she threw her arms around him, believing he had rescued her again.

"Good to see you," he said, returning a loose hug and stepping back. "You're not easy to find. Sorry we had to do this, but you have something of mine. I need it. Let's go inside and I'll tell you about what's happened."

Anita believed he meant the hard drive, but why was he at this mansion? With Mike? She tried to absorb these facts but remained baffled. Something wasn't right.

Inside was a sitting room with a fire blazing behind the glass enclosure around a brick fireplace. Dark leather sofas and chairs rested atop a pale wood floor, and soft light came from the hunter green shaded lamps on the tabletops.

Off to the side was a wet bar with wine bottles and glasses laid out along with three small trays of canapés.

"What's going on here?" Anita asked.

"You're our guest, and we thought you'd be hungry after the flight, not to mention thirsty. Red or white?" Paul walked over to the wine and held a glass toward her. She shook her head no and he placed it back on the bar.

"Whose guest? Who lives here?"

"You'll meet him later. For now, it's just us, so you can relax. Mike won't be staying."

At that, Mike nodded, turned, and left.

Her brows drew closer. "Quite a step up from Newport. Is this your new bed and breakfast?" Anita asked with obvious sarcasm.

Paul laughed. "I wish. No, I don't live here. I'm visiting too."

"So have I been rescued or kidnapped? On the way here, I assumed kidnapped, but then I saw you and . . ."

"You have the ability to turn this whichever way you want. I hope you pick 'rescued.' This can work out for both of us."

Anita paused, considering these conflicting messages. "Do you know where I was when they kidnapped me? I was at the detention facility where they're holding my husband." Her voice rose as the heat of anger began traveling up her neck. "Whoever this is, they know about the facility. They probably run it, and they have my husband imprisoned—without any charges, bail, or legal representation. This man is not a friend."

Cheeks flushed, Paul opened his palms toward her like an offer. "You can talk to him about it when you meet him. With any luck, he can fix it. I bet he can. Then your nightmare will be over, and you can go back to the life you had before this all started."

Anita frowned. "I'm not sure that's possible now that I know what's going on."

Paul poured himself a glass of red wine and looked over at her, raising his eyebrow in a question. She decided a little wine would help her nerves.

"Ok. Give me a glass of red."

He poured a second glass and handed it to her. "Have a seat. There's nowhere to run, and nothing to run from. Might as well enjoy it while you're here." Retrieving a tray of canapés, he placed them on the table between two chairs, sat and looked up at her. "Please. Sit."

Anita was starving now that her stomach had settled. The last time she'd eaten was hours ago, and she'd vomited what was left. Thoughts of how hungry François must be haunted her, stranded back in Coal Creek. And what did they feed

Julian in that horrible place? Guilt didn't keep the hunger away, however. She needed to eat.

The chair let out a puff of air as she collapsed into it. First, she ate a puffed pastry filled with gooey blue cheese and ripe pears. Next, she ate the sliced turkey on toast topped with horseradish sauce. The poultry was still warm, and the tanginess of the fresh grated horseradish tickled her nostrils. Anita washed it down with the silky red wine full of soft tannins. For the moment, the tempting victuals seduced her. She ate several more before agreeing to listen to Paul.

"I know you have the hard drive because I was in the kitchen when you talked to Caitlyn on the phone. I tried to have her give me the phone, but she wouldn't. If she had, I'd have asked you to give it back to me, instead of leaving it in Canada. That's all I want. After all, it is mine."

"What does that have to do with this place?" Anita folded her arms.

"This man's an investor. Energy, and he wants to break into clean fuel. It's the future, after all. I mean, this is what we want, right? For someone with this kind of money to develop it and put it into use all over the world?"

Anita tried not to scoff. This administration had made sure clean fuel wasn't a future anyone could fathom, so she had trouble believing anyone as wealthy as this was suddenly a big investor in it. "What makes you think he will? All the laws in this country are turning away from clean fuel."

Paul nodded. "True. But he wants to make money, and this technology will. My company never got the patents approved. He has the power and influence to do just that. He can bring it to market."

Anita nearly spit out her wine upon hearing him suggest this man own the patents. "Paul, don't you see what he's doing? When he owns the patents, he can charge exorbitant prices so it's not financially feasible or, more likely, he can prevent it from being developed at all."

Paul shook his head. "No. Not true. Because he's having me run it. I'm going to make sure it gets developed."

Anita sighed in frustration, remembering what Caitlyn had said about her father being a poor judge of character and easily duped.

"Maybe you don't believe me," Paul continued, "but this is a huge opportunity. This guy has more money than God, and he knows everyone. His reach is worldwide. Since he can do whatever he wants, isn't it best if he wants what will benefit the world? Isn't that what you want?"

Anita shook her head and set her wineglass on the table, looking into Paul's eyes. "I don't trust him. I don't trust anyone who locks people away, hides them in some hole in West Virginia, and pretends they don't exist. Do you?"

Paul's mouth opened, as though to speak, but instead he closed it again and glanced down at his watch. "Looks like it's time to meet the big guy." Paul stood. "Follow me."

Mike thrust his chest out and walked upstairs from the reception room where Anita and Paul were talking. He was pumped and couldn't wait to see his father's face. Between delivering Anita from Coal Creek, his hunch about Paul and the hard drive, and turning Paul into their ambassador, his ideas had fallen into place. His father would have to acknowledge his value, hopefully by giving him a position in his company with status and respect. They'd work together on his special projects and become close, like a father and son ought to be.

At the top of the stairs, Mike found his father in his office at the end of the hall. Doug was reading his laptop on an otherwise empty cherry desk. Besides the desk, the stark office contained only two plush chairs and a table with a fax machine and printer.

"Hey," Mike said, greeting him. "I brought her here. She's with Paul downstairs right now listening to his pitch."

"Good job," Doug replied without looking up. "Give me a minute. We need to talk."

Mike was a twinge disappointed, but not enough to slow the drumming in his chest. His father was a busy man. He stood in the doorway and waited.

After a few more minutes, Doug acknowledged him. "Come in and have a seat. I've got great news."

Mike's chest pounded in anticipation as he sat across from his father. He leaned forward.

"I got a call from my friends in Washington. Anita fucked up. She logged into her Google account early this morning. We got an address of where she was in Gettysburg last night. Gives us someone you can lean on if she doesn't cooperate."

"Okay," Mike replied with an air of uncertainty, his eyebrows dipped together. "Hopefully it won't come to that if Paul convinces her you're the good guy."

Doug scowled. "She's done a hell of a job eluding U.S. intelligence for the last week. I don't see that happening."

"She didn't elude me." Mike's body tensed.

"You're right. You're a hell of a good detective. I appreciate it."

"I'm good with cracking computers and tracing data, too. Remember I have a computer science degree. Maybe that never impressed you, but I can be a big asset to you. The reason I found Anita was I hacked into one of those climate activists' email accounts and took it over after he was detained. When I received her email, I knew I was onto something."

Mike searched Doug's face for agreement, a reinforcement of his value, but Doug frowned.

"I know, Mike. I know. But it works a lot better if we keep our distance. You should keep doing what you're doing, and I'll be in touch when I need you. You're a very valuable asset, and I appreciate that. But what I want you to do isn't always, shall we say . . . I can't be associated with those things. Knowing I have your loyalty and we can't be connected is what works. You understand, right? And I'll make sure you're well compensated. I had a bag of cash put in your car. I think you'll be pleased."

Mike pushed down the lump in his throat which threatened to humiliate him. Putting on the well-practiced face he'd always used with his father, he thought about the bags of money his mother stashed in her closet, how she'd kicked them across the room and cried after his father left, and he'd never understood why. Now he fought the urge to kick the desk and put his fist through the wall. Instead, he pushed his shoulders back and replied, "Of course, sir. I understand completely."

"Oh, and one more thing," Doug went on. "I want you to go with her to retrieve the drive and bring it to me personally. Once you have it, get rid of her."

Mike stared at him, not sure how to respond. Was he hearing this correctly? His father expected him to kill her even if she cooperated? Maybe he could have killed her before, when his anger drove him to the edge, and she clearly deserved it. But not like this. Not at his father's command, like a contract killer. This just proved his father disrespected him. "I'm not some goon. That's not what I do."

"Hey. Don't wimp out on me now, huh? That's not how I raised you. I know you can handle this. You're not like your mom. You're special. Like me. You can do what needs to be done. The bag of money in your car reflects that." Doug winked at him and gave him a big grin.

His father hadn't raised him at all, but he did remember one thing from his childhood about the man. "Whatever you want," Mike said, the feel of Doug's belt on the back of his thighs echoing through the years.

CHAPTER TWENTY-NINE

TRUTH

Paul led Anita upstairs to a spacious conference room with several plush baby-blue chairs around a cherry wood table. Matching wood panels lined all walls except the video wall. Anita observed cameras above them, pointing at each chair.

Paul motioned for her to sit and joined her.

"I guess I don't need to ask if anyone is listening to us here. I assume anything we say is being recorded," she said.

Paul was silent.

Doug entered the room, followed by Mike. Paul stood and smiled, then introduced them.

"Anita, I would like you to meet my good friend John St. Claire. He's the man who makes things happen."

Doug walked over and reached out to shake Anita's hand, which she accepted. Appearing cooperative felt like the safest response. Her chest tightened as Mike stopped behind him, watching her, reminding her of her vulnerability. The connection between the three men puzzled her.

"I am thrilled to meet you, Mrs. Forester. I've heard so much about you. May I call you Anita?"

"Of course," she replied in an agreeable tone, relying on her business instincts to portray confidence even though her mouth was going dry.

Doug positioned himself across from Anita, and Paul sat next to her. Mike took a seat farther down the table, where he used a remote to raise a computer keyboard before him.

Doug smiled at Anita. "Did you have a nice ride here? I'd have picked you up myself, but I've been busy today. I do enjoy flying those birds. It gives you a whole different perspective on the world."

Anita gritted her teeth. Was he trying to get under her skin? He certainly realized where they'd picked her up and what her ride entailed. She decided to abandon the fake pleasantries. "I had an unexpected perspective of all the damage being done to the mountains of West Virginia."

Doug placed his elbows on the table and interlaced his fingers. "You see damage. I see progress. Men don't die in mines anymore. It's far safer for the workers. You value trees over people?"

"Without trees, you won't have people. And we don't need coal anymore. There are plenty of good alternatives."

He leaned back in his chair and grinned. "Which is why we're here. I assume Paul told you about our plans for developing his technology."

For a moment, she had a flicker of doubt about her assumptions and considered his sincerity. "He did. Frankly,

I'm not buying it. You didn't offer a reward for finding me to share your business plan. I'm here to get schooled on what you want from me. Am I right?"

Doug tilted his head to the side with a frown. "That's a bit harsh, isn't it? You don't even know me. How about we start over, and you give me an opportunity to explain how this can benefit us both. You have the hard drive, which is what I want, and I have something you want."

Anita contemplated what that might be. It had to be Julian, right? If Doug buried this technology, the harm he would do to the world would be massive.

"Let me ask you, Anita, what is your price for this hard drive? Because I can afford anything. Look around you. You can see it's true. Tell me what you want and it's yours. I'm a fair guy. I'm not trying to cheat anyone. You're a businesswoman. Let's negotiate."

Listening to him was an assault on her common sense, but she'd dealt with his kind before. The others in the room were riveted by him. Paul had the look of every brown-noser she'd ever met, ready to concur with whatever came out of his mouth. Mike was hypervigilant. He reminded her of a schoolboy vying for his teacher's attention.

"Unlike some people, Mr. St. Claire, I don't have a price." Anita's arm muscles tightened as she made fists below the table. "I'm not willing to trade away a solution to reducing carbon to someone I don't trust. I guess you'll have to do to me what you do to those who don't comply with your wishes. Do I go back to Coal Creek so you can dump me into your detention center?"

"Funny you should mention Coal Creek," Doug said.

"Paul, would you wait downstairs for us? Anita and I need to discuss this privately. Order up dinner if you like. Mike, you can stay."

The hair stood up on Anita's arms. With Mike in the room and Paul banished, she feared what Doug might do to her. She turned to Paul, hoping he would stay. Catching her glance, he hesitated. Doug's lips tightened as he leaned forward, staring at Paul with a furrowed brow. Finally, Paul rose and left the room, shutting the door behind him with a bang. Anita stifled a shiver.

Doug tapped his fingers on the table as he focused on Anita. Her stomach churned with fear. The room remained silent, but she was determined to appear composed.

Mike leaned back in his chair with an unblinking gaze at her.

Shifting her eyes between the two of them, each of them staring, goosebumps traveled up her arms. She folded her hands on the table, studying the two men.

"You were snooping around Coal Creek when we found you," Doug said.

This is the part where he offers to trade Julian, Anita thought. *Predictable. Hopefully François can free him.*

"Why do you have protesters locked up? They're harmless. Just a bunch of nobodies with big mouths."

"See how little you know? Their voices are dangerous. One voice becomes two, two become two hundred, two hundred become two million. Two million people can't be silenced, and they can swing an election. The way to prevent this is to stop the leaders one at a time. Then the rest lose interest and forget about them, don't they?"

He admitted he is responsible for locking up protestors, and he's doing it to affect elections. Anita clenched her fists again, wondering which elections he meant. Was he responsible for those now voting against clean energy?

"No. They don't forget. I will never forget." She repressed the urge to shout. Men like him enjoyed watching a woman break. They push and push, hoping a woman will become emotional and lose credibility. Then they can dismiss her. She would not allow that.

"I believe you," Doug said. "You're such an ideologue. But I believe everyone has their price, including you."

"Why do you want this drive so badly? Are you actually going to develop clean fuel? I don't think so, because if you were, you wouldn't need to imprison demonstrators."

Doug rolled his eyes. "I'm going to do whatever makes me the most money. I'm just an oil man, sweetheart. The person who keeps this economy cranking while the rest of your kind gather around for handouts, and I will make damn sure nothing gets in my way, including you. Now, let's move on and find out what your price is, shall we? Because I plan on having this hard drive tonight."

Anita shuddered, fearing what threats, or actual violence, he would use to convince her.

Doug nodded to Mike, who activated the computer, which appeared on the giant wall monitor, launching a web conference named Coal Creek. Anita saw her face was the only one on camera in this room. The Coal Creek screen was dark. A voice came over the speakers.

"Are you ready to begin?" the voice asked.

"Yes, we are," Doug replied. "Turn on your camera."

Anita held her breath, fearing what condition Julian was in, wondering if she could stick to her convictions if she saw him suffering.

The screen came to life in a room where a man looked back at her. The blood drained out of her face and her pulse rocketed. Before her sat a ghost, his unkempt beard nearly disguising his too-thin face.

"Surprised to see your son alive?" Doug asked. "Want to keep him that way?"

Anita's heartbeat pounded in her ears while she studied this face she'd loved from his first breath, the mouth she'd fed from her own body, the hands she held to lift him up when he fell, the fingers that had wrapped around hers, secure in the knowledge she'd keep him safe.

"Mom! Where are you? Do they have you, too?" Steven asked from the computer screen.

He was struggling to breathe, his wet eyes focused on her. She wanted to scream. Or cry. Wanted to leap up and pull Steven through the screen and into her arms. Then she would kill these two men with her bare hands, squeeze the life out of them in seconds.

Instead, she gripped her hands together and held her arms tight to her body to hide her shaking. "I thought you were dead," she said to Steven. Tears welled up in her throat, but she caught them in time. She would not let these men see her cry. "I'm going to help you. You'll be okay. I love you."

"Be careful. Dad's here, too," Steven replied in a low voice, like he didn't want anyone to hear. "He came for me, but shouldn't have. You shouldn't either."

A wave of nausea flowed through her when she realized

that Steven was the reason Julian got himself captured. She burned with shame over cursing Julian for his foolishness. He'd literally risked torture, maybe death, to save their son.

"I think we're done here for today," Doug said. "End the call."

When the screen went dark, Anita's heart imploded, turning into a black hole.

"Have we found your price?" Doug asked with a smile on his face. "I think we have."

Staring at the darkened screen, Anita was unable to breathe. One thought ran through her mind, blocking out all else: Steven was alive and only she could keep him that way.

"I don't have it with me," she said.

"Yes. I understand it's in Canada. But I have a jet and we can be there in a few short hours."

Anita shook her head. "It's not in Canada. I can drive to where it is from here. Give me a car and you'll have it tonight."

Doug laughed. "Mike will take his car and you two will go together. Tomorrow all the detainees are leaving Coal Creek forever. Leaving the country in fact. After tomorrow, you'll never see either one of them again. So make it hasty. Otherwise, I'll send you those family shots from your husband's phone so you can remember what they looked like."

Anita nearly choked hearing those words and tried to slow her breathing. Until this moment, she'd never known how deeply she could despise someone, and it made her nauseous realizing she must comply with his wishes. Although she didn't trust Doug, she couldn't risk doing nothing. Maybe once he had the hard drive, he would have mercy and let them leave for Canada. Or maybe it would buy time and she could devise another escape plan. Sitting here under his scrutiny was hopeless. Riding with Mike was her only chance.

Doug's phone rang. "Hi there." He paused. "I'm sorry. I got tied up . . . I'll be at the house in ten . . . I know this is your big night, son, how could I forget? . . . Of course. See you in a few."

"You have a son?"

"I do. Why do you ask?"

"Do you think your money will protect him when the planet is so toxic that he can't breathe the air? When nothing grows because of the severe heat? Can you imagine the pain I've been through thinking my son was dead? You never want to experience that kind of pain."

He laughed. "You people overreact to everything. Doug Jr. will be fine. You don't need to worry about him or me."

Anita tilted her head and frowned. "Doug Jr.? Not John Jr.?" She shook her head at Doug's frown. "I'm not surprised. Who are you, Doug? A man like you wouldn't have a son named after someone else."

Doug recovered his arrogant façade. "I already told you. I'm an oil man, and I'll be here long after your kind is forgotten."

"Even an oil man must love his son."

Doug glared at her, then turned to Mike. Anita thought Mike's self-assured demeanor had evaporated, his shoulders slumping forward, as he looked at his keyboard, avoiding Doug's face.

"Mike, I need you now. You're the only one I trust to handle this. You with me, buddy?"

Mike's eyes shifted to Doug, then away. "Yes, sir."

The three of them stood and started for the stairs, Anita

walking ahead as Mike and Doug hung back. She turned to see Doug talking to Mike in a low voice and giving him a playful shoulder punch that looked harder than necessary. Mike winced and nodded, joining Anita and walking her to his car.

CHAPTER THIRTY

FRIENDS

IKE HELD ANITA's handcuffed wrists as he fastened her seat belt on the passenger side of his BMW. He opened one handcuff and threaded it through the armrest on the door. The sound of Mike clicking it shut again made Anita wince.

Deep breaths forced her to stay calm, despite being trapped. Her brain was her only defense weapon now.

Mike started the car and spoke Stacey's address into his GPS. Panic slammed into Anita's chest, causing her to miss a few breaths.

"Why are you taking me there?" She had not mentioned Stacey, intending to go to her own house and figure out a way to have Stacey drop it outside, unseen.

"Your Google account was accessed from this address this morning at 4:13. Must be where you left the hard drive since it's not in Canada."

Nausea filled her. She'd never wanted to endanger Stacey, but that was exactly what she'd done with her thoughtless computer use. "It's not there. I stopped and hid it at my house."

"No you didn't. We've had cameras on your house for days."

A flush crossed Anita's cheeks as she cursed her foolishness. Lulled into a sense of safety in François' arms and her friend's familiar house, she'd acted stupidly. Her head began to throb. She leaned her face against the window to cool herself and counted her breaths as a distraction.

The drive should take an hour and a half, but she guessed Mike would make record time as he pounded on the gas pedal. Tractor trailer trucks disappeared into her side mirror. The thought of being in a crash while she was handcuffed to the door was terrifying.

"Could you please slow down? I want to live long enough to see my son again."

Mike was silent and continued.

"What if your mother were in the car? Would you drive like this and risk her life?"

"Shut up about my mother," he replied.

Anita made note of his reaction. "Sorry. All I mean is she probably worries about you. Mothers do. Do you visit her?"

"We talk, but I haven't seen her in a long time. She's too far away."

Anita noticed his driving was less aggressive, as if the thought of his mother might be calming him. "That's sad," she continued carefully. "My son lived far away, too. I'm so grateful he's alive. Your mother must be thankful she gets to talk to you."

"She got us phones to make it easier for us to speak to one another since she's in another country."

"It's wonderful to have that kind of love." Anita watched his face morph into a pained expression. "Is your father there too?"

Silent, Mike once again accelerated as he stared straight ahead.

"Maybe you'd rather not talk about him."

In the darkness, the highway stretched out ahead like a runway as they hurtled toward the next set of taillights. Anita tried to figure out how she would escape this time. Being alert for an opportunity was probably the only way, but she also feared Doug might hurt or kill Steven and Julian if she did.

First, however, she had to prevent Mike from hurting Stacey. She couldn't while handcuffed. Maybe she and Stacy could overpower Mike together. Inside, she smiled a little at the thought and her stomach started to unwind.

Her mind shifted back to Steven. Only a few hours ago she'd been in the same building with him. Maybe in the next room, or a floor or two away, and she hadn't known he was alive. Her heart silently screamed from the pain.

"What will happen to me once you have the hard drive? Will Doug let my son go? Let us both walk away and leave the country?"

Mike didn't answer. She feared he knew Doug wouldn't hold up his end of the deal.

"My son is almost your age. My heart broke seeing his face, discovering he was alive, imprisoned. All this time when I thought he was dead, I felt like I was dead, too. What kind of person does that? Who makes a family, a mother, think her son is dead? Steven didn't break any laws."

"How do you know?" Mike asked.

"You heard him. That man Doug, John, whoever he is. He said their voices are dangerous to him. He can't get his way if they speak out."

"Maybe they should shut up and they won't have a problem."

Anita shook her head. "Shut up so his greed can poison the planet? Look how much money he has. He doesn't even care about his own son. That's selfish and cruel."

Mike flashed his high beams at the car ahead as he crawled up to its bumper. Before Anita could scream in fear, it moved over.

"What do you want? Is it the money? I can pay you. Not like him, but I have enough money for you to walk away from this man and never have to bow to him again."

"I don't bow to him," he said with disgust. "We work together. He needs me and respects me."

"Bullshit," Anita said, knowing how risky it was to criticize his idol. But she sensed he might be wavering based on his conversing with her. "He doesn't respect anyone. He lied to Paul. I expect he is lying to me. He's probably lying to you too. What did he promise you?"

"None of your fucking business."

Mike laid on the horn at the car ahead, which wasn't pulling over despite his flashing his high beams. After a moment, he pulled to the right of the car. As he did, the car accelerated, racing him. Mike took the bait and raised his speed until the two of them were locked in a drag race. Anita watched him in terror as his mouth curled into a smile, his eyes lit up, and he leaned closer to the steering wheel, glancing back and forth at the other car. A slow tractor trailer suddenly appeared ahead in their lane leaving no time to brake. Mike veered right onto the shoulder. They hit the rumble strip sending a roaring vibration through their seats as their car swerved before stabilizing. He sped past the truck, pulled in front of it, then cut into the left lane ahead of the racing vehicle. The driver flashed his high beams at him and slowed down. Mike was grinning now. Anita's head was pounding from clenching her teeth.

"You're going to kill us both before we ever reach his precious hard drive. If you want to die, don't take me with you. I want to hold my son again." She lost control and sobbed.

"Christ almighty. Shut the fuck up." The anger she expected didn't materialize. Instead, it was like he was pleading with her as he slowed to a more reasonable speed.

Before long, they had reached Gettysburg. Mike followed the GPS to Stacey's house and turned into her long driveway. A floodlight came on as they approached, illuminating a black sedan with tinted windows parked by the garage. Anita's legs shook, and her lungs suddenly tightened. *Calming breaths,* she thought.

Mike opened her door and unlocked one handcuff to remove her from the armrest, then fastened the cuffs together behind her back. Lights shone from the windows inside. Steering her toward the front door, she stumbled, recovered, but her feet refused to move. Mike shoved her forward until they reached the entrance.

"I can't look," she said to him in a whisper, burying her face into his shoulder, as though touching him would change his mind. Anything was better than walking through Stacey's door. "Please," she begged. "Don't make me."

He didn't move. "This will be over soon," he said in a soft voice.

The door opened from inside revealing two men in ski masks wearing black leather gloves. Anita trembled as Mike looked them over.

"I don't know what your jam is, but I'm here for a hard drive, then I'm leaving," Mike said.

"We're here to help," the taller of the two said. "We were told you were coming, and he sent us for support."

"Who sent you?" Mike asked.

They both laughed.

"Same man who sent you. Said you're the boss though. We got a head start while we were waiting. She doesn't know anything about a hard drive. We made sure. But hey, she can tell you herself. She's in the other room."

Anita held her arms against her body to stop her shaking and studied Mike. His eyebrows drew together, and his face appeared softer. The anger she'd been used to wasn't there.

"She doesn't need to see this," he said quietly, nodding toward Anita. "One of you can stay here with her."

"I think it might be an incentive if she does," the shorter one said.

Anita inhaled deeply, knowing she had only a slim chance of saving Stacey and herself. "I know exactly where the hard drive is and I'll tell you. But first, let Stacey take her car and leave, or you get nothing."

Both masked men laughed, but Mike stayed silent.

"I don't have to do anything," the shorter one said. "I'll get it out of you."

"I can make this take a long time. Remember who you're

keeping waiting. If you kill me before I talk, you're all screwed. It will take you a long time to tear this house apart and you may never find it."

"Everyone talks eventually."

Anita shivered. "You're wasting time. She hasn't seen your faces. What do you care? Aren't you paid to satisfy him?"

The two men huddled together for a moment, then consulted with Mike. The taller one left the room.

"Take your car keys and get the hell out of here," she heard him say from the kitchen.

Stacey coughed and whimpered. Keys jingled. Anita breathed like someone had wrapped their hands around her throat as Stacey limped past in the hallway on her way to the garage, turning briefly to Anita. Her face was swollen, one eye all the way shut, and blood dribbled from her nose and lip. Anita gasped. Mike steered her to the window, where she waited until Stacey's car lights disappeared from the driveway. She turned and vomited into a ceramic planter holding a begonia.

"Your turn, babe," the short man said. "You talking? Or are we playing?"

"In the office, top shelf of the bookcase, behind two volumes of Shakespeare."

He left the room. A chair scraped across the floor in the office. Books tumbled to the ground. A few minutes later, he returned with the hard drive.

"I'll take that," Mike said. The man hesitated, but handed it to Mike. "You two are done here. Thanks for your help. I'll take care of the rest."

"Can we watch?" the tall man asked.

"Fuck off. This is my party," Mike replied.

The two of them laughed and left the house. Anita watched their headlights leave and ground her teeth. She'd tangled with Mike too many times already, and she knew she couldn't out-wrestle a man his age.

"Who do you aspire to become?" she asked, visibly trembling. "The boss of those assholes? Men who beat women your mother's age?"

He was silent. Instead, he grabbed her arm and led her back to the car. Once again, Anita was handcuffed to the door. Inside, Mike slid the hard drive under his seat. Ten minutes later, they were at the on-ramp to Route 15 and heading south. Anita looked for Stacey's car, hoping she'd made it to the hospital, hoping she wasn't passed out on the side of the road from her injuries.

Mike made a call over his car speaker and Doug answered.

"You're on speaker and she's in the car," Mike said by way of greeting. "I have the hard drive. She cooperated. No problems."

"Good," Doug replied. "Make the stop we discussed, and I'll see you when you arrive."

"Doug?" Anita asked, attempting to join in the call. "Will you release . . ." Before she could finish, the call ended.

CHAPTER THIRTY-ONE

SCOPE

EVEN WITH THE headlights, the return ride from Coal Creek was slow in the dark. François was unusually silent while Erin peered into the woods, alert for sets of animal eyes and lights from patrolling rangers. Her throat tightened when an opossum suddenly froze in front of her vehicle. She hit the brake, and it scurried across the trail and disappeared. She shut off the engine and removed her helmet to scan for sounds. In the distance, the deep groan of machines echoed through the valley, and an area of light illuminated the sky, reminding her of the map with the Xs marking off mining locations. Some were not far. Her gut ached with the realization that beyond these woods, destruction of the mountains was taking place night and day.

Erin glanced over at François who was silent, his forehead resting in his hand. Restarting the engine, she navigated back to Billy's ATV resort. The two of them rolled the vehicle across the parking lot to prevent Billy hearing her arrival, and parked it near the barn. To Erin's relief, Billy didn't come outside and yell at her for getting back after dark. She unlocked the cooler and retrieved the camera bag and Anita's handbag, then they sprinted to her car. Once inside, she flipped on the air conditioning to dry out the mugginess.

They drove in silence. François squinted under furrowed brows, concentrating. When they reached the main road, he finally spoke.

"Turn right. We need to go back to Coal Creek and interrogate those guards. Plus, I left my suitcase behind a building, and it has the passports in it."

Erin's jaw slackened. "You mean, you're just going to walk up to them and say 'Hi, guys. Can you help me out?' Way ballsy, but why would they do that?"

"The flyer Mike passed around said there was a five-thousand-dollar reward. Whoever is at the gate right now is angry he is working while the other man got the reward. And Anita has money in her handbag she brought for this purpose."

Erin nodded and drove toward Coal Creek. "That makes sense. I wish I'd found more information before you arrived."

"You had no time. By the way, my rental has a flat tire, and we are not near anything. I am hoping I can retrieve it. Did you bring Fix-a-Flat like last time?"

Erin gave him a thumbs-up. "Two cannisters every time since Nevada. They're in my rucksack."

When they reached Coal Creek, Erin parked along the curve in the road hidden from the detention center. François removed several hundred-dollar bills from Anita's handbag and slid them into different pockets.

"How much pepper spray do you have?" he asked.

"Five canisters. What do you have in mind?"

"I'll talk to them alone, but back me up with pepper spray and stay hidden."

Erin put two cannisters in each pocket and crept along behind him, staying hidden next to the high fence, her mouth getting dry. François held his gun behind his back and sneaked through the shadows by the edge of the road. Sweat beaded up on Erin's forehead.

François approached the guard shack. Empty. Erin spotted three young men, camo-clad, sitting against the chain-link fence and barely visible in the dull light from the parking lot. Burning cigarette tips lit up when they inhaled, and Erin smelled pot as well as tobacco. The men were passing a bottle between them. One of them appeared to be nodding off in between gulps. No guns were in sight. François stopped before they saw him.

"So what the fuck we gonna do with no job no more?" one of them said.

"Fuck if I know."

"I'm pissed they hired those guards from the prison to move these guys. We could do that. I mean what the fuck, all you gotta do is drive. I can fucking drive."

"You can't even fucking stand up."

"Fuck you."

"No. Fuck you."

The silent one fell sideways onto the ground and lay still.

"I'm so fucking broke. This job sucks ass anyhow."

Erin held her breath as François stepped out of the

shadows to face them. "Sounds like you guys need to make some money. I'm here to help."

One of them jumped to his feet, while another struggled to rise, moving onto his hands and knees and grabbing the fence to pull himself up to standing. The third remained motionless on the ground.

"Who the fuck are you?" asked the one already standing.

"I'm the guy who wants to give you five hundred dollars to tell me what you know."

"Five hundred, huh? How 'bout we beat the shit outta you and take it instead?"

Erin tensed and grabbed a spray cannister with each hand.

François pulled the gun from behind his back and pointed it at the speaker. "Bad idea. A better idea is I give you this money, maybe a little more, when you answer my questions, and we all stay quiet. You go back to doing whatever you are doing but with money in your pocket. Who is going to know?"

The young man stared at the gun, shifting his eyes briefly to the guard shack.

"You try to shoot me, and I shoot you first. Then who's going to pay you? Them?" François nodded toward the detention center.

"Fuck 'em. Gimme six hundred dollars."

"Deal."

"Wait. What do I get?" the other standing man asked.

"Six hundred for you too. And both of you never knew I was here." He turned back to the first speaker. "Here is my first question. I heard you say you lost your job here. When are they moving the detainees?"

"Ten tomorrow morning. I'm working 'til then. Then these sorry-ass losers go to hell."

"Where is hell?"

"All I know is the airport, not which one. But I heard where they're going, they ain't never coming back." He nodded as though satisfied and looked at his buddy, who nodded along with him.

François reached into his jacket pocket and pulled out two one-hundred-dollar bills, handing one to each of them. "Do either of you have access to this facility? A key or a pass to get inside?"

"Yeah, of course."

"How many guards are inside?"

"What the fuck? You breaking in here or something?" the tallest asked with a frown.

"Not necessarily. Why should I when you can walk right in? I can pay a lot more if you bring me a detainee."

The tall one looked over at his buddy, shuffled his feet around, and glanced toward the detention center and back.

"How much more? It's gotta be a lot so I can blow this town 'cause that's fucking dangerous." He peeked over at the detention center again and rubbed the back of his neck. "I seen these guys come and go. They ain't no amateurs. Today they had a fucking helicopter."

"How much do you want?" François asked.

"Twenty-thousand." He looked over at his buddy. "Each."

"I guess four-thousand each is not enough? It is all I have right now."

The taller one shook his head. "You outta your fucking

mind? I can't disappear on that. Gimme my six hundred dollars and get lost."

"How many guards?" François asked again. "That is the last question."

"Two, besides me. They hang around the office bullshitting all night."

"What about these guys?" François nodded at the other two men with him."

"They're just my buds. We're all hanging here."

François reached into his jacket pocket and pulled out the rest of the bills. He counted out five hundred more to each of the two men.

"Thank you," he told them.

The guard grinned. "Come back with that money and we'll talk more."

Back at the car, Erin drove to the end of the street with François to retrieve his suitcase and throw it in the trunk.

They sat together quietly for a few minutes, until Erin broke the silence.

"Tonight is our only chance to break out Julian."

"What would you suggest?"

"What if we tie up these three guys and take that guard's pass? I've got rope and duct tape. With only two guards inside, I think we can do this."

"Maybe. But something is bothering me. All of those detainees are flying somewhere tomorrow where no one can find them. And they are all innocent protestors or activists, not only Julian. We need to break all of them out. We are their only hope."

Erin's pulse sped up. "I know. After tomorrow, no one is

left to rescue. It must be tonight. But if we're successful at breaking them out, what will they do? Hop a freight train? Run through the woods? We can only fit three in this car, maybe one in the trunk. Five more with your rental car when we fix the flat tire."

François nodded. "Whatever happens, they have a better chance than they do now. I counted five windows across the front of the building on the second floor. If we assume ten rooms per floor and two in a room, we have potentially forty people inside—more if they have several in a room."

Erin rubbed her forehead, as though clearing her mind, desperate for an idea. His sad eyes stared back at her.

"School busses!" Erin almost shouted. "I saw a school bus garage on my way here from the prison town."

François raised one eyebrow. "Can you drive a school bus?"

"How hard can it be? There's no clutch, no stick shift. It's just a long, wide car."

"On a winding, hilly road in the dark."

"Hey. I drove an Expedition in the Rockies during a snowstorm at night. That was way worse. All I saw was white—white road, white shoulder, white drop off a cliff. A bus will be easy. How about you? You ever drive a bus?"

François shook his head. "I hoped one of us had."

"Don't worry. I got this. As long as we can find a key, I can drive it."

"Okay. It's Sunday morning now. They won't even miss it until Monday."

CHAPTER THIRTY-TWO

CHOICES

ANITA SPOTTED THE road sign for the exit to Owen's Creek right before Mike turned on his signal and slowed down. "Why are we getting off here? Do you need gas?" Her heart pounded. She recognized this area. The following exit took you into Cactoctin Mountain Park where she, Julian, and Steven had often hiked, a place of waterfalls, rocky cliff faces, and steep mountain vistas—an easy place for someone to disappear.

Mike didn't answer but turned right at the end of the off-ramp. She'd been on this road too. It wound along the top of the park through an often desolate area that crept through the mountains. No gas stations or convenience stores were this way, just a school and a few houses before you hit the woods.

Oh shit, Anita thought, the pulse in her temples throbbing. *This is it. He's finally going to kill me.*

"Is this the stop Doug asked you to make?"

He continued to drive in silence.

She began to cry. "I'm never going to see my son again. I did all this for nothing. I should have let those thugs kill me instead of giving you the hard drive to save my son. What was I thinking?"

"You had no choice, just like I have no choice."

"Of course you have a choice. There's always a choice."

"You chose betrayal."

Anita snapped her neck around and glared at him, her eyes wild and unblinking as she shouted: "I chose my son. That's what mothers do. Women sacrifice themselves for their children. I'll bet your mother did too."

Mike squinted and spoke in a low, deliberate voice. "She saved that asshole's money so I could come to this country and go to college. Let herself be his whore. Let me be his punching bag. She thought he'd help me when I got here because I was educated and could speak perfect English. She was wrong too, like you. He doesn't give a shit about me. That part you're right about. About him not caring about his son."

He slammed on the gas pedal. The curves increased and he steered through them, slipping into the oncoming lane as he sliced off the turns.

Suddenly, Anita made the connection, and everything became clearer. "You're talking about Doug, aren't you? Doug is your father."

In the light of the dashboard, she saw his frown deepen and his eyes narrow. As he accelerated further, she spotted the glowing eyes of a pair of deer through the trees and shut her own eyes, bracing for the impact.

None came.

His voice pulled her attention back. "His sick-fuck blood runs through my body, and it makes me a sick fuck too, just like him. But he has never been my father."

The turns of the road became sharper. The motion of being tossed side to side as he played chicken with the road made her nauseous. Her stomach lurched.

"I'm going to throw up. I get motion sickness, you know."

He jerked the car to the side of the road, slammed on the brakes, and raced over to Anita's door. When he yanked it open, her arms flew out as she was still handcuffed to it. She heaved what little was left in her stomach, then heaved again while she shivered in the icy mountain air.

Mike unbuckled her seat belt and motioned for her to stand. Her knees nearly collapsed, trembling. After unlocking the cuff attached to the car, he locked her hands behind her back again.

"Are you going to shoot me?"

"Shut up." Pushing her ahead of him into the woods, the darkness enveloped her, cutting off her vision. Several steps later, she stumbled on a rock and fell sideways, extending her elbow to break her fall. Instead of stopping it, her hipbone hit a partially buried rock and her shoulder slammed into the ground.

She howled in pain. "I can't . . .walk . . . like this . . . can't . . . balance . . .can't see . . ."

He fished the key out of his pocket, leaned over and unlocked one handcuff, then reached out his hand to pull her up. Gripping onto his arm, she summoned a burst of energy. Using the momentum, she sprang to her feet and swung her dangling handcuff at his head, striking him across his nose with the open hook. He screamed in pain and grabbed his nose as blood flowed into his eyes and down his face. She swung again, hitting the side of his head, causing him to stumble backwards. Tripping over a tree branch, he landed with a thud as his head hit the ground. Dazed, he wiped the blood flowing into his eyes. She dug into his jacket pocket where she'd seen him stash the car's key fob and snatched it. As she pivoted away, he swiped at her ankle, narrowly missing, then rose to his feet. She dashed for the car, popped open the lock for the driver's door, and scurried inside, locking it. Seconds behind her, he tried the locked door handle, then whipped his jacket off one arm and wrapped it around his hand, punching the side window as she started the car. It didn't break. The rear tires kicked up gravel as she floored the accelerator and was gone before he could hit it again.

After putting several miles between them, Anita pulled over to check if Mike had left his phone in the car. Still shaking, she searched under the front seat and, finding the phone, powered it off. Next to it was the hard drive, safe again. For now. As though it had a purpose to keep returning to her.

This road led to Interstate 81 right outside of Hagerstown, where she could buy coffee energy drinks and another pre-paid phone. She was grateful they'd never found the money in her boot when they nabbed her at the detention center. From Hagerstown it was a straight shot down to Lexington, VA, where she would cross over into West Virginia.

Hopefully, she would reach Coal Creek before the police got a report that she had stolen this car. She had to rescue Steven—even if she had to die doing it.

CHAPTER THIRTY-THREE

TOOLS

ABOUT AN HOUR south of Hagerstown, a cell phone rang under Anita's seat. She startled, certain she'd shut it off. The ringing stopped for several minutes, before starting again. At the next exit, she pulled into a truck stop and reached under the seat, finding both the hard drive and the cell phone she'd already powered off. A phone chirped. She got out of the car and felt around from behind the front seat locating another cell phone. A text message across the screen read:

HIM: Where the hell are you? You should be back by now. Call me.

Curious, she swiped open the screen, discovering the phone wasn't password protected. She tapped on contacts and found only two. One labeled MOM. One labeled HIM. MOM's phone number was formatted for a foreign country. Then HIM must be Doug. His direct, private line that only the three of them knew.

She sighed with relief. Apparently, Mike hadn't been in contact with Doug yet, and this phone wasn't tracked as Doug didn't know where he was. Powering it off, she searched the rest of the car for any more surprises. Only an ice scraper and snow brush were stored in a back seat pocket.

Next, she popped the trunk and found a bulging gym bag. Unzipping it, her eyes widened, and her jaw dropped. Piles of twenties, fifties and hundred-dollar bills were fastened together with rubber bands. Obviously from some illegal activity.

On top of the money was a metal case with the initials SIG on the front. She unbuckled the clasps and lifted the lid. Inside was a gun the size of her hand. Next to it were two more cartridges. Her heart was racing. Mike had a gun but didn't bring it with him into the woods. Maybe he'd thought about having the choice and decided not to kill her.

She closed the case, scanning the parking lot for anyone that might be watching. Shoving the case back in the bag, she reached around inside for anything else. Her hand stopped on a neoprene holster for the gun. Leaving it there, she closed the zipper and shut the trunk.

Back on the highway, she ruminated on her new acquisitions. A gun might protect her, and it might give her a way to rescue Steven and Julian. Or, with all this money, maybe she could buy their freedom. Either way, she had a few more hours of driving to devise a plan.

High beams from a car behind Anita flashed in the rearview mirror. She punched the BMW's accelerator and easily passed two tractor trailers before pulling over, relishing the shot of adrenaline. No wonder Mike liked driving fast. Speeding gave her a sense of power despite her life being out of control.

The hypervigilance was exhausting, however. Opening another can of coffee energy drink she'd bought back in Hagerstown, she took a long gulp.

Seeing Steven on the conference call kept invading her thoughts, causing a knot in her stomach—his hair had been straggly and unkempt, his face thinner than she'd ever seen it. Either they were starving him or torturing him, or both. When she imagined the pain he must be enduring, her breathing grew shallow.

Her thoughts turned to Julian, the man who tried to save their son—a hero. Yet something nagged at her. He'd known Steven was alive, known he was captured and in a detention center. Why hadn't he told her? Steven's death devastated her. Julian's silence about the truth was . . . horrible. There was no better word for it.

The nerves of her arms and legs crawled with restlessness from the caffeine and her jaw clenched tightly. After rotating one stiff arm, Anita switched to the other. Rage at Julian spread like heat through her body until she pounded the car's steering wheel with her fist, shouting. "How could you? How could you? How could you?"

If only she could slam on the gas pedal. If only this drive would end. If only she could unleash revenge on Coal Creek for mistreating her son. She had way too much time to seethe over all this.

When her mind drifted to Stacey, her anger turned to shame. She'd been wrong and selfish to put Stacey in danger.

Anita reached for her new phone on the passenger seat,

entered Stacey's number, and hit Speaker. It rang several times before rolling over to voicemail and beeping to record her message.

"Stacy, it's me. I'm so sorry. I used your computer, and they were tracking my account. I was stupid. Very, very stupid. Can you ever forgive me? I understand if you can't. You've always been the greatest friend and I put you in danger. It's my fault they hurt you and I'm sorry beyond words."

She disconnected, staring ahead at the road, not letting the tears come. Instead, she let this pain burn inside her, knowing she didn't deserve the release tears would bring.

Thinking about François, she feared what had become of another innocent party in the drama of her life. The person who put her needs above his own life. The one she'd let go of years before because his desire to save the world conflicted with her desire to own it. How ignorant she'd been of what truly mattered. Her heart ached, imagining what she'd lost.

Just then she remembered he had her handbag and dialed her Canadian phone number, hoping he would answer. Voicemail again. Weary of her solitude, she left a message in case he checked her phone.

Signs appeared for Lexington. That meant about three more hours to Coal Creek. She pulled off the highway at an all-night McDonald's and ran to the restroom, careful to tuck the dangling handcuff securely in her sleeve, then ordered food and water.

An hour later, she made one last stop on the winding road through West Virginia, at a remote spot in the woods. She popped the trunk, walked around back, and took the gun from the bag. Before tonight, she'd never held one, much less fired one—so she practiced. Stretching out her arms with the weapon in both hands, she aimed it at the bank on the opposite side of the road, took a deep breath and squeezed the trigger. It didn't budge.

She exhaled and held it under the trunk lights. There was a lever above the hand grip which she assumed was the safety. Turning back to the hill, she used her thumb to push it down. With more pressure, the trigger moved this time. At the snap of the bullet, her arms sprang up from the recoil. The pounding of her heart was louder than the bullet firing. *Deep breaths. In, one, two, three; out, one, two, three, four, five.* Once more Anita lifted the gun with her outstretched arms. This time, she spotted a neon green dot at the end of the barrel for lining up with the sight. She aimed at a tree on the bank and held the gun firmly, ready for the recoil as she fired. The sound of the wood splitting informed her she'd hit her target—a large target, she admitted, but no wider than a man.

She slid the safety on again, grabbed another magazine from the case, retrieved the gun holster, and closed everything. Before stepping into the car, she slipped the holster around her waist, slipped in the gun, and adjusted it so her dominant left hand could easily reach it. Her chest fluttered with determination.

This would all be over before morning. She would make sure of that. Over for the captors or over for her. She was done crying.

CHAPTER THIRTY-FOUR

TRANSPORTATION

CELL SERVICE KICKED in as Erin and François left the valley, and Anita's phone dinged.

François rummaged through her handbag until he located it. "She bought this in Canada a few days ago. I think only I have this number."

Erin considered this, while François tried to access it. "Maybe Anita called it herself to reach you."

He moaned and shook his head. "It is useless. I do not know her pin. It is already disabled for one minute."

"Try her birthday," Erin suggested, not surprised that he knew it.

"Nothing. Maybe it is Julian's or Steven's." He slammed the phone on his thigh. "I do not know either of those."

"Try your birthday."

"Why would it be my birthday?"

She smiled. "Just try it."

When he punched it in, the phone came to life.

"Told you. I know how women think." Erin winked at him.

He raised an eyebrow at her as he played the message over the speaker.

"It's Anita. François, I hope you get this and you're safe. I escaped and I'm on my way back to Coal Creek. I'll be there around four. I'm driving a stolen car with a big bag of cash and a gun. I'm going in to get them one way or another. Meet me if you can."

"She is alive!" François threw his head back and closed his eyes, then leaned over and kissed Erin's cheek as she continued to drive. But a moment later he was frowning again. "She worries me. What will she do with a gun? We must arrive before her. We cannot let her do this alone."

"Can Anita shoot a gun?"

"I doubt it. Two nights ago, just seeing my gun made her weak in the knees."

"Sure it was your gun, stud?"

François blushed and shook his head. "Be careful what you say. We are here to rescue her husband. We must not forget this."

Erin cleared her throat. "I haven't forgotten. I'm worried about you. You don't hide your feelings well." After witnessing him fall apart earlier in the evening, she needed to know she could depend on him.

"When he is with us, I will hide them perfectly. It is what I must do." Shifting in his seat, François checked his watch. "We have time before she is here. We should go to the town with the prison and find an open store. I am starving."

"Me too. The sandwich I ate at Junior's feels like days ago." Her stomach was so empty she salivated imagining salsa and Doritos.

Erin slowed down as they passed the bus garage. About a dozen school buses were parked out front. Only one small floodlight lit the entrance of the prefab steel structure.

"I hope they keep the keys inside," François said, looking it over. "If they do, this part will be easy."

Fifteen minutes later, the road straightened and commercial buildings appeared. The valley widened and distant lights from the prison illuminated the night sky. Ahead on their left, an Exxon sign shone like a beacon over three aisles of gas pumps beside a brick convenience store. A neon sign in the window read, "OPEN." Erin pulled alongside the pumps to top off her gas while François walked inside. She hoped the tank in the school bus would be full, or at least have enough gas for them to reach the highway, where they could buy fuel without drawing attention to themselves.

When François returned with three bulging bags, they moved to the back of the parking lot.

"I bought all the phones they had. Once we break them out, they will need to make phone calls. We will activate them after we eat. I bought several rolls of firecrackers to make a distraction. Oh. And food. I am sorry about the meat and dairy. It is all they had."

François tore open a ham and cheese sandwich and handed her half, which Erin devoured.

Weary from the long day, she reread the phone activation instructions several times, while a problem gnawed at her stomach.

"They're coming for the detainees at ten o'clock, maybe earlier," she said. "We can't reach the Canadian border before it's discovered they're gone. And even if we could, we have no way to take forty people across it. Where can we take them?"

François' shoulders slumped and he shook his head. "All I know is we cannot leave them here. And they probably have my picture on the security tape in this store, so I may not get back into this country again. Drive somewhere else. I do not want to sit around here."

Erin started the car and drove back the way they had come, stopping at an abandoned parking lot near a streetlight to finish eating and activating the phones.

Afterwards, they drove to the bus garage, parking behind the building next to a steel door with a keyed deadbolt. No one could see them from the road.

She handed François the electric lock pick from her rucksack, and he assembled it. As she trained the flashlight on the lock, he shoved the pick into the door and pushed it open.

Erin returned to the car and listened for slowing vehicles. They'd seen no traffic on the way from the convenience store, but now she heard several cars drive by.

"Dear God, don't let them stop. Don't let them find us," she mumbled, her eyes wide.

After a couple of minutes, François emerged with a handful of keys and they ran out front to the buses. He read off the numbers on the tags while Erin scanned for the matching bus. The first one she found was in the front row, blocked in by the bus behind it.

Car headlights sped down the hill. They hid, moving around behind the nearest bus to avoid being spotted. The car passed by. Moments later, another set of headlights appeared, and they repeated the routine. When it was clear again, François read a couple of more tags, eventually getting to one standing right next to Erin.

Unlocking the door, she stepped inside with the flashlight, found the ignition, and turned the key to accessories. The dashboard illuminated. She flashed François with two thumbs up and he ran back behind the building with the remaining keys.

As she familiarized herself with the controls and examined the gauges, she was happy to discover the fuel gauge read full. She forced the side window open to let in air, but after a couple of inches, it stuck.

Headlights crested the hill to her right. This time the bubble lights of a police car were heading in their direction. Turning the key and her flashlight off, she slid onto the floor under the steering wheel and listened. The police car slowed, then turned into their driveway and stopped, idling by the front of the building.

The pounding of Erin's heart was explosive. Resting her face on her hands, she inhaled the odor of the rubber mat while the floor grit dug into her palms. The police car's engine stopped, but the car door did not open. Had François spotted him? She lifted her head slightly and put her hands together in prayer, then begged God to keep him safe.

An eternity seemed to pass, the silence occasionally broken by the crackling of the police radio, but the occupant didn't reply.

What if he's taking a nap?

Eventually, a car door opened. From where she was curled up, she saw the darting light of a bright flashlight. She hoped

François had time to cover his tracks and nothing suspicious was visible through the window of the building.

The searching light continued shining, moving slowly over the buses nearby. When it reached hers, his footsteps approached as the light beam bounced off her partially open window. She squeezed as close to the wall of the bus as possible, took a deep breath, and buried her face in her arms so he wouldn't hear her breathe. The flashlight flitted around inside the bus but didn't reach her motionless body. Then she heard him bang the window shut, causing her throat to tighten as she suppressed a gasp.

Circling the bus with his light, it shined through the door toward the driver's seat, flashing around without landing on her. A moment later, the light moved on and Erin allowed herself to breathe again.

After a while, she heard the police car door open and shut, followed by the sound of it starting and driving away in the direction of Coal Creek.

Erin left the bus and ran around behind the building to where the rental car was parked. François was nowhere in sight. She tugged on the driver's side door, but it was locked.

"François?" She gazed around from the building into the darkness.

The steel door opened, and François stepped out as Erin expelled a breath of relief.

"You were inside the whole time?"

"On the floor, under the desk. I only had time to shut the key cabinet."

He unlocked the car and got into the driver's seat. "Are you ready for this?"

"I'm ready. But a bus will be hard to hide in Coal Creek. Plus, the police car went off in that direction. What if he went to the facility?"

"I was thinking that, too," François said. "You should park the bus near the facility, but not where the guards will see it. If it's in plain sight on the road, people in the neighborhood won't find it suspicious."

⅋

Erin climbed onto the bus and moved the driver's seat forward. When she started it, the rumble of the engine gave her goosebumps of excitement and nervousness. She maneuvered out of the parking spot, satisfied with the way the steering responded.

François' headlights appeared from behind the building, and Erin pulled onto the road, with François following. Before long, the sway of the massive bus around the curves felt natural in her hands as she commanded the steering wheel and her muscles relaxed.

Fifteen minutes later they were in Coal Creek. Nearing the facility, Erin shut off the headlights, eased the bus over against the chain link fence, and parked. Thanks to the bend in the road, she could see neither the facility nor the guard shack. François pulled up behind it. When she joined him, he handed her firecrackers and a lighter.

"Anita should be here soon," he said in a low voice. "I doubt any other cars will be coming. I am going to take a walk and look for the police car. Stay here and watch for her."

It was three thirty in the morning as François disappeared, slinking along the fence.

Erin always grew anxious when the time neared to begin, like a swarm of bees invading her stomach. At this stage, anything might go wrong, and she had to be prepared to improvise. Exhaustion permeated every inch of her body. Sleep was still a long way away, so she opened a bottle of iced coffee which had grown warm. It had a slightly sour flavor but didn't spoil the caffeine effect she needed.

François reappeared as stealthily as he'd left.

"No police car. Just the same guard sitting on a chair in the parking lot. The other two are passed out on the ground."

He snagged the other iced coffee bottle through the car window, then leaned against it to drink.

Fifteen minutes later, a vehicle approached. François ducked behind the car. Erin peeked over her seat. A white BMW with Massachusetts license plates approached. The headlights obscured her view of who was inside, but as it got closer to theirs, they shut off, and it pulled over to a stop. The door opened, and a figure emerged.

"It's Anita!" François jumped into the road and waved. Anita walked forward as François ran to her and pulled her into his arms.

CHAPTER THIRTY-FIVE

TEAMWORK

Anita basked in the comfort of François' embrace, allowing all her muscles to unwind.

"I was so worried about you," François whispered into her ear. "I am sorry I put you in danger. I had no idea."

Anita relaxed her head onto his shoulder and breathed him in, calmed by his familiar scent as warmth spread through her body. "I thought they would catch you too. I was coming to free all of you."

"All of us?"

Lifting her face to him, she stared into his eyes.

"Steven is alive. He's here too. I saw him on camera."

François' eyebrows dipped, and he cradled her face, looking at her like he might say something.

She pulled away, her eyes darting past him in the direction of the facility. "I will die getting him out of here if I have to."

He hugged her close to him again and rubbed her back.

"Not necessary. All these prisoners deserve to be free, and we must rescue them before they come to take them in the morning. We will do it together."

They held each other a moment longer, until François turned his attention to the BMW.

"Where did you get this?"

"It's Mike's. He drove me into the woods—I'm pretty sure to kill me, but I escaped. The trunk was full of money and a gun."

"Did he hurt you?"

Anita shook her head. "No, but a couple of thugs beat up Stacey because I used her computer to access my Google account. They traced it back to her house. I'm afraid for her. I've tried calling but she didn't answer."

"When we are finished here, we will try to find out."

Erin joined them. "Nice to finally meet you in person, Anita. He's been a wreck waiting for you."

"Erin had to rescue me first." François blushed. "I was a mess after they took you. Thank goodness she showed up and brought me to my senses."

Anita smiled at her. "I'm grateful." As she reached out to shake Erin's hand, the handcuff dangled from her wrist. Erin smirked.

"Mike's handiwork."

Erin examined it. "Easy stuff. I'll have this off you lickety split." She returned from the car with a paperclip which she twisted inside the lock. It popped the handcuff open.

"Wow. You're amazing. Thank you." Anita opened her jacket to reveal her gun. "This is my plan. I practiced in the woods on the way here."

Erin's eyes widened.

François frowned. "Shooting is always the last resort. If you miss, you give them time to shoot you."

"I don't care. Whatever it takes to bring them down. I've seen what they did to Stacey, and Steven looked terrible on the video call."

François nodded, but his forehead stayed creased.

"First, tell us what you saw inside, please. This will be the most help. How many guards? How many locked doors? Were you in the area where they keep the detainees?"

"No. I didn't see any detainees. The guard by the shack swiped his ID and took me inside. In the entryway was a guard behind a glass window. Another one came out of a locked metal door and frisked me. None too nicely."

François groaned. "This was all my fault."

"Hush. Let her finish," Erin said.

Anita continued. "He took me inside a small room with a few chairs and had me sit there. Eventually, Mike arrived. That's all I saw. I asked to use the restroom, but they had one in the same room, so I couldn't go anywhere else."

François nodded.

Erin pulled her backpack from the car and removed duct tape, rope, and scissors, handing Anita the roll. "We're taking the night guard's access card. You tape his mouth, I'll tie his hands, and François will hold a gun to his head so he cooperates. Then we'll do the ones on the ground. We'll have to share the scissors."

"We must be very quiet," François said.

Anita zipped up her jacket, so her gun was hidden. She crept along the fence behind François and Erin until they reached the guard shack. François raised his hand to signal "stop." Anita's heart raced, her mind laser focused as they prepared for the ambush.

The guard was smoking a cigarette. It dangled from one hand as he slouched back in his chair. No weapon was in sight.

François slipped behind the shack. In a flash, he leapt toward the guard and stuck the barrel of the gun against his temple, placing his hand across the guard's mouth.

"Do not move," he said in a stern voice as he gripped the guard's jaw shut.

Anita ran around in front of him and plastered a strip of tape across his mouth. The guard's eyes widened and shifted back and forth as Erin pulled both his arms behind him and secured him to the chair, knotting the rope three times, then bound his feet. Anita rolled more tape completely around his mouth and head.

Before the other two men awoke, the trio bound and taped them too. Their groggy bodies shimmied in the dirt as they tried to maneuver free.

François grabbed the guard's semi-automatic weapon from the shack, checked the chamber and emptied it, pulled the magazine out and handed it all to Erin.

"Put it in the trunk," he said.

Anita searched the guard's pockets and pulled out a plain, white card with a clip on the end. "This is like the access card the other guard used to enter," she whispered.

"I want both of you to stay back here until I signal it is safe to join me," François said as he pointed behind the fence.

Anita glared at him, the heat of fury crawling up her back. "Not on your life. I'm going in with or without you. It's not for you to decide."

Frowning, François pushed his hair away from his face. "At least stay behind me. Erin, when we are at the front door, light the first set of firecrackers and toss them into the parking lot, away from us. When they come out, we go in. Toss the second and third set as you see fit but stay back here until I give the signal."

"Ok, boss," she replied.

François maneuvered around the edge of the fence as Anita shadowed him. They moved in spurts, pausing when they reached shadowy brush as they circled the outer perimeter of the lot.

Anita scanned for any other movement each time they stopped. When they had circled halfway and were in line with the back of the building, they bolted to its side and froze flat against the dark wall, creeping along it until they reached the front. François slid his gun from his jacket pocket and held it in front of him. If she did the same, she might shoot François, so she took out her gun and pointed it at the ground, double checking that the safety was on.

They scurried across the front of the building. When they reached the front door, the firecrackers exploded like gunfire from across the parking lot. At the sound, the door sprang open and a guard emerged, carrying a semi-automatic weapon like the one François took from the shack. Before the guard turned toward them, François had his pistol at his temple.

"Drop it," he said. The guard moved his head slightly toward François, but François dug the pistol harder against his skin. "Do not move. I cannot possibly miss."

The guard let the weapon fall to the ground. François kicked it behind him, where Anita picked it up and hid it in the shadows. She didn't have a clue how to use it and this was not the time to learn.

"We are going back in, and you are going first," François said. He wrapped his other arm around the man's neck and shoved him to move forward as he shifted the pistol into his back. Anita took a step back and gripped her gun in both hands, still pointing at the ground but ready to raise it if François had trouble.

Inside, the guard behind the glass ducked. When they reached the metal door, Anita pulled the ID from François' pocket and swiped it against the security lock. The door clicked open. As François forced the guard through the door ahead of him, gunfire erupted. The guard collapsed against François, who stumbled backward from the weight. He shoved the body forward into the gunfire as he backed out through the door and slammed it shut.

"Get down," he said. His arm covered Anita's head as they scrambled to lie flat on the floor. She turned her face to him and saw beads of sweat on his lip.

"You should not be here," François said. "I risked your life once already. I cannot do so again."

Anita gasped as she noticed a blood spot growing on his other sleeve. "Oh my God. You've been shot!"

"Shhh. Just a graze, I think. It only stings a little."

Anita's stomach lurched, but she swallowed back her panic—and the bile threatening to rise. She couldn't fall apart. Too much depended on her staying levelheaded.

She slid away from him and began to stand, but François grabbed her hand and yanked her back to the floor.

"No! Stay here. Wait for Erin to set off the firecrackers again and he comes out."

A moment later, another round of firecrackers exploded outside. They both held still on the floor with guns drawn. Nothing happened.

"Shit," François said. "I think he is not fooled."

"I'm going in." Anita stood, gripping the ID she was preparing to swipe.

"Not alone." François pushed himself up, grimacing. "We're going in together."

"Me first. I have an idea."

Anita pulled out the wad of hundred-dollar bills she'd stuffed in her jacket earlier. She swiped the card, opened the door slightly, and flung the money inside as more gun shots were fired. She slammed it shut again.

They leaned together, breathing in each other's air as they waited for a sound. After a few minutes, Anita shouted, "Can you hear me? I have a lot more money. Come out and it's yours."

Silence continued behind the door.

"I have more in my pocket too," François said. "We should give it another try."

"Give it to me. I think he may believe a woman more than you."

François handed her another wad of bills, and she swiped the door again. When it clicked, she tossed the money in. There was no shooting.

"We want to talk," she shouted, keeping the door opened a crack. "I have a lot more money. You can have it."

"I have an AR-15. Give me the rest of the money and I'll go. Fuck with me and you're dead."

"Give me five minutes, and don't shoot," Anita shouted back to him, slamming the door closed.

Nodding at François, she sprinted outside to the BMW. She grabbed stacks of money from the trunk and stuffed it into one of the plastic bags from the convenience store. Minutes later, she was back inside.

She pushed the bag of money through the door, biting her lips together to stop them from trembling. The blood patch on François's shirt now saturated a growing area, and his skin looked ashen.

The metal door opened, and the barrel of a rifle pointed out. "Slide your guns through the door, handle first. Then I'll leave," the guard instructed them.

François shook his head, but Anita pushed hers through the opening. One eyebrow dipped and he shook his head furiously.

"Both of them," the guard shouted from behind the door. "I saw two pistols."

Anita nodded at François, her sad eyes begging him. This was their only chance of getting inside.

Sweat dripped from François' forehead. His eyes were wet as he held her gaze. "I do it for you, my dear."

As he slid his gun in after hers, transfixed by his demonstration of love, she hoped they were making the right decision.

"Lie face down on the floor. Move and I kill you," the guard said.

François and Anita obeyed. From the floor, she watched his boots walk through the door and stop next to her. The barrel of his weapon jabbed into her back. She suppressed a scream but couldn't stop shaking.

CHAPTER THIRTY-SIX

COLLABORATION

IKE WALKED FOR over two hours after Anita abandoned him, taking his car. His jacket was encrusted with blood, but his nose had stopped bleeding. It didn't move when he tried to wiggle it, but it hurt like hell.

When he reached the twenty-four-hour convenience store in Thurmont, Mike bought a cell phone, an energy drink, and an assortment of snacks. The cashier kept his head down and didn't look him in the eye. Mike was glad. His fingers were gray from clenching his hands into fists and he didn't want to have to punch this cashier for some snarky remark.

Outside, he sat on the curb, popped open his drink, and gulped down half of it. He tore open packages of chips, beef jerky, and granola bars and devoured them while activating his phone. Having lost his car, the hard drive, Anita, two cell phones, and a bag of cash, his father was the last person he wanted to talk to. This was, without a doubt, the worst screw-up he'd ever made. His father would be infuriated.

Not that Mike gave a shit anymore. Whatever he accomplished would never be enough. That was clear. He was nothing more than the dirty secret in his father's life, a secret he surely regretted.

Hunting through his wallet, he located the business card for the Howard Street Bed and Breakfast with Paul's mobile number and called.

The first three times, it rolled over to voicemail. On the fourth try, Paul answered in a groggy voice.

"Who's this?"

"Mike. You're still at the estate, right? In the guest house?"

"Yeah. I was sleeping. Why are you calling me at this hour?"

"My car was stolen. It's a long story. I'll tell you about it when you pick me up. Don't tell anyone I called. And bring the laptop in the office at the end of the hall upstairs. If the door's locked, the code is 7734."

"This better be good," Paul said.

"Better than you can possibly imagine." Mike smiled as he disconnected. This might work out after all.

⁂

"What the hell happened to you?" Paul asked.

"Anita happened. She took my car and the hard drive."

"Damn. Hop in and tell me about it."

Mike slid into the passenger's seat and buckled in. "Not much to tell. I pulled over to the side of the road because she was going to be sick, and she attacked me. While I was bleeding, she made off with the car and the hard drive."

"Did you report it stolen to the police?"

"No. I know where she took it. We can take another ride to pick it up later. Right now, I'd rather not have anyone realize it's missing, or exactly where I am. Catch my drift? Let's keep this between you and me."

"So you found the hard drive?"

"I had it in my hand. Right here." Mike tapped on his palm to show Paul. "I was so close. But I am not a man who gives up. Ever. I *will* get it again. You can count on it."

Mike took Doug's laptop from the floor and placed it on his lap. He rubbed his fingers across the cover.

"There's something I've been meaning to tell you about John. I was going to tell you before, but I didn't have the opportunity."

Paul's eyes narrowed as he gave Mike a sidelong glance.

"His name isn't really John St. Claire. It's Douglas Hayes. He's not really interested in clean fuel because he makes money from fossil fuels. But I am. I'm very interested in clean fuel. I thought I was steering him in that direction, but I've given up. I think he wants to prevent it from being developed. Instead, I want to take over his role and we'll bring it to market together. I think we'd make great partners."

Mike always found that mixing truth with lies made them more believable. What was most important, however, was telling people what they wanted to hear. While he didn't care about clean fuel either, he recognized the data on this hard drive was his ticket to wealth. First, however, he would have to distance himself from his father to convince Paul to work with him.

Paul's mouth dropped open. He glared over at Mike a couple of times. "Wait. You lied to me about who this guy is, and now you expect me to trust you as my partner?"

"Those were his terms, not mine. I'm not a person who lies. He wanted anonymity, so I had to go along with it to convince him to put up the money."

Paul's eyebrows squished together as he grimaced.

"I swear on my father's grave," Mike said, suppressing a smile over the image. Paul didn't reply. Mike clenched his teeth and began tapping a beat on the laptop, impatient for a reply.

"If we drop him and become partners, who will finance this? There aren't grants anymore."

"I will." Mike stopped tapping. "I recently inherited well. That's why I can tell you this now. It might take me some time to move the money around, but I absolutely have it. Besides, you and I will both make a lot more money without Doug in the middle. I trust you to run this. All of it. I'll work on the financing. You'll be the brains of the operation."

Paul smiled. Mike was satisfied his flattery was working, along with his promise of wealth. People always fell for that shit. They pretended ideals mattered, but what they really wanted was money. Big money. Money that made you forget you ever had ideals.

"Won't we run into the same problem my employer had? Where the government shut us down and defunded us?" Paul asked.

"I have connections. You'd be surprised. No one will come

after me, I guarantee it. And if we run into delays, we'll take it offshore."

"Let me think about it," Paul said.

Not good. I need his commitment now, Mike thought.

"Listen. If this opportunity isn't for you, I can look for someone else. You'd be the best, but I don't want to force you. I can find another EnerGeLabs leader to run the company. We need to take advantage of the opportunity while it's hot. I know people who will jump on this now, once we have it together."

Paul shook his head. "No. Not necessary. I'm the right person. If you can get my hard drive, I'll be your partner in this."

"Excellent. We're going places, you and me. This is going to be huge."

Adrenaline pumped through Mike's body. He had a few more preparations to put into place, then he'd be unstoppable.

Opening his father's laptop, Mike logged into his own cloud account, downloaded a keystroke capture program, and installed it so it'd upload data to his cloud.

His watch read 4:07 AM. His father must have figured out all did not go well, and Mike would have to deal with his anger. No biggie. Like one of his business professors at college used to say, every risk is also an opportunity. What matters is identifying when the opportunity outweighs the risk.

He understood there was plenty of risk, but the opportunity was massive.

When they reached the estate, Paul parked his car near the guest house.

"I might need another ride later today or tomorrow," Mike said. "Are you good with that? To get the hard drive?"

"Yeah, sure," Paul replied. "Whatever it takes."

"I'll text you the details once I know. Remember, this is all just between us for now."

Paul smiled. "Absolutely."

The two of them went inside, Paul to his room, Mike to his father's office, where he replaced the laptop on the desk and plugged in the charger. Back in his own room, he grabbed his backpack and returned to the office with his tools.

He picked the desk lock. Inside, he found several dead phones, which he plugged into chargers. When he examined the first one, almost nothing was on it, not even phone numbers, calls, or texts. Then he opened the photos and instantly understood their value. The first three photos showed an easily identifiable senator and a naked woman kneeling between his legs.

Priceless.

He sent copies to his own phone, then checked the rest.

SEARCH

ANITA CREPT BEHIND François into the detention center, still shaking from the guard poking his weapon into her back before he flew out the door. The immediate area was clear, but she feared who else might be waiting to ambush them.

The guns they'd pushed through the door were lying on the floor. Anita froze at the sight of the dead guard who François had used as a shield, lying in his own blood. The stench of urine and feces rose from his body, and his blank eyes stared out from his pale face. She squeezed her nose closed with her fingers but couldn't tear her eyes away. François retrieved both guns and shook her shoulder, pointing to the next door ahead, motioning for her to follow him as he handed her gun to her. They passed the room where Anita had been held earlier. At the next door, he pushed it open and peered around it, pulling Anita after him. She pointed her gun at the ground, worried that her jitters would accidently set it off, and made sure the safety was on.

The door led to a long empty hallway lit by florescent lights shining through the panels of a drop ceiling. In place of the classroom doors, sliding metal doors with single windows and electronic locks had been installed. A small red light shone on the lock above the keyhole. Anita peered through the first window into darkness. The outline of four bunk beds, three of which contained sleeping people, could be seen, but not their faces.

François leaned over her shoulder. "I'm going to the office to find the keys."

Slipping her gun into her holster, she continued down the hallway, becoming more frantic as she strained to see the others without success. Finally, she too, returned to the office, where François sat at the computer.

"I am hoping I can find the system to unlock the doors."

"I wonder if the room lights are controlled here, too. I didn't find any switches in the hallway," Anita said.

After he examined a few screens, François rose from the desk. "I am not getting anywhere. You are probably better at this than me. I am going to the car for my lock pick. It's 4:45 already and we need to go before the others arrive."

Anita sat at the computer and changed the settings to make sure the screen wouldn't time out and lock her out. Next, she hovered over each icon on the screen until she read Artemis Access Control System. She clicked it open, and it asked for her password.

"Shit!" Grinding her teeth, she tugged open the narrow desk drawer above her lap, hoping the guards kept their passwords written. She shuffled through pens, pencils, packets of sugar, salt and pepper, paper napkins, colored plastic push pins. Grasping pads of Post-it notes, crumpled napkins, and coasters, she flung them on top of the desk. One by one, she leafed through the Post-it notes, front and back, uncrumpled the napkins and flipped over the coasters. Nothing. She banged her fist on the desk.

Again, she reached into the drawer, exploring the grit in every corner, every loose dime and penny, methodically covering the area once more to ensure she'd missed nothing. She caught herself holding her breath and exhaled. While sliding her hands out, something tickled the top of her knuckle. Flipping over her hands, she ran her fingers across the top of the drawer. A tiny Post-it was stuck to it. She ripped it off and laid it on the desk.

8f773gr!, it read. Holding her breath, she entered the characters into the box labeled password and hit enter.

A menu appeared. She was in.

The sound of a car interrupted her. She ran to the door and peeked outside. François was stepping out of Erin's car with her backpack, while Erin followed him in the bus.

Back at the computer, she examined the options. Settings. Lighting. Change Start and End Times. Anita tried to move the start time to now, but it wouldn't let her. The earliest available time was in thirty minutes.

Damn. In the upper right-hand corner was an option for Advanced Settings that she clicked on. Enter Security Code. Using the same password, a new screen appeared with an options list and boxes to select each one. At the bottom was a selection by itself: Override Default Settings. She selected that option and hit continue as Erin and François arrived at her side.

Like magic, everything she needed appeared.

Unlock / lock all doors

Turn all lights on / off

Sound Alarm

No alarm please. Within seconds, the system confirmed she had unlocked all the doors and turned on all the lights. The three of them rushed into the hallway where lights blazed from the rooms. François, Erin, and Anita rushed down the hall, pulling open doors and shouting.

"Wake up."

"You're being rescued. Get up now!"

"We must leave immediately."

Groggy people appeared in the hallway. Some looked dazed. Others began to run for the exit. Anita's pulse leapt as she raced down the hall, yanking open door after door and scanning the occupants. No Steven or Julian. She shouted to the detainees in each room and moved to the next one, her stomach twisting into a knot. At the end of the hall, she bounded up the steps to the second floor two at a time, while she examined the faces of those passing her on their way down. Once at the top, she swam against the tide of detainees, frantically searching the rooms until she reached the end. By then, the hallway was empty. She ran down the opposite stairway, becoming light-headed by the time she reached the bottom. No one remained in the first-floor hallway.

As her toes went numb, Anita spun around and leaned against the wall, hyperventilating, her eyes wide with fear.

"They're gone," she whispered and slid down the wall.

CHAPTER THIRTY-EIGHT

POWER

ANITA SAT AGAINST the wall of the detention center with her eyes closed, taking slow, deep breaths, counting three breaths in, five breaths out. Her heartbeat slowed and her concentration returned. She had to regroup and continue her search for Steven and Julian. Believing they were gone was her fear talking, not the truth, she reminded herself. She needed to find the truth.

Outside, Erin was ushering people onto the bus. One of the detainees was sitting in the driver's seat. Anita scanned all their faces again to make sure she hadn't missed them, but she hadn't.

François was nowhere in sight. Back in the office, she found him sprawled across the desk as two detainees worked on his arm—one holding it still while another was sewing stitches. François' face was pale. He grunted and squeezed his eyes shut with each stitch.

"Is he okay?" Anita asked.

"He's lucky," the woman stitching replied. "The bullet nicked him pretty good but didn't damage anything critical. He'll be fine in a day or two, but he needs to replace the blood he lost. He needs lots of water. Thankfully, I found antibiotics in the first aid cabinet. Painkillers too. Both of which he needs to take. And he needs rest."

"I'm thankful you're here to help," Anita said.

"I'm an ER nurse in real life, so I've stitched up plenty of gunshot wounds." She tied off the end of the string and put a bandage across the entire wound.

"Have either of you seen a man named Steven or Julian? A father and son? Steven was on a videoconference yesterday. Do you know where they hold those? I didn't find any computers when I walked around."

"I'm sorry. I don't know either of them," the woman said. "They kept us locked in our rooms so we couldn't talk to each other."

The man holding François' arm shook his head. "Me neither. But keep looking. I haven't heard about a conference room."

Anita walked back outside where Erin had finished loading the bus. She walked over to Anita with her head down until they were close, then held Anita's shoulder. Anita felt a lump growing in her throat.

"I have bad news," Erin said. "The people who shared the room with Julian and Steven said they weren't there last night at lights out. They haven't seen them since yesterday evening."

Anita pushed Erin away while shaking her head, close to tears. "No. They have to be here. Steven was in a conference room, which we never found. It has to be in this building. I'm going to find it."

Anita turned and ran back inside, her breaths growing shorter. There had to be another room, a closet, a door which didn't unlock and light up along with the rooms on the access system. But where? She'd seen no other stairs, and no other doors on the two floors she had scoured. She walked over both floors one more time and checked inside each room for doors she may have overlooked, but nothing. When she reached the office again, Erin was standing by the door talking to François, who was sitting alone.

"Nearly everyone is on the bus," Erin said. "I put five others in your rental car to drive to Vermont, after I filled the tire with Fix-a-Flat. They have one phone between them and three hundred dollars from Anita's handbag. They left."

François frowned. "Why?"

"You can't drive with your injured arm, and we already have fifty-four more on the bus. Thirteen are sitting in the aisles between the seats, and one is driving. I handed out the rest of the phones and whatever food and water we had. They can share, but they'll need more. Meanwhile, they need to get moving. It's almost sunrise. But without money and IDs, what will happen to them?"

"I still can't find Steven and Julian, and I'm not leaving without them," Anita said.

"Me either," François said. "I made Anita a promise and I will keep it. We will stay here and keep looking. You should go, Erin." François stood for a moment before turning pale and flopping back into the chair.

Erin teared up as she looked at François. "I don't know

where they should go or how to help them. And I am afraid to leave you here. You don't look good."

The three of them stared at each other in silence. Anita was deep breathing again to stay calm when she was struck with an idea.

"I know what to do," she told Erin. "Follow me."

She walked outside to the BMW with Erin trailing her and opened the trunk. Removing the money bag and placing a couple of stacks of bills on the floor of the trunk, she shut it. With the bag in hand, she and Erin boarded the bus.

People were talking loudly, arguing with one another, while two women were crying a few seats back. The driver had his arms tightly crossed against his chest.

"Can I have your attention?" Anita shouted, but her voice didn't carry over the noise. The driver handed her the bus's PA microphone.

"Attention, please." Her voice boomed through the speakers and the bus went silent.

"I have two announcements. The first is this bag contains a lot of money. Put enough aside for gas for the bus, then pass it around and share it, please. Make sure everyone gets some so you can buy food and transportation to wherever you are going once you get away from here."

"What will they do if they capture us?" a man asked.

Other voices acknowledged the same concern.

"They had plans to put you all on a plane and take you out of the country today. I don't know where, but it didn't sound good."

Their voices exploded with anguish as they spoke, shouted, cried out, or whimpered.

"Please. I need your attention a little longer."

The noise trailed off.

"I know who is behind this," Anita continued. "A fossil fuel tycoon with deep pockets and friends in high places. He told me your voices are dangerous to him—"

"Good," a man shouted, and several replied with whistles or howls.

"He locked you up to silence you. Because people forget the damage he's doing if they don't hear your voices. Do you want to bring this man down?"

The bus roared with agreement.

"Okay. You need to make yourselves as loud as possible. Americans need to know what went on here. You are the proof. You have the power to prove the truth."

"Take us to Washington, D.C." a man shouted. "I want my life back. I want my country back."

"Me too," another replied. "Washington, D.C. or bust."

"D.C., D.C.," a few began chanting. Fists started pumping in the air and another stood and motioned for the rest to join in.

A Black woman with matted hair in a stained T-shirt stood up from the front seat and took the mic from Anita.

"We were all detained because they feared us. We all had the guts to stand up to them before. I have a lot more guts now. We know what they're capable of. We have to say no more. I'm going to Washington, D.C."

The group cheered.

She handed the mic back to Anita.

"Is there anyone here who doesn't want to go to Washington, D.C?" Anita asked.

"I'm scared to go," came a man's voice from a few seats back. "But I'm going. We can't let them get away with this."

Anita looked behind her at Erin, who was grinning and fist pumping along with the rest. They hugged each other. Others around the bus were embracing one another, too. The driver gave Erin and Anita a thumbs-up and started the bus.

Anita and Erin got off the bus and waved as it departed. Erin returned to the building, but Anita walked straight to the guard they'd left tied up in his chair by the guard shack. She ripped the tape from around his head and mouth.

"Fuck! That hurts!"

"Where's the videoconference room?"

"How the fuck would I know?"

"It's a room with a computer where they use a camera and a microphone to talk to people over the internet."

"Untie me and I'll show you."

Anita pulled her gun and jammed it into his temple. "My son is in there. Tell me where it is, and I won't blow your head off. Otherwise, you'll be the next to die here today."

"Okay. Okay. Fucking chill, okay? It's around the back, in the basement. There's a metal door and you need the key. It's locked in that office cabinet."

Anita replaced her gun under her jacket and sprinted to the office. Erin was waiting with François, whose color was improving.

"We need to break into this cabinet for a key to the metal door in the basement out back."

François turned and banged his fist against the steel cabinet, which gave off a solid metal thud. "If we must break into this for a key, I should just break into the door to the room instead. Hopefully my pick still has enough charge left in it." He stood. "I am better now. I can walk."

Erin grabbed her backpack.

Behind the building, four steps led to a basement door. Electrical and cable wires were strung from the entryway to a nearby electrical pole. François sat on the step, adjusting the tools for this lock, while Erin held the flashlight. He cringed with pain as he maneuvered the electric pick through the keyhole. After a minute, he stopped and pulled the door open.

Erin shone the flashlight inside, where two motionless bodies were asleep—each curled up across two armless straight back chairs side by side. Switching on the light revealed a desk with two computers and webcams attached against the wall.

"Steven?" Anita said, and the bodies stirred. By the time Steven rose to a sitting position, Anita had dropped to her knees and had her arms wrapped around her son. Silent tears streamed down her face while warmth tingled through her body.

"What are you doing here?" he muttered. "Are you okay?"

"I'm okay now," she replied, rocking him back and forth as she hugged him.

"I love you, Mom," Steven said, his voice cracking.

She broke into sobs, euphoria racing through her and making her heart pound.

Julian struggled to rise from the other set of chairs, stumbled over to Steven and Anita, crouching to wrap his arms around them. "I knew you'd find us. You're our hero, Anita. My love and my hero."

Anita let him hold her, but she tensed at his touch.

Erin interrupted their reunion. "We have to go," she said, still holding the flashlight. "We're out of time."

The four of them walked up the stairs. Anita scanned for François, but he was gone.

This is the end of us, she thought.

In the midst of her joy at finding Steven, a hollow pain burrowed into her stomach.

CHAPTER THIRTY-NINE

CONFESSIONS

ANITA DUG THROUGH Mike's BMW and collected what she needed. The hard drive, both of Mike's phones, and the remaining cash from the trunk went into her pocketbook. She removed her gun and dropped that in, too, but left the holster in his trunk. Then she slid into the back seat of Erin's car next to Steven, who sat between her and Julian. François was in front of her and didn't turn around. Erin settled into the driver's seat.

"I'm deeply grateful for your help, François," Julian said. "My family owes you our lives."

"I am honored to have helped."

Anita gazed out the window, trying to pretend this man whose back was to her was no one special, just a benevolent colleague. Not her lover who was near enough to touch.

François raised his phone to the window. "Once I have a signal, I will call Zack. I expect I will wake him."

"Knowing him, he probably just went to bed," Erin said.

Anita turned her attention to Steven and leaned against him, warmed by his presence. "Have you been here for two years?" she asked. "You look starved. Did they hurt you?" Brushing his hair away from his face, she saw thick, red scar tissue running down the side of his neck, under his shirt, and into his hair, creating a patch where no hair grew. She shuddered and wrapped her hand around his arm, allowing his hair to fall back to cover the area.

Steven smiled, put his arm around her and gave her a squeeze. "I'm okay, Mom. It hasn't been the best, but I'm fine."

"Tell me everything. I need to hear it all." She clasped Steven's hand between hers and rubbed it, needing to feel the blood pumping through his body, to be reassured he was here and not a dream.

"You remember I emailed you to tell you I was doing some meaningful work?"

"Yes, of course. It was the last email I had from you."

"I was helping this small company in San Francisco that was making huge progress into developing clean fuel. I was compiling statistics and modeling scenarios for their product so we could show the costs and benefits. They had to find private investors after the government cut all their funding."

"Bastards," Anita said. "The damage they did by defunding is reprehensible."

"No shit. Anyhow, we heard how research was being confiscated from green companies which received grants. So we closed the office, moved some servers into my house and everyone worked from home. A couple of days later, I got a text threatening me, telling me to destroy the data. It was all backed up between the servers, but I figured I should make a copy, too. So I started downloading it, but before I finished, someone broke my window and threw a firebomb inside." Steven's hands swept into the air like an explosion.

"Someone tried to kill you?" Anita touched her neck, imagining the pain that caused his scar. Her breathing sped up and she felt woozy. *Stop it. He's here. He's okay. Get yourself under control.*

"Me and the data on those servers. I barely escaped through the screen door to my patio. By then, the wind was blowing flames everywhere, but I rolled in the grass, screaming, 'cause my shirt was on fire. Fortunately, my neighbors spotted me as they pulled out of their driveway. They covered me with their fire blanket and threw me into their car."

Anita leaned into his shoulder. "Thank God. You were very lucky."

Steven nodded. "Once I was listed as presumed dead, I figured I should stay dead so whoever tried to kill me wouldn't come after me. Unfortunately, I had to stay dead to you, too." He took a deep breath as he looked at her. "I'm so sorry."

She sighed. "It wasn't your fault. Don't apologize. I'm just glad you survived."

Anita was exhausted. Her muscles were unwinding after too many hours of caffeine, adrenaline, and no sleep. She started to drift into sleep but was jolted awake by François' voice.

"I've got a signal," he announced as he tapped a number on his phone.

Daylight was spreading through the hills as Erin guided the car along the twisty road, while they listened on speaker phone.

"Zack here," a groggy voice answered.

"Zack. We have had a huge success, but we need your help. Not only did we rescue Julian, we rescued all of them. An overflowing school bus is on its way to Washington, D.C. to show the world what happened to them."

"Holy shit. How did you manage it? Never mind. Tell me later."

"I need you to send high-priority press releases from our foundation to every news service. Ask them to go and bring cameras. Then notify every pro-climate organization we track in the D.C. area to wait for them to arrive about ten o'clock. We need huge publicity to keep them safe. Get this out fast."

"Gotcha. I'll need to call in media assistants. Do I have approval?" Zack asked.

"Yes. Approved. In the press releases, say that more detainees are being transported from the Nevada and Montana detention centers to airports today as well. Provide those addresses. Maybe we can save them, too."

Julian released his seat belt and leaned over the front seat to speak. François held the phone for him. "Contact Richard Stryker at American University for help. I'll have François text his number. He can round up a group on short notice, hopefully a large group. Tell him I asked."

"Okay," Zack replied.

"And we need lawyers and people from the ACLU," François continued. "We must make a lot of noise so the detainees stay safe."

"Okay," Zack replied. "Is Erin with you?"

"Sure am," she shouted. "I'm the sucker driving."

"Keep on truckin'. Good luck to you all," Zack said.

François ended the call, turning around to face Julian and Steven and handing his phone over for Julian to text Zack the phone number.

"Now we must discuss next steps. Erin and I cannot go to Washington, D.C. We are not American citizens, and we are here on illegal passports—a felony with a ten-year prison sentence. The three of you have not committed any traceable crimes. You are free to decide what to do next."

"I'm here on an illegal passport, too," Anita said. "But I won't go anywhere without Steven. Whatever he's doing, I'm doing."

"If you choose to stay, just ditch the passport." François faced forward, watching her in the visor mirror. "You are a citizen and there is no record of you leaving or reentering the country."

Anita considered this and realized it was true. She had simply disappeared, but what she'd done with her time couldn't be proven. As she tried to interpret François' feelings through the mirror, he flipped up his visor. That stung. Maybe he was pushing her away because Julian was free. The hollow sensation in her stomach returned.

"I don't believe it's safe for me to stay," she said. "I'm sure Mike will be coming for me." She studied Steven's face. "What are you thinking? I think you should leave the country with me. We can be in Canada today or tomorrow."

"Agreed," Steven said. "Canada sounds like the best option until I can figure out what's next."

"Also agreed," Julian said. "We should all go to Canada, then sort it out. How can we cross the border?"

"I have passports for everyone but Steven," François said.

"The border agents may be looking for you, and possibly Anita too. I think the safest way is for the three of you to cross through the woods with Odina. Erin and I can drive over the border and pick you up on the other side."

"Who's Odina?" Julian asked.

"Someone I met through Paul, the owner of the Howard Street Bed and Breakfast in Newport. I went there after you disappeared."

"Wait. You went to Newport? To the bed and breakfast? Why?" Julian voice was anxious.

Anita leaned forward to look around Steven at Julian. "You wrote it on the paper you gave me with the email addresses. I thought that's where you wanted me to go."

"Oh shit," Steven said. "Dad, why did you give her that name?"

"I didn't. I never wrote it with the email addresses."

"Yes, you did." Anger made heat crawl up Anita's neck. "On the back, in pencil. What was the problem with going there?"

"This isn't good," Steven said. "Not good at all. What does he know?"

"Would you please tell me what's going on?" Anita yelled. "Paul tried to help me, that's all. Then his hard drive was stolen, and I tried to buy it back for him, but everything went wrong. And for some crazy reason he is now working with Doug."

"Seriously?" Steven asked. "Where is this hard drive now?"

"In my pocketbook."

Steven's eyes widened, and he turned to stare at his mother. "You have it in this car, right now?"

"Yes! What the hell is this about?"

"Holy shit," Steven said. "I've been trying to find it for two years. Those servers that burned up? They belonged to EnerGeLabs. Before I started my download, the security log showed someone else had downloaded it already. But no one knew who, and after losing the servers, I had no way to figure it out."

"You think it was Paul?" Anita asked.

"Probably. I've spent the last two years locating as many former employees as I could, getting some of them into Canada, and trying to figure out who has the data. My last information suggested a man who ran the Howard Street Bed and Breakfast. That's when I was picked up and thrown in the detention center. They must have been watching people who'd worked for EnerGeLabs and saw me approaching them."

"Why? The company wasn't even in business anymore."

"The company was on the shutdown list. That's why they burned my house down, 'cause I had the servers and they wanted them destroyed. I found that out when I learned about the list."

Anita shook her head. "This is taking corporate espionage to a whole new level. More like corporate search and destroy. But how did this bed and breakfast get on the back of my email list?"

"I wrote it there when Steven told me that's where he was going next. I guess it got mixed up with my other notes," Julian answered.

Anita's mouth dropped open, and she glared at Julian. "Wait. How long did you know Steven was alive?"

He turned away and looked out the window.

"Don't you be silent with me anymore. I've had enough of that." Anita's anger burned all the way to her skull. "Julian! Tell me the truth!"

"Mom, please," Steven said softly. "Please don't fight about me."

Anita's eyes welled up, and she lowered her voice. "I'm sorry, but I have to know."

Finally, Julian turned to her. "Almost the whole time. We couldn't risk getting you involved. We wanted to protect you."

Her anger flared again. "We? Who the hell is we?"

"Steven and me. We thought it was too dangerous for you to know."

Her eyes shifted from Steven to Julian and back as the hurt from their betrayal struck deep into her stomach.

"Who the hell do you think I am? Some delicate little flower who can't handle real life? You let me believe my son was dead for two years? Two years! You let me suffer and grieve with a sorrow I would never have believed possible . . . because you wanted to protect me? Steven! You went along with this?"

"Dad said it was necessary to keep you safe. I hated doing it." Steven's lips trembled.

Anita leaned over and glared at Julian. "How could you? What right did you have!"

Julian's expression was calm.

"It hurt me to see you in pain. I just didn't want to put you in danger. Besides, I knew Steven and I could handle this ourselves. You never gave me credit for what I was capable of, but this we did better on our own."

Anita gaped at him in disbelief. "Right up until you couldn't," she said, shaking. She wanted to scream. Instead, she closed her eyes and took a few deep breaths, counting three in, five out. When she was in control again, she spoke quietly but vehemently.

"Go fuck yourself, Julian. I want a divorce."

CHAPTER FORTY

SHUTDOWN

DOUG SLEPT RESTLESSLY after waiting half the night for Mike to return with the hard drive. He'd fallen into a deep sleep an hour before dawn, so dozens of text messages beeped alerts now. Rolling over toward the nightstand, he realized someone wanted his attention. The clock read 8:06 am. More beeps erupted from his phone.

He slipped on his readers and picked it up. Staring at him was a stack of messages and several breaking news alerts. He shook his head to clear away the grogginess.

The most recent text was from Senator Colton:

Are you watching this? What now?

Doug frowned and picked up the remote. His wife was already up, as usual, and had left the room. He leaned back against his pillow, also grabbing hers to stuff behind his back, and turned on the television.

One news channel was showing live coverage from

Washington, where a crowd gathered near the Capitol waiting for a bus to arrive. Multiple camera crews and news services were set up near the crowd and streams of people were moving toward the mall. They cut to an aerial view of a school bus on a highway.

"Fifty-seven missing people surfaced early this morning, claiming they were illegally detained in West Virginia without due process, some for months," the young, blonde announcer reported, sweeping her hair away from her face in the blowing wind.

A sharp pain stretched across Doug's chest. "Shit."

He switched to another cable news channel where the caption read "From Inside the Bus." The picture blurred while a phone was passed around. A Black woman with matted hair appeared. Turning the camera, she panned more passengers behind her before turning it back to herself.

"I've been at this facility for seven months. Never spoke to a lawyer. Never had any contact with my family. Never given a phone call. I was leading a protest at the Capitol in D.C. against a new law designed to favor fossil fuels. As I left the mall later that day, two men dragged me into a van. I was bound and gagged and driven for hours. This morning we were rescued. We are on our way to Washington to show Americans how they violated our constitutional rights."

A White man behind her took the phone. He had a short beard, looked to be in his mid-thirties, and was wearing a dirty hoodie.

"I'm Ryan Mathews. I was detained a couple of weeks ago right after my email was hacked. I was walking home from work when a van pulled over ahead of me and three guys jumped out and kidnapped me. They drove me to this pseudo jail in the middle of nowhere. I wasn't charged or given an opportunity to contact a lawyer or anyone. They just shoved me in a locked room with three other people. Guess what, folks at home: all of us are climate activists! Every. One. Except for a few climate scientists."

He turned and passed the phone to a man behind him. Doug switched the channel to where a dark-skinned man was standing with a microphone lit up by cameras against the night sky. Behind him was a fenced-in warehouse. The caption read "Jasper, Montana: Site of a Second Detention Facility." Doug's fingers grew cold.

The iPhone vibrated for an incoming call from Senator Colton. Doug groaned, then answered.

"What the hell happened?" the senator shouted into the phone. "I've got planes sitting in airports ready to fly these people to Haiti! I've got the President calling me on my private line demanding we sacrifice someone to take the fall for this! He will deny any knowledge. Who organized this attack and why weren't we alerted about it? I am *not* taking the fall for this!"

"Take it easy. I'm doing damage control and this conversation needs to cease. Give me fifteen minutes to reach my office. I'll send you a fax with information."

"Okay. As long as you're on top of this, I'll be waiting for your fax. We've already destroyed the Shutdown List. Wiped that server clean and any traces of who used it."

"What if someone made copies?"

"Not possible. We had it locked down tighter than the launch codes. Some people could read it, but no one could copy it."

"Okay. Ending this conversation."

Doug disconnected and scanned his other messages. Retrieving his private phone from the drawer in the nightstand, the one he used to communicate with Mike and Elena, he saw no missed calls or messages. Pain spread into his jaw from clenching his teeth.

Where the fuck was Mike?

⁓

By the time Doug reached the guest house, more than fifteen minutes had passed. In his office, he booted up his laptop.

He couldn't fathom what had transpired since last night when everything was cruising along the way he liked it—his way.

Grabbing a sheet of paper and a pen from inside his desk drawer, he wrote down the phone number of his Argentine phone. This is what he would fax to the senator, to ensure their communication flew under the radar. Meanwhile, he needed to devise a response, which was difficult considering he had no idea what had happened.

Instead, he called the kitchen to bring him coffee.

Another text from the senator arrived:

WTF.

"Fuck," Doug said. He sensed Senator Colton was unraveling, which could be dangerous. He fished around in his pocket for the key to his desk drawer and unlocked it. Inside were several phones, including the one from Martina, with photos of the boy's night out in Argentina. Once he located the most compromising ones, he selected them and forwarded them to the senator, along with a message:

"Your continued loyalty is appreciated. I need time. Talk soon."

He logged into a succession of bank accounts he controlled, none tied to him personally. From each he paid a few hefty, supposedly outstanding bills to the accounts of seventeen foreign corporations that didn't exist, which he also controlled, managing to shift that money out of the country. Everything he was doing, including his account IDs and passwords, were captured and logged to Mike's account in the cloud.

CHAPTER FORTY-ONE

WANTED

ANITA AWOKE IN the back seat of Erin's car. They had stopped moving. She checked her watch. 10:37 AM. They'd been driving for nearly five hours and were parked next to a Walmart; Erin was pumping gas. François was in a deep sleep as he leaned on the window in front of her against his jacket. Steven and Julian were nowhere in sight.

Anita sat up straight, stretched her arms, and took a deep breath. *Need to find the restroom fast,* she thought. She hurried into the Walmart, asked for directions to the facilities and located them.

As she washed her hands at the sink after using the toilet, she glanced in the mirror and recoiled. She probably hadn't brushed her hair since leaving Stacey's house. It looked like a tangled wreck with bits of leaves from when she'd fallen in the woods. She wished she had a hair tie so she could pull this mess into a ponytail, but she'd left her handbag in the car. Instead,

296

she washed her face and rinsed her mouth with water. Leaning into the mirror, she winced at her puffy, red eyes and stuck her tongue out with disgust.

In the food section, she cruised the aisles for something appetizing, fondling the twenty-dollar bill she'd found in her boot. What she wanted most was a real meal—a plate of grilled salmon and mashed sweet potatoes over a pile of sauteed spinach and garlic. Her mouth watered and her stomach grumbled. As she rounded a corner into an aisle packed with chips and crackers, she nearly bumped into Julian carrying handfuls of sandwiches and snack foods. After an abrupt stop, she spun on her heel to leave.

"Anita, please. We need to talk." His voice made it clear he was begging.

Her whole body tensed as she turned to face him.

"I don't want a divorce." Julian's eyes were wet and desperate. That look proved he was hurting, but this time Anita had no empathy. "I know things have been bad, but we can make a new start. We can fix this."

Anger burned in Anita's chest, flushing up her neck and into her face. "You have no idea what I've been through since you pulled this stunt. I was nearly killed twice. Stacey was beaten up. My Google account was tracked. I had to assume a new identity. And the entire time, I didn't know why. Plus, I'm not even touching on the two years of hell before this. You saw how tortured I was believing Steven was dead and said nothing. What kind of man are you?"

He nodded. "Ok. You're right. I've made mistakes. But everything's different now. Steven is alive and safe. We can go back to how we were before the fire."

She glared at him. "You're right; everything is different. I'm different. I've seen you for what you are and I'm not settling for your crumbs anymore. I don't want to be with a man who abandons me when I need him most."

His face frozen, he backed up a step. "This is about François, isn't it? I should have never asked him to help you."

Her mouth dropped open. "What would have happened to me if you didn't? Thank God he was here to help me. No. This is about you and me. Just so you're aware, if François hadn't helped, you and Steven would be on an airplane right now to God knows where because he was the only one who came forward to help. In fact, I would have left you there to rot. Now excuse me."

"I'm sorry I disappointed you by trying to rescue our son," he said as she walked away.

Tears choked Anita as she snatched a bag of potato chips and moved out of the aisle, glancing around aimlessly. Julian's confrontation shook her, and she couldn't focus. He was right: She was grateful he'd gone after Steven. Maybe, however, Steven wouldn't have been captured in the first place if she'd known about this.

She grabbed a bag of cashews, made a cup of coffee, then walked over to the cash register. After paying for her items with the cash in her pocket, she turned away and left the store.

Outside, the others were all sitting in the car with it running. The back door was open.

"Get in, Mom. Hurry," Steven shouted and waved his arms to beckon her.

Anita rushed into the back seat, but before she could shut the door, Erin sped off.

"What the hell?" Anita asked. Steven gripped her coffee so she could buckle up as the door slammed from the sudden momentum.

"It's bad," Steven said. "They found a murdered guard in the detention center and are claiming you killed him. Your picture is all over the news saying you are wanted for murder. Why do they think you killed him?"

"Oh shit!" Anita shook her head. "None of us killed that guard. The other guard shot him when he was trying to kill us."

"We have to escape all this congestion," Erin said, turning up the onramp and back onto the highway heading north. "They're showing the photo Mike passed around of you on the flyer. Maybe it's the scumbag we left tied up at the guard shack."

"Damn. I did threaten to blow his head off. I guess he believed me." Anita slumped back against the seat.

"You have a gun?" Julian leaned forward to look at her.

"Yes. In my pocketbook. The bullets won't match the ones that killed the guard. But if Doug is behind this, it may not matter. His power seems limitless. He was able to imprison all of you. Now that all eyes are on the bus in Washington, D.C. I doubt he'll stop at anything to direct those eyes elsewhere. In this case, to me."

"Who's Doug?" Julian asked.

"The fossil fuel tycoon who owns our government, who wants to have me killed."

"Is that so?" Julian asked. "You aren't exaggerating your importance here, are you?"

François winced in the visor mirror.

"Seriously? This is why I want a divorce. My picture is on national television saying I'm wanted for murder. Twenty-four hours ago, I was a captive at his estate after being flown from Coal Creek in his helicopter. He's the one who arranged the conference call with Steven, then told his lunatic son to kill me. And you think it's my ego talking?"

Anita breathed slowly in and out, trying to calm her pulse and keep from exploding. Gazing out the window, she sipped her coffee.

François was reading his phone. "Turn off at this next exit," he said. "There is a rural road continuing in our direction. We are less likely to be spotted."

Erin turned off Interstate 81 onto a lightly traveled country road, and they continued north. François stayed immersed in his phone while the rest were silent.

Steven was flipping between streaming news channels while using Erin's headphones. His eyes suddenly widened, then he turned to his mother.

"One channel is still talking about the bus, but another has stopped," he said with trembling lips. "They're only talking about the guard who was murdered, and they're reporting a nationwide manhunt for you. They're claiming you are armed and dangerous." He wiped his palms on his jeans.

"That means they can shoot you on sight," François explained. "We have to hide you and find a different vehicle."

The hair on Anita's arms rose along with goosebumps. She crossed them against her chest and shivered.

"Home Depot rents cargo vans," Steven said. "We used them all the time moving our friends out in California. With a giant Home Depot logo on the side, they look totally benign. Mom could ride in the back."

"Better get me a sick bag, too," Anita said.

François studied his phone. "The closest Home Depot is twenty minutes north of here. In the meantime, Anita should ride in the trunk." Looking back at her in his visor's mirror, he added, "Sorry."

"No problem. It's become my travel mode of choice the last week," she said, facing Julian. "First time was crossing the border, when I was on my way to Switzerland for money to save you."

Julian turned away, silent.

Erin pulled over and opened the truck, pushing the semi-automatic weapon François had taken from the guard off to the side. Anita climbed in and curled up, bringing her pocketbook with her and a doubled-up plastic bag in case of illness. While the car bumped along, she rummaged inside her pocketbook and located her gun, confirming the safety was on. Then she shoved the pocketbook under her head and tucked the gun near her breast where she could grab it in an emergency. Next, she positioned the plastic bag near her mouth in preparation for the vomit already stirring in her stomach. Perhaps it was good she hadn't eaten. It meant less to regurgitate. Moments later, she was spitting up her coffee into the bag.

When the car stopped, Anita heard car doors opening and shutting. Light and air streamed into the trunk when Steven folded down one of the back seats. She breathed deeply.

Leaning against the door, he stooped down to see her. Erin was still in the driver's seat, but Julian and François were missing.

"They went inside to rent the van," Erin said without turning around. "François brought a fake passport, driver's license, and insurance card for Julian, so he'll rent it. François can't drive with his injured arm yet."

Steven leaned over and held out his hand to Anita. She squeezed it in both of hers, wishing to wrap him in a hug.

He let out a heavy sigh, squeezing her hand back. "Mom, I'm sorry I let you think I was dead. I deeply regret it. I wasn't going to tell Dad either, but François thought it best that I did."

Anita dropped his hand and started to sit up but hit her head on the roof of the trunk. "What did you just say?" She flinched as she rubbed the new bump. Her chest tightened. "What do you mean, François thought it best?"

"When I first went underground, someone suggested I contact this foundation in Canada who helped climate activists, so I did. It was François' foundation. He smuggled me into Canada, but I wanted to find the rest of the company's scientists, so I got a fake passport and came back to the U.S."

Her breathing accelerated until she was seeing spots, like the world was spinning too fast.

"He helped me find them and transport them out," Steven continued. "At least the ones on the West Coast. There are three of them on the East Coast I still need to locate. Dad was doing research for me on his college computers so it wouldn't get traced back to us."

"François knew you were alive?" Anita shouted. Her face grew damp.

"Please," Erin said, her voice panicked. "You have to be quiet."

Sweat beaded on Anita's upper lip as she scrambled to recall every word he'd spoken. She wanted to remember the exact words he'd used when he'd lied to her. Lied and lied and lied.

Her stomach lurched and she dry heaved into the plastic bag.

"Mom, are you okay?" Steven asked, frowning.

Anita didn't answer. "How about you, Erin? Did you know Steven was alive?"

"I only know François and Zack. François keeps us all apart, so we're safer. I never heard of Steven before this."

Anita stared at Erin's image in the mirror.

"You're probably lying, too," she said, and rolled over onto her back, her stomach churning as much as her heart. Like a mirage that was just out of reach and grew fainter the closer she got, she now knew François' love for her was only an illusion.

CHAPTER FORTY-TWO

CAGED

When the trunk popped open, Anita was looking into the back of an empty van parked right up against Erin's car.

François leaned around the van's door. "It is clear. Move quickly into the van. Stay away from the front, where they might see you through the window."

She slid her gun into her pocketbook, pulled the strap over her shoulder, and scrambled from the trunk into the van, not looking at François as she did. Julian was already in the driver's seat and Steven had joined him in the front. A metal grate separated the front seats from the cargo area, almost like a cage to lock in animals—or prisoners. As the back doors slammed shut, the echo jolted her nerves. She closed her eyes and an image appeared of sliding metal doors all closing at once, locking her in. That's what happens to convicted murderers, isn't it? Unless you received the death penalty. Her stomach ached from vomiting, hunger, and fear.

François opened the side door slightly and peeked in at Anita. "You are safer with them now than with me. Odina can lead you across the border, and Erin and I will pick you up on the other side. You should be safe when driving on the highway. Steven and I have phone numbers to stay in touch. Call me if you need help."

He held out her phone to her and she snatched it from him, glaring. All she wanted to do was scream *liar*. Instead, she sat against the cold metal side of the van and focused on the wall across from her.

"We'll be fine," Julian replied. "Thank you so much for everything. We'll see you in Canada."

When the door shut, it blocked out most of Anita's light. In the shadows, she told herself she was okay, despite the pervasive emptiness creeping through her. She closed her eyes and envisioned padlocking the door to where her love for François had lived. It was the only way she could still breathe. Better to be empty then to feel the pain of his betrayal. Better to forget the lies from someone she'd trusted. Better not to acknowledge her life might end with the next police cruiser driving by.

Her son's voice in the front seat spoke with Julian about where they should stop to buy food. She was filled with longing to be sitting beside Steven, to be part of their conversation. Julian had shared two years of his life that she'd missed. Tears welled up in her eyes. It hurt her face to hold them in. A few leaked down her cheeks. Even now, with him sitting a foot away, she wasn't part of his life.

But he was alive, not burned to death in a forest fire. She needed to focus on what she had, not what she'd lost.

He is alive and safe. Nothing else matters, she repeated like a mantra.

❧

Anita was dozing when her phone rang. It took a moment in the darkness to remember she was in a Home Depot van. Checking the phone, she recognized Stacey's number and rushed to answer it.

"Thank you for calling."

"What the hell are you doing?" Julian shouted back at her. "You'll give away our location."

"It's Stacey. I need to talk to her," she said, holding the phone against her chest. "Besides, we both have unregistered account numbers, so calm down."

"Sorry about that. My husband's driving," she said to Stacey, covering her other ear to avoid listening to him complain.

"You rescued him! What a relief," Stacey said. "I got your message from last night, so I wanted to tell you I'm okay. And it looks like you've got those crooks in Washington trying to finger-point their way out of the hot seat. Can't wait to find out who's the last man standing."

"I'm so sorry I got you involved in this. Deeply sorry. I've been sick with worry about you."

"They bandaged me up in the ER. I told them I fell down the stairs. No one was fooled. They probably thought a boy-friend beat me."

"I feel terrible you were subjected to this. Are you in pain?"

"It could be worse. They wanted to give me opioids, but I opted for Tylenol and ice packs. I can't drive on opioids. And I need to be alert if they come looking for me again. My nose is broken but they pushed it back into place. That stung. They said I'll heal, but my face has seen better days."

"Oh my God. Ice as often as you can stand it. Your face will be beautiful again, I'm sure of it. I hope you're safe."

"I got a hotel room until I figure out what's next. So I have room service."

"If I can help in any way, if you need to move or go somewhere safer, tell me. If I can't physically reach you, I can help financially. I owe you. Big time."

"You don't owe me anything. But I'll remember you offered. Meanwhile, what the hell is this about you being a cold-blooded killer?" Stacey's voice conveyed indignation.

"I'm not. I didn't shoot anyone. A guard shot another guard by accident. They're framing me because they want the damn hard drive."

"Tell them to go fuck themselves. Even if I'd known where you hid it, I wouldn't have told them. But you should have asked me, you know."

Anita's face grew hot with shame. "You're right," she replied. "I thought I was protecting you by not telling you."

"You should have given me a choice."

Anita realized she'd just said exactly what Julian had said about protecting her. This wasn't the same . . . was it? "You're right. You deserve better," she said. "I've been an asshole."

"At least you're an asshole who knows she's an asshole."

Anita broke out laughing as she remembered the old joke they'd shared back in college about three kinds of assholes. The first kind is an asshole who doesn't know they're an asshole. The second is an asshole who knows they're an asshole. The third is an asshole who brags about it. They'd repeated this many times to each other as they described people they'd met.

Anita moved into a crossed-legged position to relieve a pressure point. "By the way, my son isn't dead."

"What?"

Stacey's shocked reaction confirmed this was news. "Yep. He's here right now."

"You must be flipping out. I want to ask a whole lot more, but it's probably not a good idea. I don't know if we should be talking this long. Call me when you're safe and we'll talk."

"Absolutely. Heal fast and stay under the radar. I've memorized the new phone so I'll stay in touch. Hugs."

"Hugs."

Steven turned around and faced her.

"Don't look back there," Julian said. "It can't look like you're talking to someone in back."

Steven reversed position and faced forward. "Mom, I wish I could speak to you face-to-face. Are you mad at me?"

Anita took a second before answering. "No. I was never mad at you. Leaving me in the dark about all this was wrong. But I'm happy you're alive. At least you never lied to me."

Julian glanced back at her in the rearview mirror. "I guess I'm the liar here. How could I tell you the truth when I had no idea what might happen to Steven? What if he died trying to rescue the other people from EnerGeLabs?"

Anita pulled her knees up and hugged her legs, gritting her teeth. "You should have given me a choice. You had no right to make that decision for me. I'm not a child. I guess that's how men are. Even François lied to me."

"Not really," Steven said. "François said I should tell you too. Now I understand I should have, but I was torn over what was best. He would never betray the choice Dad and I made by telling you himself. He insisted it wasn't his place to come between our family."

Her brow scrunched up as she tried to process the full meaning of this. "He acted like he had no idea who we were rescuing besides Julian."

"He didn't," Julian said. "I guessed Steven was being held near D.C. because we all stopped hearing from him while he was in that area. So I took the risk, hoping I would find him. What if I was wrong? How could I tell you Steven was alive, only to have him turn up dead? I never told François why I planned this either."

"No one knew I was in the detention center because I was using a different name," Steven said. "I used an alias after I entered the U.S. this time. It wasn't the one François gave me. I didn't want to put him at risk if I got caught. His insider only had a list of detainees, and my name was never on it."

Anita sighed and leaned against the side of the truck, her stomach fluttering. Nothing was black and white, and her own guilt gnawed at her—putting Stacey at risk by using her computer, assuming the worst about Julian while he was sacrificing himself for their son. She'd even betrayed François years ago by moving on with Julian, and herself for never admitting Julian was not the man she really loved.

"Oh no." Julian slowed the van. "Traffic jam."

"I'll check on the delay." Steven used the phone François had given him.

He studied it for a couple of minutes while he adjusted the map. "This doesn't look good. There's a long, red, line ahead of us and no exits." He continued examining it. "Shit. It shows police activity where the traffic ends. Let me check the notes."

He tapped the phone and his eyes widened. "It's a roadblock."

CHAPTER FORTY-THREE

SOLUTIONS

ANITA PRESSED UP against the grate separating the back of the van from the front seat, so she had a view out the window. The southbound side of the highway wasn't visible. Hills covered in trees lined both sides of the northbound lanes.

Julian stopped with the traffic. "There's nowhere to cross over the center divider. Looks like we're stuck here."

"Do you think we can pass through a roadblock with mom hiding in the back? Who would suspect a Home Depot van with a giant 'nineteen dollar rent me' sign on the side?"

"It's too great a risk," Julian said.

"Murder is serious enough to make them open the back," Anita said. "Probably with guns drawn."

"Is there a road running parallel to us nearby?" Julian asked. "Maybe you can both get out and walk past the roadblock. I'll drive through and pick you up after."

The vehicles ahead of them inched forward while Steven searched.

"Yeah. This undeveloped area on our right leads to a road a few miles east. If you get through the roadblock and take the next exit, right-hand turns will lead you to an unpaved road. Follow it south. I'll text you once we reach it."

"Let's do it." Anita was itching to escape the confines of the van. Had she been able to pace in circles, she would have.

Julian inched his way into the right-hand lane, pulling onto the shoulder. "Walk away from each other like you're going to take a leak, okay? I'll wait awhile, then drive away."

Steven got out first and walked to the left, behind a thick stretch of mountain laurels. Anita slid her pocketbook under her jacket and pulled up her hood, stuffing her hair inside, and left through the side door. There was a steep uphill climb into the woods. Low-lying brush and thorny branches blocked her path as she wove around them. Still exhausted from lack of sleep, she breathed heavily, struggling to maintain the pace. The trees held little foliage to hide her. When she finally crested the hill and wasn't visible from the road, she stopped.

Damn. When did I get so out of shape? Anita used to be able to hike ten miles without a thought. Panting, she counted her breaths in and out to slow them down.

"Mom?" Steven shouted.

"Over here." She plucked thorns from her jeans. Branches cracked as Steven pushed them aside to rejoin her.

"Your battery's dying," he said, handing her phone back. "I can't use the phone François gave me because we need it charged when we cross the border. It's the only way they can locate us. I hope we're walking in the right direction."

Anita slipped it into her pocketbook. She hunted for Mike's phone, which contained Doug's personal number and turned it on.

"This one has a good charge. And I don't think it's being tracked, so we can use this for our GPS. Also, I just got an idea that may help us." She opened the contacts where only two numbers were listed and selected the one labeled HIM.

After three rings, a voice answered. "Who the hell is this? Not Mike."

"It's Anita. I have Mike's phone. This one that calls you and his mother, but you know that. This phone has plenty of calls from you, and text messages as well. Plus, I'm sure if I call his mother, she will tell me plenty. Wouldn't your family find this interesting?"

"No one can trace this number to me. My phone will be trashed as soon as you hang up."

"I'm pretty sure these voicemails can identify you. Your voice print is as unique as a fingerprint."

Silence.

"So. We're back at the negotiating table. What is it you want?"

"I didn't shoot anyone. Another guard did. Of course, I'm sure you already know that, too. I want everyone else to know as well. Stop this manhunt of me and let the police do their job finding the real shooter."

"What guarantees me you won't blackmail me again?"

"How do I know you won't try to kill me again?"

"Touché. Frankly, sweetheart, you are in no position to send your message into the world, or to my wife, so you don't frighten me. In the spirit of good faith, however, I'll have the media kill this story, and tip off the police about the guard. But if you ever threaten me again, you can say goodbye to your son, Steven, while you watch. Do we understand each other?"

"One hundred percent," Anita said. She cringed at his mention of Steven but thought it likely the manhunt would end. The muscles in her chest eased up.

§

"You fuckup!" Doug yelled at Mike as he sat across from him in his office. "You fuck up everything you touch. Any ideas about how to fix this mess?"

Mike crossed his arms and straightened. "I did not fuck up everything." His tone was defiant. Doug hadn't heard him speak like this before. "I had Anita and the hard drive in my car, heading here. If you hadn't asked me to kill her, you would have everything you wanted and there wouldn't be a bus in Washington, D.C. right now."

Doug scowled and his eyes narrowed. Mike's attitude threw him. This entire day was one damn problem after the next and he hated not having control over events. Mike's loyalty and support were things he'd always been able to count on. He couldn't allow this to go awry.

Mike continued. "But once again, I do have a solution. I have a GPS tracker on my phone case. Let me use your laptop to log in to the site and we'll find her."

"Well, why didn't you tell me this four hours ago?"

"I just found out she had my phone. I hid it in my car."

Doug was encouraged by this, the tension in his head easing. He turned his laptop around for Mike's use. After some typing, Mike rotated it back to Doug, showing a map with a dot in an area off Interstate 81 in Pennsylvania.

"She must be on foot. I don't see any roads."

"Perfect." Doug examined the map. "You and I are going for a ride in my helicopter. Have Paul drive you five miles north of here, then leave. I'll put down in the field and pick you up. I don't want anyone seeing us flying out together. Let's go get the phone and the hard drive and be done with Anita."

Doug unlocked his desk drawer, pulled out two pairs of gloves, and gave one to Mike.

"Put them on," he said, sliding them over his hands. Mike did the same. He produced a gun and a magazine, handing them to Mike. "You'll be needing these. You won't fuck it up this time."

Mike put them in his pocket, shut Doug's laptop and placed it under his arm. "I'll need this too, if I'm going to track her."

Doug frowned. "Take your own laptop."

"My battery's dead."

"Can't you use your phone?"

"This website doesn't work right on a phone. You want to take the chance we'll lose her again? With your laptop, I can pinpoint her exactly."

Doug hesitated, staring at Mike while neither of them moved. "Fine. We'll take the laptop. Give it to me and I'll put it on the helicopter."

Mike handed it to Doug, who gripped it to his chest. "Now go find Paul and get moving. I'll make sure they call off the manhunt, so the police don't find her first."

"Yes, sir," Mike replied.

CHAPTER FORTY-FOUR

TRAPPED

Anita's journey through the woods with Steven to bypass the roadblock was taking far longer than she had expected. Prickly branches caught on her clothes when she passed through brush and ducked under tree limbs. She fought exhaustion. Her thighs burned. Each step sent a jolting pain from a blister rubbed raw on her ankle. Desperate to sit and rest, the nagging ache in her shoulder and hip, caused by falling when Mike dragged her into the woods, reminded her of why she needed to push on—she could be killed at any time.

Steven stopped repeatedly to untangle her from wild briars, never complaining. She recognized his frustration from the way he squeezed his lips together before continuing on.

Finally, they came to a clearing. Ahead was a farmer's field, filled with ruts from the season's plowing. Dried corn stalks lay half cemented in the soil in the high spots, and puddles lingered in ditches. Anita dreaded crossing this daunting stretch of land leading to yet another hill and more woods.

"Where's this road?" She was nearly in tears. "I don't know how long I can keep going. Maybe you should go on ahead. I'm taking too long."

"Don't be ridiculous. I'm not abandoning you. You're going to make it. You never give up."

Hearing his words, the faith Steven had in her, boosted Anita's determination and gave her a shot of adrenalin. It was important she stay strong, to show she was the person he believed her to be. Thinking of how he must have suffered in captivity caused her to push through her pain and keep moving. She could do this for him.

Steven checked Google maps. "We're almost there. It should go fast once we cross that next hill ahead."

He stuffed the phone into his pocket. Then he put his arm around her waist for support as he helped propel her forward.

Anita staggered onto the field, limping from one furrow to the next. His steady grip prevented a near fall. Recovering her balance, she carried on. A strong gust of wind hit her head on, stinging her face. She shivered as she pulled her light jacket tight around her chest. After sweating from the hike, her damp clothes chilled her.

Their footsteps crackled, but beyond them was silence.

Halfway across the field, a low rumbling disturbed the quiet. When Steven spun around toward the sound, Anita's eyes followed his gaze.

"Drop!" he shouted as he pulled her to the ground, breaking her fall with his arms, and holding her head down.

"Lie here and don't move. It's a helicopter."

The hard mound of dirt dug into her ribs, and the decaying corn stalk against her face smelled rotten. She hoped their drab clothing would blend into the field from above, rendering them undetectable. What if it was the police? Her pounding heart throbbed in her ears.

The rumble grew louder, followed by the whooshing of the blades. The aircraft flew straight at them, too close for them to reach the woods and hide.

Steven leapt to his feet and sprang away, drawing the helicopter in the opposite direction from Anita. It dropped down near him, kicking up a brutal wind with its blades. Before the skids touched the ground, the door flew open. Mike jumped onto the landing gear, pouncing forward, toward her son. Steven pivoted away, but Mike leapt on top of him and pinned him to the ground.

Anita's pulse skyrocketed as she registered what was happening. Climbing to her feet, she screamed, "Steven," as her whole body shook. The helicopter landed and went silent. From the pilot's seat, Doug stepped out and faced her, grinning like the class bully who'd just tripped a smaller boy.

Digging through her pocketbook for her gun, her eyes stayed riveted on Steven and Mike. She pulled it out and pointed it at Mike, now leaning above her son while holding his arms behind his back.

"Look out, Mike," Doug shouted. "She has a gun."

Anita aimed her pistol at Mike with her arms outstretched and slid down the safety. Her stomach did somersaults, and her arms shook. The pistol refused to stay still. Mike shoved a gun into Steven's back and yanked him from the ground, using him as a shield. She froze.

"Let him go," Anita called out. "Take me and let Steven go. I'll be your hostage. I'll do anything you ask."

No one replied.

Anita turned her gun toward Doug, certain she could hit him. He laughed.

"You aren't going to shoot me, sweetheart. Because if you do, Mike over there will kill your son. You don't want that. Women are so predictable. It's your weakness."

They stood facing one another in a triple standoff.

"You're right. I love my son and that's my weakness. Too bad you don't love yours."

Doug's eyebrows creased together in a frown.

"You treat Mike like a guard dog."

Doug turned to Mike, narrowing his eyes.

Mike looked away, back at Anita. "Give me the drive. That's what we're here for. Throw over the hard drive and you get your son."

She continued to point the gun at Doug. "Last time, you were going to kill me anyway."

"Don't give it to him, Mom. There has to be another way."

"Shut up or I'll shoot you right now!" Mike shouted at Steven.

"It's in my handbag. You can have it. I need to reach in there. Don't shoot me." She pulled it out.

"Throw the hard drive and the gun over here and you can both leave," Mike said.

Anita tossed the hard drive and it landed two feet behind Mike.

"Now the gun and you can go."

Anita's teeth were locked so tight, she could break her jaw.

Her gun was the only bargaining power she had left. But if she didn't give it to him, he might kill Steven. She stared back at her son; he had Mike's arm around his neck and the man's gun in his back. She couldn't shoot Doug and risk retaliation. There was no other choice. Replacing the safety, she tossed the gun at Mike. It landed within a foot of him. While keeping his arm around Steven's neck, he leaned over and retrieved it.

"Good work, Mike." Doug nodded toward him. "Now clean up this mess. Kill them both."

Anita's legs became weak, threatening to buckle from fear, realizing she'd made a tragic decision.

"We have what we need," Mike said, not moving. "We have everything. Why do we need to kill them?"

Doug glared and his voice rose. "Because they're still dangerous to me. Now get on with it."

Mike raised the gun to the back of Steven's head and Anita trembled in horror. She gripped her eyes shut and covered her face. The gun fired and she screamed as she waited for the second shot. There wasn't one. Slowly, she moved her hands and peeked through her fingers.

Steven was still standing.

Doug was staring at Mike with wide-eyed disbelief. Then he collapsed to the ground as blood spread across his chest.

Anita's jaw fell open.

Mike dropped his arms, releasing Steven, who ran to his mother and grabbed her hand, tugging at her to run. She stood, rooted to the spot, watching Mike as he picked up the hard drive.

"One more thing before you go," Mike said. "I need my phone. I have to call my mother. I need to tell her she's free of him now."

She nodded to Steven. "Go ahead. Give it to him."

He tossed the phone over to Mike.

"I told him I wasn't some goon. Told him again and again but he never listened to me. Now with this"—he motioned with the hard drive—"I don't need him anymore. *This* . . . is the future. And it's mine."

"But you can't decrypt it," Anita said.

"Paul and I are partners now, so it's not a problem anymore."

Anita shuddered. She tried to process the idea of the man who'd rescued her and cared about green fuel partnering with the violent man before her, a man who just shot his father. "Partners?"

"My father was kind enough to leave me a nice startup fund. You could say I inherited well. Not that he knew it. With my money and Paul's knowledge, nothing can stop us."

As Anita let Steven pull her in the direction they'd been heading, Mike called out after them.

"By the way, I used your gun to shoot him. Has your fingerprints all over it."

They halted. She looked back at him waving his gloved hands.

"No one even knows I'm here thanks to you for driving my car to West Virginia. I appreciate the alibi. Don't give me any trouble and I won't need to turn this gun over to the authorities."

Anita took a deep breath. "Don't worry," she replied. "You'll never see me again."

CHAPTER FORTY-FIVE

PROMISE

THEIR DAY BEGAN with a full breakfast of eggs, pancakes with maple syrup, fresh fruit, and coffee prepared by Caitlyn. After they ate, Odina opened a closet of used winter jackets, since severe cold had descended into Vermont. Anita, Steven, and Julian each found one that fit well enough.

Anita dumped everything out of her pocketbook onto the table and picked out what she didn't need. To lighten the load, she put aside makeup, a hairbrush, car keys to her EV down in Newport, and the remaining pile of hundred-dollar bills, all of which she donated to Caitlyn and Odina. She kept her fake passport and driver's license, her cell phone and charger, and her Swiss debit card, along with a wallet of Canadian money. After a long sleep the night before, she was ready for this trek. Until the blisters stung her feet.

"Do you have band aids?" she asked. "My feet need them. And my clean socks went on to Canada without me in Erin's car."

"Let's see the feet," Odina said, sitting in a chair facing Anita.

She pulled off her boots and socks.

Odina took a foot into her hands and examined it, frowning, then did the same with the other foot. "You won't get far on these. Lucky for you, you're in the right place. I have blister bandages and moleskin. Let's get you fixed up. I can spare you a pair of hiking socks, too. Not new, but clean."

Odina rested Anita's feet on her chair as she fetched her supplies.

Steven finished up the dishes in the kitchen while Caitlyn joined Anita at the table.

"No wonder you love this woman," Anita said. "She's a godsend."

Caitlyn smiled as she picked up the remote and switched on the television to the news. A newscaster sat at a desk with a photo of Doug behind him, alongside a photo of a burned-up helicopter.

Anita's chest tightened from confusion. She'd seen no smoke after she and Steven walked the rest of the way, and Mike was preparing to leave. If Mike was going to set fire to Doug's helicopter, he'd have no reason to warn her about her gun. Maybe someone else wanted to hide Doug's death.

"A helicopter crash in the hills of Pennsylvania yesterday took the life of Douglas T. Hayes, the billionaire executive of Claydon Industries, a conglomerate with holdings in oil, coal, natural gas, and energy. Mr. Hayes was mentioned as allegedly having involvement in the detention center scandal that emerged yesterday. His wife, Virginia Claydon Hayes, was unavailable for comment."

How convenient, Anita thought, to have a dead man to blame for the detention centers. She wondered who else was involved and how high into the government this might go. Those he'd helped get elected had reason to keep him quiet now that he was exposed.

The newscaster continued as the picture behind him switched to the Capitol building in Washington, D.C. Odina returned to her chair.

"This morning, congresswoman María Juarez of California, a member of the House Committee on the Judiciary, called for a full investigation into the detention center allegations. She stated that she has been assured that all alleged detainees are protected under the Crime Victims' Rights Act, and as such will have the right to be reasonably protected from the accused and will be treated as crime victims with their associated rights throughout the investigation and any subsequent trials."

Steven ran in from the kitchen while the others leapt up from their chairs. The five of them cheered and gave each other high fives. Anita hugged Julian briefly.

"The tables are beginning to turn," Odina said. "How high that corruption goes, however, may never be exposed."

"Do you think they'll find and convict those involved?" Caitlyn asked.

"I hope so," Anita said. "They can't all be on Doug's payroll, can they? Besides, with him gone, he won't be there to bankroll his accomplices."

"Claydon Industries and the Claydon family lives on. Don't think there aren't more just like him ready to step in," Odina said. "At least now, people may question this administration's narrative about the climate crisis and demand action.

After all, we must be getting somewhere if they'll go to such lengths to shut us up."

"Do we still need to go to Canada?" Julian asked, looking at Anita. "Maybe we can just go home."

"That's up to you," Anita said. "Other than Doug, they're all still out there. Maybe in the future it will be safe, but I'm not convinced that time is now, even with the national exposure and a pending investigation. I'm certainly not about to testify to Congress."

Odina looked stunned. "Why wouldn't you?"

"Mike is still around, and he's dangerous." She hadn't told anyone that she saw Mike murder Doug, and Steven had promised not to either. Mike had already threatened her. Staying out of his way was critical.

"I guess I shouldn't be surprised that my dad joined forces with someone like him, but I am," Caitlyn said. "How can he trust Mike after what he did to us, to our inn?"

"Maybe he thinks getting this developed is so important that it doesn't matter who he aligns himself with," Odina said.

Caitlyn smiled at her wife. "You always want to believe the best about everyone."

"If he fathered you, there must be something good about the man. I'm keeping an open mind until we see how this plays out. Maybe he can pull it off."

"Well, I, for one, want to go home," Julian said. "I still have my teaching job in Gettysburg . . . I hope. That's what I want to go back to. Along with my cohorts at American University, we can keep a close eye on this administration. We have a good group of people who are willing to keep the pressure on. I'd like to call my congressman first and make sure I'll be safe under this Crime Victims' Rights Act, however. Can I stay here until I find out?"

"Sure. For a little while," Caitlyn replied. "But you have to promise not to let them track you here. We still have to be careful, and we may still need to help activists escape the country."

She handed him the keys for the EV. "You'll need these."

Julian thanked her and turned to his son.

"How about you, Steven?" Julian asked. "What's next for you?"

"For now, I'm going up to Canada again. I'll keep working with François when he needs me. I don't think this is over yet, either. Besides, as far as the U.S. is concerned, I'm dead. Erin suggested I stay in Ottawa for a while. She can fix me up with some online work. I'd like to see where that leads."

Anita smiled, suspecting the question about where this would lead went beyond work.

"Okay, Son. I respect that. I'll miss you."

"You know we'll stay in touch," Steven replied.

Julian turned to Anita, not looking away like he normally did. "Can we speak alone for a few minutes?"

"Of course," she answered. They walked to Julian's room and sat next to each other on the bed. His face looked softer, more relaxed than she remembered seeing him for some time. He took her hand, and she didn't immediately tense up. There was a certain comfort in it that warmed her.

"I'm sorry for the way I've acted over the last couple of years," he said. "I understand why it upsets you. If a divorce is what you really want, I won't fight you." He rubbed her hand between both of his. "You've suffered enough. We've had a lot of good years, you and I, and I hope you don't regret them. I just ask that you give it some time to make sure you're doing the right thing. Please don't rush into this."

He turned to look at her, his eyes damp, and she sensed a shift in his perception, as though he were truly seeing her at last.

Anita nodded. "I can do that." She needed time to put all these experiences into perspective, to decompress and figure out where she was going from here. Maybe even have some peace in her life.

"And thank you for trying to rescue Steven." The tension in her neck was loosening and she managed to squeeze his hand to show she meant it.

"Thank you for rescuing us both," he replied, patting her hand before he let it go.

Anita stood up.

"Assuming you go back, look out for Stacey, will you? I'll call her and let her know you're there if she needs you."

"Absolutely. I can relate to what she went through."

His remark surprised her. Maybe someday they would both be able to sit down and discuss what they'd each dealt with. She realized they hadn't been close for a long time, even before they thought Steven was dead. They had shared activities, but not themselves.

It was time for her to move on. They walked back out to the great room, where Steven, Caitlyn and Odina sat waiting.

"So I guess it's only Steven and me for the hike to Canada today."

"Let's finish your feet and get on the road," Odina said.

❧

"Keep your Canadian passport handy. And take this." Odina held out a compass, offering it to both Anita and Steven as Caitlyn pulled over to the side of the road. "You'll need it. You might get away with presenting yourselves as Canadian hikers who strayed too far if you are picked up on the U.S. side. So far, no one I've led that way has been stopped. But keep your phones and any devices powered off until you reach the road in Canada."

Anita and Steven acknowledged her advice. Steven had called François and arranged a meeting point a few hours from now, where Odina told them they would end up if all went well. François and Erin had safely crossed the border separately in their rental cars.

"Come back in two hours," Odina told Caitlyn as she bundled up. "Park somewhere in the town and I'll call you."

"Be careful," Caitlyn said.

Steven, Anita, and Odina climbed over a guard rail and into the woods.

Odina used her compass to lead them through an unmarked area without trails, while Steven followed along using the one she'd given him. The trees were far enough apart, and the brush had died off for the winter, so it wasn't difficult to pass. Anita had expected to be anxious, but instead, the wooded hike was soothing. She settled into a pace with steady breaths as a sense of peace washed over her. After an hour, Odina stopped.

"Just ahead, you'll see a narrow clearing leading in both directions. That's the border. Don't stop to look. Keep your compass set at three-hundred forty-eight degrees north and you'll reach the road. Good luck. Call me when you get there."

"I'll never forget your kindness—and your guts," Anita said as she hugged Odina. "Thank you."

"I have no doubt we will meet again," Steven said, shaking Odina's hand.

Despite the frigid weather that felt more like mid-January than November, Anita maintained her stride behind Steven. The cold prevented her from getting thirsty, but she knew it was important to stay hydrated to keep warm. Every fifteen minutes she made sure to take a gulp of water. Counting down to this activity helped make the time go by.

They were sheltered from the wind while walking in the woods. After a few hours, they stumbled into an opening revealing a narrow, unmarked road. They had arrived at a place where they could be picked up. Anita moved onto the road's edge, staring around her with the realization that this was her home now, for the immediate future at least, and she could stop looking over her shoulder. A wind gust nearly knocked her sideways. She slid off her mittens and pushed them under her arms, then struggled to pull the hood tighter around her head as her fingers grew icy. Once she had the cord fastened under her chin, she blew on her hands to warm them up before shoving them back into the mittens.

Steven rummaged under his jacket for the phone. He turned it on and called François, who said he was about fifteen minutes away.

"We'll walk in your direction to keep warm," he said before disconnecting. "See you soon."

Anita's pulse quickened as she thought about seeing François. She needed to hear the truth from him about why he didn't tell her about Steven. Whatever it was, she owed it to him to hear him out, this man who'd risked his life to bring her everything that mattered. In the past, she'd judged him too quickly and wouldn't make that mistake again.

"Erin is following François in her car," Steven said. "I'll be riding with her back to Ottawa."

This announcement caught Anita off guard. A lump filled her throat. Was Steven only minutes away from leaving? It was too soon. She'd barely had a chance to get used to him being alive.

"Can't you stay in Montreal for a few days?" Her voice cracked. "Just long enough for me to see you cleaned up and looking healthy? I'll get you a hotel room. Erin too, if she wants to stay."

He stared at his feet while they walked. "I suppose I could," he said. "What's a few days after being dead for two years?"

Turning to her, he smiled, a smile that sent warmth throughout her body.

"By the way, you'll be glad to know," he continued, "that she's bringing something with her we both care about. A certain hard drive I switched with the one in your handbag when we stopped at Walmart yesterday. I bought one that looked just like it and put the real one in Erin's backpack. She drove it into Canada. It's safe. You gave Mike the one from Walmart."

Anita stopped walking and stared, gaped-mouthed, the warmth shifting into anger.

"Why didn't you tell me? What if I'd chosen to die rather than give it to Mike?"

Steven grinned.

"Do you think I don't know my own mother? I knew you'd

put our lives first. Your performance was completely convincing. We may not have gotten out alive if it wasn't."

"You could have told me when we reached Stowe."

"I couldn't tell you at the inn because I didn't want anyone else to know. The fewer people who realize this, the safer we are. Remember how I helped some of the EnerGeLabs scientists get into Canada? They'll be able to work on it here. And they've located some fellow scientists in Switzerland that they can exchange research with so they can all progress faster. But they'll never know that you are their hero who rescued it."

He paused and gazed at her, his eyes shining with pride. "Mine, too."

Anita's indignation retreated, calming her, as this knowledge sunk in. She could once again visualize a future that held promise as she locked eyes with her son. Her arms tingled as joy spread out from her chest, and she began to laugh—a great big, exuberant laugh that she couldn't control. Then Steven started laughing too, and he threw his arms around her. They rocked back and forth in the middle of the road, laughing. She laughed as tears slid from her eyes, warm on her icy cheeks. The laughter and tears flowed from deep inside her, from a spot her body had forgotten until now, sending all her anxiety, worry, and pain into the wind, blowing them to a place where they wouldn't easily find her again. A sensation she'd believed lost forever was coming alive inside. This was what happiness felt like.

ACKNOWLEDGMENTS

I must first thank Linda Schreyer, author, writing instructor, and workshop leader, whose writing prompt inspired me to begin this story. I worked with her as a member of her online group through the entire first draft of this book. Thank-you to the other group members, Paula Bernstein, Laurie Collister, and Rick Draughon, for their feedback and support throughout this process.

Much appreciation goes to my developmental editor Gretchen Stelter for her insight, direction, and commitment during challenging times. I am also beholden to Heather Knorr and Melissa Carro for the additional editorial support they provided.

For research on the scientific possibilities of the technology presented in this book, I thank Edward T. Wu, Professor of Electrical & Computer Engineering, Judson S. Swearingen Regents Chair in Engineering, and Director, Center for Dynamics and Control of Materials: an NSF MRSEC at the University of Texas at Austin.

For research on fires, my thanks to Joanna Lambert, former Certified Fire Investigator for the Bureau of Alcohol, Tobacco, Firearms and Explosives.

Others who contributed to my research for various aspects of the book include authors and experts in their field Mark

Bergin, Patrick Hyde, and Lane Stone, as well as some not listed here.

My Thursday night Zoom writer's support group run by authors Lainey Cameron and Charlotte Dune continues to be an endless source of knowledge and ideas. I am constantly grateful to both the moderators of this group, and the other members who show up to both learn and share, offering their experience and opinions in meaningful and respectful ways.

To my community of readers and writers that helped make this book possible, I thank the following: Nancy Teed, Corie Skolnick, Kate O'Brien Wooddell, Maylah Uhlinger, Valerie Taylor, Paulette Stout, Maria Matarazzo, and others not listed.

My deepest gratitude goes to those who contributed to the development of this book during its various stages, through workshops and classes, including Gayle Lynds, Wendy Goldman Rohm, and Julie Cantrell.

Many thanks go to Damonza.com for their cover design and layout.

Thank you to all the friends who have offered their support along the way, and most of all to my husband, who continues to share all his love and friendship, understanding and commitment, as I travel along this road.

AUTHOR'S NOTE

Thank you so much for reading *The Shutdown List*. I hope you enjoyed it and perhaps found it thought-provoking. If you liked it, please share that information with your friends.

I would also love it if you would leave your honest review on book review sites such as Bookbub, Goodreads, Barnes and Noble, and Amazon. Reviews are much appreciated, no matter how short or long. I read them all.

Please sign up for my newsletter. I will keep you informed of news and events, engage in discussions, provide reviews of other books I recommend, and announce specials.

https://sharondukett.com/contact-us/

If you use social media, please join me on any or all of these:

Facebook: *https://www.facebook.com/sharondukettauthor/*

Instagram: *https://www.instagram.com/sharon.dukett/*

Threads: *https://www.threads.net/@sharon.dukett*

On my website you will find my schedule of events, media links, and other information. *https://sharondukett.com/*

You can email me at: *sharondukettauthor@gmail.com*

More books are in progress. Meanwhile, you may enjoy my memoir *No Rules: A Memoir*. It takes place in the early 1970s when I ran away from home to join the hippies, and ultimately awakened to feminism and found my own strength.

Praise for No Rules: *A Memoir*

"*No Rules*, like all great memoirs, grants the reader the feeling of time travel — immersing you in the body of someone who was there to witness a now-alien era."

—*SALON*

"This illuminating coming-of-age account chronicles a young woman's counterculture journey. Dukett's revealing memoir effectively captures the restless disillusionment of many members of the generation that came of age during the '60s and '70s."

—*KIRKUS REVIEWS*

"Readers seeking a memoir that embraces personal, social, and cultural change and epitomizes the atmosphere of these times will find *No Rules* an intriguing examination of power, control, influence, and evolution. Its ability to capture the process of questioning and growth…is particularly well done…"

—*MIDWEST BOOK REVIEW*

"*No Rules* is a compelling and complex memoir and a deep dive into intergenerational trauma, family, finding ourselves despite unconventional paths, and love in all its forms."

—*INDIEREADER*

"Colorful, adventurous, and transformative . . . unflinchingly raw and unapologetic . . . *No Rules* is a thrill ride of a memoir."

—*THE NERD DAILY*

"*No Rules* does more than pull us into the adventures of a girl who finds the courage to leave home and forge a life contrary to everything she has been taught. It is also a reminder that every girl has the right—and owes it to herself—to grow, learn, succeed, and become the woman she is meant to be, no matter how difficult it is to find her way and her purpose in a male-dominated society."

—Victoria Zackheim, author of *The Bone Weaver*

"This memoir is filled with beauty and fear and fearlessness and courage and audacity and words to inspire all girls and women that life, as Helen Keller once said, is an adventure."

—Amy Ferris, author of *Marrying George Clooney: Confessions from a Midlife Crisis*

"Beyond flawless exposition, Dukett's memoir also offers an unflinchingly honest recollection of her years in late adolescence as a "hippie chick" runaway and in her competent story telling hands that is one hell of a story."

—Corie Skolnick, author of *Orfan* and *America's Most Eligible*

". . . a strong feminist success story. Bravo Sharon, a great story, well told."

—David Crow, author of *Pale-Faced Lie*

Author photo © Karen St. Denis-Piazza Photography

Sharon Dukett is an award-winning author who writes thrillers and memoir. She is a member of Sisters in Crime, International Thriller Writers, and Connecticut Authors and Publishers Association. Her memoir, *No Rules*, won a gold medal in the Next Generation Indie Book Awards in Memoirs (Historical/Legacy), and was a finalist in several other writing contests. Sharon worked in information technology as a consultant, programmer, and project manager in the private sector, and as a deputy director in government. This taught her the infinite possibilities of how plans go awry, and the creativity needed to rescue them: a useful insight for writing thrillers. Sharon lives in central Connecticut with her husband, within driving distance of her children and grandchildren, whom she hopes will have long lives in a healthy world.

www.ingramcontent.com/pod-product-compliance
Lightning Source LLC
Chambersburg PA
CBHW022011310726

48972CB00006B/1597